Wingless

Book 1 of the Wingless Series

by David M. James

Three Ravens Publishing
Chickamauga, GA USA

Wingless By David M. James
Published by Three Ravens Publishing
threeravenspublishing@gmail.com
P O Box 851, Chickamauga, Ga 30707
https://www.threeravenspublishing.com
Copyright © 2023 by David M. James

Publishers Note: This is a work of fiction. Names, characters, places, and incidents are a product of the author's imagination. Locales and public names are sometimes used for atmospheric purposes. Any resemblance to actual people, living or dead, or to businesses, companies, events, institutions, or locales is completely coincidental.

Credits:
WINGLESS was written by David M. James
Cover art by J.F. Posthumus
Edited by: Taylor Robinson
WINGLESS by: David M. James /Three Ravens Publishing – 1st edition, 2023

Ebook ISBN: 978-1-962791-29-8
Trade Paperback ISBN: 978-1-962791-30-4
Audiobook ISBN: 978-1-962791-31-1

Table of Contents

Foreword

I started writing role-playing games in 1985 and many of the best times of my life have come from sitting around a table with friends, watching sparkly polyhedral dice fly across character sheets and weaving our stories together. I even met my wonderful wife Nadina through playing one of these games.

In 2013 I started working with the ideas that would eventually become a game I called "Wingless". I ran that twelve-part game several times with different groups of friends, and each time the world became more nuanced, more alive. In the end, I knew I needed to expand that story into a complete novel, and after several years, here it is.

And so, it is vital that I thank those brilliant, funny, heartwarming, and supportive friends who created living, breathing characters in my world, and then foolishly let me play with them. You are all fantastic, and I could not have even dreamed of writing this without you.

Thank-you Nadina, Sarah, Jim, Graham, Bernard, Emma, James, Callie, Katie, Samantha, Mark, Sandra, Ryan and of course, our very own 'Joan', Ingrid.

Prologue

As the flames licked higher up her body, causing oil-soaked skin to blister and blacken and hair to flare alight, a scream of absolute agony forced its way out from between her clenched lips. Even the most steadfast of her executioners turned their eyes away at the sound of that cry, but they found little solace in the wooden crucifix on the wall that gave them their authority.

The woman tied to the stake reflexively tried to open her wings, to assume her angelic form, to show them she spoke the truth. But just like the countless number of previous attempts, they stubbornly stayed closed against her back, invisible to the men who had condemned her.

The burning was not a mortal threat to the Angel, even to one whose power had been all but culled. Her spirit would continue, and a new body would eventually coalesce for her. What drew the scream from her lips was the abject sense of failure she felt at being stopped in doing her work.

Again.

In her mind, the fire did not touch her body at all. No, what she saw was far more terrible. Before her eyes, the rest of the world was burning. Her executioners, the courtyard, the town surrounding it and all the people of the world that she had failed to save. Burning because of her, because of her failure. And through it all, through all the crying and screams, her father stayed silent.

With a muffled cry I sat upright in bed, sweat covering my body, muscles still shaking from the intensity of the nightmare. Choking back the last of the sobs, I reached for a glass of water on the bedside table.

"You do know that Angels aren't supposed to dream, don't you?"

My already exhausted muscles tensed across my back as I heard the voice. Without turning I quickly calculated where in my bedroom the interloper was standing and just what trajectory to throw the glass in my hand to strike him right in the nose. It would be futile, I knew—quite probably satisfying, but futile, nonetheless. Forcing myself instead to take a deep breath and ignore my impulse to fight, I turned to face the Fallen Angel. As I had suspected, he had mentally projected his will from wherever in the world he was currently, the tell-tale transparency to the image giving it away.

"What the hell are you doing here Azazel?" I choked out, the last effects of the nightmare still clinging to me.

"Charming. You are such a delight in the mornings." Azazel's warm smile attempted to lessen the sting from his words. "You know why I'm here. I felt your pain, just as I always do. It saddens me to see you like this, you know that. And you also know that I can help if you'll let me."

"Fuck off," I spat

Azazel shook his head, "Trazael, please. See reason."

His use of my old name reignited my impulse to fight. "Joan. It's Joan. If you can't even get that right…"

The Fallen held up his hands in supplication, cutting off the rest of my rant. He'd heard it enough times already anyway. "Okay, okay, Joan. Whatever you want. Listen, I'll go now, but do yourself a favour. Call me. Please?"

The projection faded away as I muttered, "Fat chance," and I was sure I saw his shoulders slump a little as I did so. It was always the same with Azazel. So calm, so caring, and on a certain logical level his offer even made sense. That's what made it hurt all the more.

My phone trilled its ringtone into the now silent room, 'The Mission' by the Piano Guys. That meant it was one of my compatriots. I swear, selectable ringtones and caller ID had to be about the best inventions of the last century.

Shaking off the last of the tension from Azazel's visit, I thumbed the answer button. "Talk to me, Toby."

"Joan? Did you feel it?" Toby's voice had a worried tone to it that sent a cold shiver down my spine. I forced myself to concentrate and listen to the song of the universe. It was something we could all do, but for some reason it never came easy for me. Sure enough, there was yet another note missing.

"Someone's fallen," I said into the phone.

"Of course, someone's fallen!" barked Toby in barely contained frustration. "Kateri fell. Didn't you sense it happen?"

"I was asleep. I was having a nightmare." I didn't bother to add that being asleep had never stopped me from sensing one of us fall before.

"You were having a what? Look, we'll talk about that later. We need to get together. Usual spot, tonight. See you there?"

"Yeah, usual place." I ended the call and slumped back onto the bed. The usual place. It sucked that this had happened enough times for us to even have a 'usual' place for these meetings.

Everyone knows about the great war.
Everyone knows who fought, who won, and who lost.

The shining armies of Michael and Gabriel clashed with the Lightbringer's forces, both fighting for the attention of their creator, one side confident of His plan, the other hurt to their core by His love for the humans over themselves.

You humans call the victors, 'Angels'. The vanquished became the Fallen, demons, or devils. But did you ever stop to consider that there might have been some of us who refused to fight?

There were 350 of us. The first conscientious objectors the Universe had ever seen. Perhaps it was because we were too closely tied to human affairs, but while we couldn't see the justice in the Lightbringer's argument, neither could we bring ourselves to raise a sword against those that were our brothers and sisters. If our creator had called us to battle the story might have been different, but there was only silence from Him; it was Michael who ordered us to fight.

We did not Fall, as the Lightbringer's forces did at the end of the battle. But neither were we permitted to rise to Heaven once more. For while that battle ended, the war, it seemed, was far from done. We were stripped of most of our power and left, wingless, on Earth, to wait out creation.

For the longest time we simply continued performing our appointed tasks. They were, after all, the last thing that He had ever asked of us. We were never able to stay in one place for too long though, our ageless bodies would draw the attention of too many powerful people. We can still perform some minor miracles when needed, although it is far easier when we are directly affecting our appointed sphere of influence. We can also still feel our wings, closed in tight against our backs, but we cannot unfurl them, and angels need to do that in order to access most of our powers. That, apparently, is one of the 'Rules'. We can see the wings on the back of another Wingless, but humans only see an intricate wing tattoo on our skin should they look.

Then, one by one, we started to fall. Heaven continued to be deaf to our prayers, while the Lightbringer was always present to offer us a home, a family, and somewhat ironically, forgiveness. Maddeningly, the Fallen, even after everything they had done, still have all their angelic powers, while we who stood apart have so very little left. Worst of all for us, the constant loneliness aches like an open wound. We were never created to be alone, to be kept apart from our family.

The Fallen can be quite chatty really, and out of respect, the nicer ones do try not to unfurl their wings in our presence.

Much.

There is only a dozen of us left now, eleven with Kateri choosing to fall. This modern world and its technology has meant that we can at least keep in closer contact with each other, but now that only seems to highlight how few of us there are left.

Chapter One

It was after 10pm when I climbed the steps towards the old observatory. I knew that I'd be the last to arrive out of those that could, but I didn't care. For the last 300 years or so we'd all gained some solace at this old place, when things seemed at their darkest. Using the public telescope to stare out at the vastness of His creation, into what the humans once coined 'the heavens', helped to calm the anxiety we all felt when one of us fell.

Somehow, I didn't think it would help tonight.

As the centuries passed and our numbers dwindled, we often found ourselves quite alone and scattered across the globe. Those close enough to London to make it here tonight will have done so, the others would be using Skype to take part in the conversation. We lacked the power to send a mental projection like Azazel had this morning, so modern technology had become quite a boon in helping us feel less alone and isolated at times like this.

I started to run through who would be here tonight and their realms as I climbed the steps. I was taking stock of our assets. When you've spent as long looking after soldiers as I have, that sort of thing is a hard habit to break.

Toby would be here obviously, probably still fussing over whatever internet connection the others would be using to Skype in. Toby's realm was all about the messengers, originally the couriers who would run messages between towns, then the postal service and more recently programs like Skype on the internet. He was always the first to have any new phone the humans had come up with and was rather pleased when he discovered that the engineers who created those gadgets fell under his purview and not Lennox's.

While Toby would be fussing over the Skype connections, Lennox would be running wires, routers and modems like some modern spider web. Lennox has looked after inventors since the first mechanical lever; computers and the internet were truly her plaything.

Adelita would definitely be here, having taken a plane over from Holland. She found it easiest to use her influence for the innocent by basing herself at The Hague and having access to all the various humanitarian organisations there.

Damien would attend so long as he wasn't needed in surgery. Having healers as his realm, he found it easier to pass himself off as a surgeon in order to do his work, and over the centuries he had become quite adept in as many forms of medicine as you can imagine.

Orfael had a sixty percent chance of being here, by my calculations. The youngest of us, Orfael was also the only one not to have taken a human name, and her refusal to do so aggravated me possibly a lot more than it should have. She looked after creatures of the air, and took pilots under her wing, pun intended, when manned flight was invented. I blame Toby for encouraging her.

Beatrice would show if she were able to get a flight from Paris in time. I hoped so, as I knew she would have my back when the inevitable argument started. Her realm of Law Keepers made her the perfect judge, and we had all, at some point, turned to her for the final word on some legal or moral decision. Our own personal Angel of Judgement.

If Beatrice were here, Silje would be as well. The two of them had been nearly inseparable for the last century or so. Silje had the hardest time adapting to the ever-increasing pace of the modern world, and each time I saw her she seemed a little more detached. Her realm was music, and she would often just stare off into space, listening. She can sense all of us, all the time, hearing our 'notes' as she describes it, and the discord caused by Kateri falling would be affecting her deeply.

Admonae had only a small chance of being here. She is our truth-seeker, and a mystery such as Kateri's fall would have her scouring the 'crime scene' for clues if she were able to get there. We didn't always see eye-to-eye if, truth be told, her need for evidence sometimes clashed with my need for action, but once committed to an investigation there was nothing anyone could do to dissuade her.

And then there would be Gary – blessed be his coffee. Gary ran a little café in Soho and made the most heavenly brew. I never quite understood why he did this however, seeing that his realm included the sages and oracles - those that attempted to understand the nature of the human condition. Whenever the topic came up, he would just put on that quirky little half-smile of his and make some pithy comment about the truths that could be discovered in the bottom of a good cup of coffee.

And then there is me. Being the only Wingless left who used to be able to summon a good old-fashioned flaming sword should leave little to the imagination about what my area of concern is.

That Kateri had chosen to fall was, unfortunately, not too much of a surprise. She had been given the realm of the environment to look after, and she had been steadily losing faith in humanity's will to take care of this little blue globe for some time now. Azazel had probably used that to tempt her to take that last step and join them.

"Bastard."

"Muttering to yourself again Joan?" Gary's calming tone penetrated my reverie, and I slowed my march up the stairs, allowing him to fall in beside me.

He was still dressed in his coffee-stained apron, and I found myself returning his ready smile despite my sour mood. "Good to see you brother," I said, pointedly looking his clothes up and down. "Inspire any new philosophies recently?"

"Ha!" Gary's natural exuberance was contagious, even on a night like this. "Always sis, you know me. How about you, toppled any fascist regimes this year?"

"It's only March," I grinned back at him. It was good to see him, and I snaked an arm around his back to hug him as we mounted the last step. The comfortable camaraderie that he was always able to create had me wondering not for the first time why we spent so much time apart.

We entered the main dome to find Silje, Admonae, Beatrice and Adelita chatting to the faces of the three who couldn't make it on various computer screens set up on the main table. Toby and Lennox were discussing which connection protocol would give us less lag in the conversations, ignoring the conversations happening around them. Like a family that has not seen each other for months we all embraced, laughed, and hugged in greeting, forgetting our troubles for a few precious minutes. I was the first to pull away, scanning the dome for the missing figure I knew would be here.

"So." I pitched my voice to cut through the small talk. "Where is he?"

It was Silje who answered first. She cocked her head slightly in that way she did when tuning into the symphony and did not bother to hide the derision in her voice. "He's not here. None of us have heard from him actually. *They* wanted to phone him, but I thought it was better to wait for you."

Gary's brow furrowed in thought. "He's never been late before. Usually, he's waiting here for us."

"To gloat, you mean," I spat.

"Now Joan, be fair," Gary admonished. "He's never gloated."

I allowed a dismissive snort to be my reply.

Toby, ever the practical one, spoke up to try to break the tension. "I've already asked the others," he said, motioning to the faces of our fellow Wingless on the various computer screens and those in the room, "And we think that you should call him. You know he makes sure that his number is in any phone you have, Joan."

The temptation to immediately crush my phone into its component parts was almost insurmountable at that point, but I paused to look at the faces on the screens, and then those of my friends around me. They were worried. Some were even scared. And right then, they were looking to me for strength.

I gave in. "Okay, but this is under protest."

"So noted," Damien added unhelpfully from the operating theatre he was Skyping in from.

I pulled out my latest burner phone, and sure enough, there in my contacts was Azazel's name and number. Listed under 'Family'. Cheeky sod. I plugged the phone into one of Lennox's computers and dialed the number.

The screen lit up to show a bright blue sky framed against what was, if anything, an even bluer ocean. As Azazel brought the phone up to him it was clear he was lying back on some sort of recliner on a tropical island beach. The drink by his chair even had an umbrella in it.

"Joan!" The delight in Azazel's voice was genuine and infectious. "What a wonderful surprise! To what do I owe the pleasure? One moment, I'll come to you."

"Stay right where you are Azaz!" The bitterness in my voice and my refusal to use his full name stunned the Fallen Angel, and even my friends involuntarily took a small step back from me. What some people don't realise is that the 'el' at the end of our names literally means 'of God'. Our kind do not take lightly to the removal of that honourific from our name. Not even the Fallen.

"Don't give me that crap," I continued while I had him off-balance, "You know why I've called. Where the hell are you?" The look of honest surprise on Azazel's face made me pause in my rant, however. The Fallen are many things, but easily surprised is not one of them.

Azazel spluttered a reply, "Joan, I'm sorry if breaking in on your nightmare this morning was an intrusion, but you were in pain. By the way, how did you…"

I interrupted, "Not that Azazel. Kateri has Fallen. Why aren't you here to show off your latest prize recruit like all the previous times?"

"Now, Joan," Azazel started taking on the tone of a parent addressing a petulant child, "You know that I am the one tasked with helping your people choose to join our family, you really can't pull this kind of joke on me. When did you decide to develop a sense of humour, anyway?"

Ignoring the jibe, I kept my voice level. "Listen to the music asshole."

On the screen I saw Azazel pause, close his eyes, and truly listen to the universe, to creation, to the music of the spheres. And as I watched, I saw true despair come over his face. "Kateri's gone?" he whispered.

"Yes, she's Fallen. That's why we called you. That's why we're here"

"No," Azazel shook his head and with the confusion I could swear I saw a tear form in the corner of one of his eyes, "You don't understand. She didn't Fall."

I'd had enough of his games, "Don't treat me like an idiot Azazel, I know she fell, I don't know what game you think you're playing but…"

The screen went blank, and Azazel was suddenly in the room with us, black wings fully extended and his full power blazing forth like a miniature sun.

"I'm not playing!" His bellowing voice rattled the centuries old glass of the observatory in their frames. He belatedly extended his power to keep them from shattering as he regained control of his outburst.

Slowly, Azazel folded his wings back and became more human-like. "I'm sorry Joan, but Kateri has not Fallen, at least not in the normal sense. Believe me, if she had, I would have been the first to know. I have never lied to you—to any of you. Please know that I am telling you the truth now."

"Okay," I begrudgingly admitted, "I believe you Azazel. But I still don't trust you."

"Don't be silly Joan," the Fallen Angel started, "We need to find out what's going on here."

I shook my head and moved to block him. "No Azazel, we need to find out what happened to one of our own, you need to butt out and leave."

Throwing up his hands in exasperation Azazel went on. "Oh, come on Joan, be serious, you need my help!"

My right hand moved suggestively over my shoulder, right where the hilt of my sword would be if I still had one. "Leave. Now."

Azazel's shoulders slumped and he looked around the room for some kind of support from the others, but they either kept their eyes on me or otherwise avoided his gaze. "Very well, Trazael, I will go. But I will come if … when you call. Take care." And before I could take him to task for using my angelic name again, he was gone.

Adelita, normally the quiet one, was the first to speak. "Joan, I know you don't like him, but we could have used his help."

Lennox and Toby joined in, talking over each other, "If Kateri hasn't fallen... He could help us find…"

"No," I said with determination.

Gary, ever the peacemaker, stepped closer and placed one gentle hand on my shoulder. "Joan? Are you sure?"

Placing my hand over his, I paused to let him know that it wasn't just my anger at Azazel speaking, "Yes Gary, I'm sure. You all feel it. Something is different this time.

Something new is coming. Kateri was one of us and ... I can't help but feel that she still may be. This is something we have to do ourselves."

"Correct," Beatrice quietly added.

Chapter Two

The sun was rising lazily over London when we could finally stand to part from one another. An early morning mist blanketed the city, adding to the depression we all felt as we left to start another day alone. Lennox did manage to trace the internet account she had set up for Kateri and found that she had last accessed it in Johannesburg, South Africa, just two days ago. So that was where we would start our search.

During the evening, we had decided to split our group to try to find out what happened to our sister, with one group following Kateri's trail while the other would separate to cover those places around the world she was known to frequent. First, however, we needed a day to get our 'ordinary' mortal lives squared away and purchase plane tickets. If I hadn't sent him away, Azazel would have offered to help by using his power to teleport us to various points around the globe, but getting miraculous help from a Fallen was, as far as I was concerned, the start of a very slippery slope. In the end we pooled what little money we had to buy some plane tickets. Gary pointed out that he thought it was ironic that we felt, in this case at least, that money was the lesser of two evils.

There would be six of us going to South Africa. Admonae, Beatrice, Silje, Damien, Orfael, and myself. Toby and Lennox would stay in London to coordinate things and most of the others were to start checking out the other possible locations Kateri might have gone to. Gary elected to stay at the little café he ran in order to be a friendly, easy-to-find face for Kateri should she come looking for us. Our flight was set to depart tomorrow morning.

During the night I had argued that it would be safer if I went alone, but Beatrice had put her foot down. "You're not going alone, Joan! What if the same thing that happened to Kateri happens to you?"

"I'm more than capable of looking after myself, Beatrice," I replied, "I could take all of you together right now. Besides, there is no way I'm about to Fall."

Beatrice dismissed the point with a wave of her hand. "According to Azazel, neither did Kateri."

"And you believe him?" I challenged.

"He's never lied to us before," Beatrice countered.

"You mean you've never caught him out doing so," I bit back.

Admonae had crossed her arms across her chest and scowled at that. "Joan, do you honestly think he would be able to lie to *me*?"

I raised my hands in mock surrender. "Alright, alright. You can come with me. Just don't get in my way if things get nasty."

Orfael piped up, snapping to a very badly arranged attempt of being at attention. "Yes, drill sergeant!"

Adelita, bless her, chose that moment to snatch a thermos of coffee from Gary's backpack and some donuts that she had brought for just this circumstance. It's not as if she was prophetic or anything, she just knew how agitated and angry I got around Azazel, and from experience understood when the best times were to exploit my weakness for sweet doughy goodness. It gave us the breathing space we needed to calm down, start planning our trip, and to eventually say our goodbyes to the others and those Skyping in.

Now, out in the chilled air, the enormity of what we were about to try to uncover settled on me. Kateri was gone. It felt to us like she had fallen, and yet apparently, she hadn't. So, what happened to her? Where had she gone?

We can't die, not the way humans can anyway. Our bodies can be destroyed, and trust me, that is not pleasant in the slightest. On top of the pain, it can take months or even years to materialise a new body, but even during that time we're not really dead. While our fellow Wingless can't communicate with us, they can 'feel' that we are still there. Silje would say that our note in the symphony was still playing.

This was different. Kateri was no longer one of us. And if she hadn't become one of the Fallen, who, or should I say what, was she?

Or... and this was not a concept I wanted to consider, what if she was truly gone? The consequences of that even being a possibility were enormous.

"No," I said to the rising sun on the horizon. "She's still somewhere. I'll find her, and I'll bring her home."

A quick tube ride later I was feeding Noah, my rather imperious cat, and steeling myself to let my neighbour know I was going out of town. She was a lovely old woman and would be happy to look after Noah for me, but she was convinced she was psychic and was always trying to get me to meet some nephew of hers or the son of one of her friends. Or daughter. She didn't care who people were with, just so long as they weren't alone.

It was sweet really, but just not what I needed right now.

I packed light, cuddled Noah once more, and locked the door behind me. Key in hand, I knocked on the door across the corridor from mine.

"Coming dear! Just hold on, my legs aren't what they used to be." The door opened and Margaret looked me up and down quickly before reaching out and pulling me into her apartment. "Oh, I knew you were going on a trip!"

"You can see my overnight bag in my hand Margaret."

She smiled knowingly and shook her head, somehow managing to make me feel five years old with a glance. That was quite a feat, because when I was five, humans hadn't developed fire yet. "No dear, I *saw* it. You're going to see a man."

"No Margaret, it's nothing like that."

"Of course, it is! You just don't know it yet. You'll meet him, trust me dear. And he's going to do something that completely surprises you, I can feel it. Now, you have a plane waiting for you, so don't fuss about Noah, he and I will get along just perfectly."

Surrendering, I put Noah down on her couch. "Okay Margaret, just don't overfeed him this time."

Margaret made a dismissive noise. "Oh, you worry too much dear, it will give you wrinkles before your time, you mark my words."

The all-pervasive human worry about wrinkles. I guess immortality has some perks. I nodded and tried to smile in response, and whatever expression my face held seemed to satisfy Margaret and I soon found myself back out in the corridor and heading for the elevator.

Orfael was practically abuzz when we met up at Heathrow, running from window to window like a little girl as the planes took off. I never understood how she maintained her childlike wonder at anything that flew, but then again there was little of her that I did understand.

I started to say to myself, "When we had wings, we could all fly…" but I clamped down hard on that line of thought. That way lay only pain, one long buried but never forgotten. It did occur to me though that being the youngest of us, Orfael had far less time on Earth before the war and hadn't had as many opportunities as we did to experience life as a full Angel on this world. I made a promise to myself to cut her a bit more slack in the future.

"Planes!" Orfael's shrill shout just inches from my ear startled me out of my reverie. I drew a slow, deep breath before turning to her. I had just promised I'd try to be gentler with her - I never promised myself it would be easy.

"Yes Orfael, planes." Her answering pout told me that I hadn't quite succeeded in keeping all the disdain out of my voice, but she brightened up as the others arrived and she ran off to greet them in a similar manner. Oh well, it was a start, I guess.

We checked in and were soon bundled into our seats. Somehow Gary had wrangled us an upgrade to Business class, and we settled in for the long haul. As the plane took off our conversation turned to the topic of Kateri herself, and we decided to share memories of the last time each of us saw the missing Angel.

Orfael, still grinning inanely from the take-off, jumped in first. "Kateri was cool! She always found time to listen to me."

"Is cool," I interrupted.

Orfael barely skipped a beat, screwing up her face and sticking her tongue out at me as she continued. "Unlike *some* grumpy people, Kateri cared."

That simple statement resounded through us all. She did care. She always had. That's why the idea of her falling troubled me. If she could fall, then what hope was there for the rest of us?

I tuned out the rest of the stories as the others continued to share, my thoughts instead shifting to how Azazel had reacted. The Fallen may not care for humans, but as misguided as it was, and loath as I was to admit it, their affection for us was honest and real. Azazel was hurt at first with the thought that we would play such a horrid joke on him. And then, when he realised we weren't joking, he was worried.

No. Not worried.

"He was scared!" My outburst cut across the conversation and turned all heads towards me.

Damien turned his body in his seat to slightly screen us from the other passengers. "Joan?"

I swallowed, collecting my thoughts. "Sorry, I just realised. Azazel was scared. Honestly scared. And I don't think he's ever felt that emotion before. That's why he reacted so oddly."

Damien nodded, casting an eye to the others to see their affirmation as well. "And so," he stated in his measured voice, "that means this is something new. Something completely outside his experience."

"Something new…" Orfael muttered in awe, before glancing timidly in my direction and quietly apologising for interrupting. "Sorry."

I smiled at her, reaching out to gently hold her arm. I'd obviously been far too rough on her recently. "It's okay, Orfael. We're all thinking it. Go ahead, say it."

She blinked at me, and then smiled back. "Do you think it could be from Him?"

It had been so long since any of us had heard from our Creator that even alluding to him caused us all a pang of loss. Hope however, for better or worse, is an integral part of an Angel.

Damien quietly replied, his voice soft and wistful, "Maybe, Orfael. Maybe."

Each of us retreated into our own thoughts at that, and the rest of the flight occurred in relative silence.

Chapter Three

To a bunch of Londoners, stepping off the plane in Johannesburg was like stepping into an overheated sauna. You could watch the passengers visibly wilt as they trudged across the tarmac to the terminal, and we mimicked them so as to not draw attention. With passports checked and our bags collected, we headed for the taxi rank.

Lennox had organised our passports and entry visas on our last day in London. We could have each used some of our miraculous power to simply step through all the security, but as Wingless, our power was severely limited. Rather than start our investigation, already down on our normally meagre reserves, Lennox had used hers, combining it with her knowledge of computers to create the paperwork we needed. Not only would we arrive rested, but all our paperwork was also now real and perfectly legal, making any future travel much easier.

It was probably something we should have been better at keeping up, but immortality comes with the need to change your name and details every so often. With modern governments and integrated information systems, this had gotten harder in recent times. Damien had an up-to-date passport, as he often travelled the world working with Médecins Sans Frontières. The last time I had done a lot of travelling, passports had not been a thing, and besides, that journey hadn't ended so well.

It was 9am local time, and since jet lag was not something that would impact us, we decided to head straight for the internet cafe that Lennox had traced Kateri's last email to.

From his complete lack of reaction, either our taxi driver was secretly a Zen Master, or the insanely chaotic traffic that he wove in and out of without seeming to even turn his head was just a typical Monday in this city.

The radio news reports were anything but ordinary, however, and had all of us listening intently. The news was a couple of days old now, but still sensational enough to have shock jocks baying for blood and asking, "Who is responsible?" to every politician they could con on to their programs.

It seemed that the day Kateri disappeared, a major traffic incident occurred throughout the city. Simultaneously every traffic light, pedestrian light, train and tram signal, as well as the control boards of the seaport and airport control tower all lit up green. Not only that, every engine in the city that was already running—from the car and aircraft engines, to simple devices like blenders and sewing machines—all surged to full power.

The result was pure chaos. Cars surged forward at top speed, tires squealing on the pavement, only to have their drivers desperately try to dodge around pedestrians stepping off the sidewalk as well as the cars from the cross-streets that were doing the same thing. Aircraft coming into land suddenly overshot their runways, causing their pilots to desperately pull up to avoid the high-rise buildings of the city. Trains slammed into each other, and people had to jump out of the way of speeding trams.

Sadly, something like that can't happen in a city as populous as Johannesburg without casualties. According to the reports, nearly a hundred people had died and four times that amount had been injured, some critically.

News agencies were trotting out scientists and conspiracy theorists in equal measure to try to explain what had happened. Popular theories ran the gamut from a Terrorist EMP device to the side-effects of a solar flare.

As we listened and watched the traffic flow past us, I marveled once again at the human creature. "That was all just two or so days ago, and yet the streets are full, and people continue on with their lives as if nothing happened."

Admonae half nodded with agreement, but said, "Not exactly nothing. Some still strive to understand. That is their light."

Beatrice sighed and added from the back seat, "But others merely strive to blame. That is their darkness."

Damien chuckled from beside her. "Jealous?"

Beatrice frowned at him, confused

"Light, dark, indifference, love. Whatever they do is their choice. Free will, my dear," Damien said.

Each of us spent the rest of the trip alone with our thoughts. The thing we dared not say aloud was that we could feel that the real culprit was not among the reasons the humans had thought up. It had been a miracle.

Of sorts.

The internet cafe was in one of the better suburbs in the west of the city. Nothing too flashy though, and frequented mainly by locals. We didn't bother to enter the cafe, however; with Lennox still in London there was nothing any of us could do to trace Kateri's movements from the computers even if there were any traces left behind. No, we were more interested in what was around it.

Silje spotted it first. Just a little way down and across the other side of the road was a church. If Kateri had in fact been here, she would have gone in. And there we would find a trail.

I should explain about Angels and places of worship. The simple fact of the matter is that there is no one 'correct' religion. Or what might be more accurate to say would be that they are all correct, from a certain point of view. Our creator is wonderful, but even we, his first creations who stood in his very presence, do not completely understand who and what He is. Humans, sadly, don't stand a ghost of a chance.

But any place that humans gather regularly to worship or commune with whatever they consider the higher power to be, builds up a resonance of sorts. How, I have no idea. Faith is a confusing concept to Angels; we don't have faith, we *know*. The best we've been able to guess is that it is somehow tied up with their free will.

The important point is that Angels inhabit a place between humans and our creator, so if we ever enter a place of worship, be it church, temple, synagogue, mosque, or even a druidic grove, we get a sense of everything that has occurred in that place. If a place of worship hasn't been used for a while the resonance fades away, but it can be quite a rush in some of the older churches in Europe I can tell you. In a way it can be quite addictive for us, especially since the Creator had been so silent since the war. It helps us to feel connected.

So, Kateri would not have passed up the chance to visit this church.

We walked across the street and through the mostly empty car park out at the front of the church. I braced myself for the usual rush of information that would come with entering any place of worship for the first time, but I was completely overwhelmed by the sheer agonising pain that flowed through me the moment I crossed the threshold.

A scream was ripped from my lips as I collapsed to my knees at the doorstep. It had never happened like this before – there had never been even the slightest hint of discomfort with all the centuries of travel and countless experiences such as this one. So unexpected was this rush of pain that it took a moment for me to realise what was causing it.

For the briefest of moments, in a mere fraction of the blink of an eye, my wings unfurled. They opened! The pain I experienced was the pain of muscles not used for several millennium suddenly being able to stretch, and then being cruelly slammed back into place. The sensation was as wonderful as it was excruciating, but, even through the pain, it seemed to carry within it a hint of promise.

I opened my eyes as my mouth closed, and I realised that I had only just stopped screaming. I was lying on the floor of the church, looking up into the concerned faces of my friends, and the confused and angry face of the priest trying to get my friends to pay attention to him.

He was rebuking them as I lay there: "I've had it with you youngsters continually causing trouble! Breaking things, stealing things, scaring my congregation!"

"Father," I croaked out, somewhat surprised at the roughness of my own voice. That had to have been some scream. I cleared my throat and tried again. "Father, I'm sorry. Migraines, they just hit me sometimes. My friend, Damien, is also my doctor - he has my medication and can explain."

Damien quickly stepped up and continued the deception, bending down to slip me a tic-tac from the packet in his pocket and then motioning Beatrice and Admonae to take care of me as he put a comforting arm about the priest, leading him away deeper into the church and talking to him in that quiet, earnest way he takes with his patients.

When they had moved away far enough to give us some privacy, Admonae whispered, "What happened? You terrified us!"

I almost told them. But obviously it had only happened to me, and somehow it seemed cruel to hold out the hope of our wings returning on the evidence of an experience I still wasn't sure I understood. "I'm … not entirely sure, sorry. Did either of you see what has happened to the Father?"

The history of the church that I received as we entered was fairly unremarkable, nothing special that would set it apart from any of the hundreds of small parish churches in this city. The current priest however, had a very singular problem.

He had lost his faith. Actually, that was not quite true. He hadn't lost his faith; it had been stolen - ripped out. And I could sense the ragged edges surrounding the hole in his soul that the theft had left behind.

Beatrice looked at the back of the priest with suspicion in her eyes. "He's missing part of his soul, if that's what you mean. Sold it probably."

Silje snorted. "You can't sell part of your soul. Look again. It's been torn out."

Orfael looked, a frown forming on her face. "It's icky. All ragged and ripped. What was taken?"

"His faith," I replied. They both turned to look at me. "And that wound in his soul won't heal by itself."

"That's very true," Damien called out from near the altar. "I've made him sleep for now, no drugs, just a minor miracle. But you're right, Joan. He's dying."

Chapter Four

Damien took Orfael by the hand and led her back to where he had laid the priest— 'Eshai' was the name the church's history had told me— down on one of the pews at the front near the altar. Admonae had stayed behind to help steady me when she suddenly stiffened and turned towards the main doors and carpark outside the church.

"He's coming," she practically snarled.

I tensed, and from force of habit reached out with my senses to try to identify which of the Fallen she had heard. Unfortunately, that meant I was completely unprepared, for the second time in as many minutes no less, for the sheer blast of heavenly power that washed over my mind as Michael touched down outside.

"Argh. What the...?" My head rang like a bell with the power he allowed to flow out from his wings over the entire area. Normally, Angels are quite circumspect when they unfurl their wings, marshalling and channeling their miraculous power like a precious resource, and only for very specific purposes. However, as he would be the first to point out, Michael is not a 'normal' Angel.

It was Michael who led the host in its war against Lightbringer. It was Michael who closed the gates of Heaven at the beginning of that war and still today guards them zealously. And it was Michael whom we had disobeyed when he called us to arms.

He never really let that one go. Let's face it, the guy could hold a grudge. But while Michael was many things, subtle is not one of them.

"Joan." Admonae moved to try to block the door. "Don't go out there. You don't have to talk to him."

I pulled myself up and took a moment to center myself before placing a hand gently on her arm. "No, Admonae, we have to. With the priest in his current state, we can't afford Michael coming in here. The church will be all he sees right now, but if he enters ..."

"He'll know," Admonae finished.

"Exactly." I squared my shoulders, my back muscles moving as if my wings were there. Admonae cast an odd look in my direction, and I could see her file that observation away for a later discussion. "Okay then," I said, "We'd better not keep the All-High Archangel waiting."

Admonae nodded, and silently walked with me out to the carpark. She kept in step with my wider stride, so we walked shoulder to shoulder on our way to face Michael, providing me with solidarity and friendship. Two things I honestly didn't think Michael understood.

To anyone just passing by, Michael would look like a normal man, probably dressed in a suit that would be far too expensive for the people who lived around here. They wouldn't see the wings he purposely left stretched out until we turned the corner, making sure that we witnessed them in all their glory before he folded them behind his back. Admonae paled and nearly stumbled at the sight of them.

Yeah, Michael was a real class act.

I've always said that a good offense was the only good defense, although if you hear Gary tell it you'd think I just liked offending people. I figured in this case either would be fine. "Michael," I started. "What has brought you down from your high horse today? Ran out of Angels to push around, figured you'd try a few humans?"

Admonae audibly gulped at my temerity, and I prayed to Heaven that Michael wouldn't notice me shaking.

Michael took a deep breath, and I could see one fist clench, but at least it didn't move towards the sword at his hip. "Watch your mouth, wingless one. Do not forget who addresses you."

"How could we?" Talking back to an Archangel was never a clever tactic, but he had pushed my buttons with the 'wingless one' comment. "You broadcasted your landing so loudly I'm surprised every Fallen between here and Cairo didn't hear it. Or was that little demonstration just for us?"

"Let them hear," Michael sneered. "What does it matter? They will not dare face me. They are unimportant now. You, however, are a surprise. What are you doing here, Trazael?"

Admonae shot me a look of surprise. "He wasn't expecting to see us," she whispered.

"It's 'Joan', asshole," I spat back. "You'd think an Archangel could remember a single name."

Admonae raised a hand to my elbow, lightly gripping it in an attempt to warn me to back off a little. I knew I was taking a risk baiting the Archangel, but I needed to keep him off balance and focused on me instead of the church.

"I refuse to refer to even one as damaged as you by a human name, Trazael. Take my civility on this point as a kindness. It will be the only one I extend to you this day." Michael looked around the suburb, seemingly for the first time since his arrival, his eyes sweeping the area like a warship's searchlight. "Admonael is correct, however. I did not expect to find one of your kind here today, let alone two. And so, I ask again, what are you doing here?"

Admonae hung her head but kept silent. She had never explained to us why she had dropped the 'l' from her name but otherwise kept it the same, rather than simply taking a new name like most of the rest of us. Now, however, was not the time to ask.

"Listen Michael," I started, raising my hands in what I hoped would be taken as a gesture of supplication, "Your arrival just caught us off guard, that's all. We're just here checking up on a friend. Why are you here?"

"There was a disturbance, I heard it." Michael hadn't stopped scanning the area, but the church, it seemed, was still considered above suspicion. "Your 'friend'," he continued, his eyes locking onto me with laser-like intensity, "It wouldn't be one of *them*, would it?"

I knew immediately who he was referring to, and to anyone who knew me it would have been obvious that my disgust at the idea was genuine. "The Fallen are not my friends."

Whatever truth Michael saw in my face seemed to reassure him, and he relaxed. Well, whatever passed as relaxed for him anyway. "Did you hear anything?"

I shook my head. "Not a thing. But then again, I am wingless."

Michael nodded to himself, completely missing the sarcasm in my voice. "True. Still, you are of God, and I expect you to inform me should anything happen that I should know about. Am I understood?"

"Perfectly, Archangel," I replied with a little mock bow. "Believe me, I understand you perfectly."

"Good." With a last look around he turned his back on us and simply vanished. It seemed that our cooperation had spared us from another display of his wings.

I let out the breath I hadn't realised I was holding and Admonae gently turned me to face her. The look on her face was one of complete puzzlement. "You just lied to an Archangel."

"Yup," I agreed. "It seems I did."

Admonae shook her head, dismissing my admission as unimportant. "And he didn't know. He couldn't tell!"

The implications of her comment were not lost on me, but I have had more dealings with Michael than most of them. "No, he couldn't. Listen, Michael is who he was made to be. I don't know how to really explain it, but the higher in power an Angel is, the less they seem to be able to deviate from how they feel the universe should be. They don't have our ability to adapt or change. His use of our proper names. for example—I think that has less to do with trying to insult us and more with the fact that he simply can't not use them. And remember, Michael isn't just an Archangel, he is the second Angel ever created.

Admonae immediately spotted the flaw in my theory. She was the truth-seeker after all. "But if you're right, then the first Angel should have been the most rigid, and... well... we all know what he did."

"Special case?" I offered, shrugging my shoulders as I did so.

Admonae frowned, obviously not convinced. "Okay, forget that for a moment. The injury to Father Eshai happened days ago, probably around the time when Kateri was last here. Michael couldn't have been talking about that when he said he heard something. He must have heard *you* when you collapsed in the entrance of the church. What happened to you? What did he hear?"

Thankfully Silje interrupted us at that point, calling from the doorway, "Damien needs both of you. If tall, dumb, and shiny has left, could you get back in here please?"

I chuckled, grateful for the delay it would impose on answering Admonae's question. She wouldn't drop it, I knew that, but I still needed time to process everything myself. "You know he's gone Silje, or else you wouldn't have stuck your head out in the first place. We're coming."

Turning to Admonae, I winked. "Can't keep the good Doctor waiting now, can we?"

Admonae fell into step beside me and whispered quietly, "Later, Joan." I nodded my acquiescence, and took her hand, squeezing it to show my gratitude that she was not planning on continuing the conversation in front of everyone.

Inside the church, Damien had moved the priest to the floor, placing his coat under the old man's head as a pillow. Father Eshai seemed to be peacefully sleeping, and somewhat auspiciously my earlier screaming fit at the doorway had emptied the church of everyone else.

Damien looked me up and down as we approached, looking for signs of injuries. "You seem in one piece Joan, you must have finally learned to control that tongue of yours. After all these centuries it finally happens, and I miss it. And what did our *better* want?"

I stuck the offending tongue out at him and made a face. "Not much, it was more of just a fly-by insulting than anything else."

Damien quirked one eyebrow at me and simply muttered, "Uh-huh." That's the problem with knowing someone for several thousand years, they learn all your tells. I needed to make some new friends.

"That aside," Damien turned his attention back to his patient, "We need to do something to stop this man's soul from completely unravelling. I don't have enough power to do it by myself, but the five of us together should be able to seal the wound."

"Will he regain his faith?" asked Orfael, her eyes pleading for a positive answer.

Damien shook his head sternly. "You know it doesn't work like that, Orfael. We cannot violate their free will. But this will heal the tear, and at least give him a chance to regain his faith himself over time, should he wish to. If we don't do this, however, that option will not be possible."

"He'll die," Orfael said quietly.

"His soul will," offered Damien. "I imagine the rest of him would probably follow soon after."

"You imagine?" My surprise at Damien's admission was obvious in the tone of my voice.

Damien sighed. "I am afraid so. I've never seen anything like this before, and trust me when I say that I can't remember the last time I said that."

Admonae was still glancing back towards the doors of the church. "But if we do this now, we will be powerless until tomorrow morning."

"And if we don't," stated Damien bluntly, "A soul is lost."

Through a lot of trial and error since we lost our wings, we had discovered that not only were we severely limited in the size of the miracles we could perform, we could only expend so much power each day. At sunrise the following day, that power would return. There were few things on earth that could threaten an Angel, even one as crippled as us, but being without that power still made us wary enough to be cautious.

"It has to be done," Beatrice said. The others looked at her, recognising as I did that her tone broached no argument. We quickly moved to sit on the floor around the priest. Perhaps there was an advantage to knowing someone for such a long time after all.

We let Damien lead the miracle, each of us supplying him with power as he wove a gauze over the poor man's injured soul. It took only minutes, but it seemed like hours, and when he was done, we all fell back, spiritually as well as physically exhausted.

"That should do it," Damien panted, sweat dripping from his brow. "Thank-you, all. That was … harder than I expected."

Admonae beat me to the obvious question. "Any idea why?"

Damien nodded. "Unfortunately, yes. It is because his faith was not just torn out and stolen, it was used. In effect, he was drained and then tossed away like an old battery. I kept being assaulted of images of crashing, twisted metal, people screaming, people being hurt. People dying."

The realisation hit me like a train, which was darkly ironic in a way. "All the accidents. Are you saying that a piece of his soul was used to power that twisted 'miracle'?"

With a sad sigh, Damien nodded. "I am afraid so, Joan."

Chapter Five

We carried Father Eshai to the little office he had in the back of the church and laid him out on his couch. Looking about the room, it was obvious that he used it for private counselling sessions with his parishioners, and I only hoped that the quality of his advice would not be affected by what had happened to him.

As was becoming a habit, Damien gave voice to my fears. "I am afraid the Father is not going to be as gentle in his advice for a while."

"Should we stop him from working?" Beatrice asked.

Damien shook his head almost immediately. "We shouldn't interfere. Interacting with his parish will be more beneficial for him than any enforced absence."

I nodded, motioning for us to leave the man asleep and head back out into the church. With everything that had happened since we arrived, I really hadn't had the chance to take a good look at the old place. The stained glass windows were fairly pedestrian in their images, but they were cared for and in good condition. Rather than expensive paintings, the walls were adorned with drawings on butcher's paper, probably from the young children who attended Sunday school here. It all gave the church a very inviting, family-oriented feeling.

It was as good a place as any to wait for tomorrow's dawn.

"We shouldn't leave the Father defenseless while he sleeps," I announced. "Damien, just how long do you think it will be before he wakes up?"

Damien shot me a quizzical glance, before casting his eyes towards Admonae, who gave an almost imperceptible nod, and then Orfael, who was looking at the doors to the outside with what could only be described as trepidation on her face.

In an off-hand way, Damien said "Oh, with what we had to do for him I'd say he'll definitely sleep through to tomorrow."

Orfael jumped on the statement. "So, we should all stay here overnight then. To protect him, I mean. Just like you said, Joan."

I'm not sure I did all that well in hiding the smirk that threatened to leap to my lips, but I nodded in acquiescence. "I did, didn't I? Ok then, make yourselves comfortable people, we're going to be here for a while."

Damien started to head back to the office where we had laid the priest down. "I'll just go make sure he's going to be comfortable enough."

"Uh-huh," Admonae muttered in my ear, "And to make sure he actually stays asleep. We are doing this for Orfael, I know, but it does mean that whatever we are chasing will get another dozen or so hours up on us. Do you really think we can afford the time?"

I honestly didn't know the answer to that, but I also thought we all needed some time to process what we had encountered so far. "We will have to, Admonae. She'd be worse than useless to us if we left now."

"At least it will give us a chance to talk about what happened earlier with Michael," Admonae added.

"Yeah." I didn't bother to try to hide my lack of enthusiasm "Great."

Admonae snorted, but as she walked off to talk to Orfael she chuckled, "Later, Joan."

Later turned out to be 4am. We had spent the afternoon lounging about the church, with Damien checking on the Father periodically and otherwise dusting and cleaning just about every surface in the building. Orfael opened the little kitchenette and made a seemingly endless supply of tea and scones for the parishioners who popped in to pray or who were looking for their priest. Admonae took it upon herself to talk to anyone who came in who was obviously upset about something, playing the role of counsellor, and simply spending a lot of time listening. She often said that most people just needed to know there was someone who cared enough to listen to them. Silje tuned the old organ that probably hadn't been played in years and effortlessly filled the church with a beautiful, almost etheric melody that brought a smile to everyone who entered.

Beatrice and I shared watch. For what, I had no idea, but it meant that the others left me alone for the most part.

By early morning, a light fog had settled on the streets, muffling the already quiet suburb into almost complete silence. It was peaceful rather than eerie, and the moisture in the air smelled sweet.

"I've always loved this time of morning." Admonae joined me by the entrance, leaning up against the open door. "It feels so full of promise, like the world born anew each day."

"I never realised you were so much of a poet Admonae," I replied, keeping my voice down so as not to disturb the others. "You did some good work yesterday, with the people who came in with problems You're a good listener."

Admonae shrugged. "Discovering the truth is what I do. And now I find it is time I listen to you. What happened?"

I had never lied to one of my friends before, and while I have to admit I entertained the thought for a brief moment, it was never really going to fly.

No pun intended.

I took a deep, slow breath, and allowed my eyes to focus on anything but Admonae. "You have to keep this to yourself, at least for now. I still need to work through what this might mean before I answer a lot of questions, especially from Beatrice or Orfael."

Admonae nodded, concern darkening her face. "You know I'd never break anyone's confidence Joan, but you are starting to scare me now. What's going on? What was Michael after?"

"Me, I think, just like you said. But he didn't seem to know that. I think he 'heard' what happened to me when I first entered the church, just as you surmised, and he came ready for a battle. I think if he had realised I was the source of what he heard he may have killed me then and there."

"Kill you? Why?" Admonae tried to work through what I was saying. "What happened to you? You weren't falling, we'd all know it if that was happening."

"I don't really know," I started. Admonae opened her mouth to protest but I signaled her that I was going to continue. "All I can tell you is what it felt like."

"Okay," Admonae offered, "Fair enough. What did it feel like?"

Despite my resolve to tell her, I stammered to a stop. It was suddenly very nearly impossible to go on. How could I admit to one of my oldest friends that I thought that the one thing we had yearned for more than anything else in creation had happened, however briefly, to me?

Admonae reached out and gently touched my arm. "We could all see how much pain whatever this was caused you, Joan. You were in agony. You had us all so scared. You've always been the strongest of us, and to have you just collapse like that was frightening enough, but to have you thinking that Michael would try to kill you because of it?"

"My wings opened." In the end I just blurted it out. I felt Admonae's fingers on my arm grip involuntarily, her nails digging into my skin. "Just for the briefest of moments," I rushed to add. "As we crossed the threshold of the church, I swear it felt like they opened, or at least they tried to, started to, and my body reacted as if my muscles had completely atrophied. The physical pain it caused was like nothing I have ever felt before, and I've been burned at the stake."

Admonae's voice broke as she strove to acknowledge my confession. "I could see that."

"But I'd go through it all again in a second." I realised that I had been staring at my feet as I spoke, afraid to meet Admonae's gaze, afraid of what I might see in her eyes as I told her. My arms were tense, my body ready for fight or flight; I had unconsciously braced myself for anger, rage, or at least disbelief.

I wasn't prepared to hear her quiet sob.

Admonae wrapped her arms about me, pulling me into a tight embrace as she silently burst into tears, sobbing uncontrollably into my shoulder.

Slowly, I returned the embrace, holding her as she rode out the emotions coursing uncontrollably through her.

There is a benefit to knowing someone as long as we have, as it turns out. You always know when words will simply get in the way.

Chapter Six

Admonae calmed and quieted after a time, but didn't let go until the sun broached the horizon, and we all felt our meagre, but oh so welcomed power, return. As one, we gathered our gear and headed out into the dawn's light.

Silje had kept up her playing all through the night, the soft music blending into the background after a while. By morning, the melody had evolved into something we all somehow inherently recognised as representing Kateri. As we prepared to leave, Silje explained what she had been doing: "Using the church as an anchor, I used the music to catch a hint of where Kateri had gone after leaving here. She headed overland, northwards from the city. The trail is quite cold now, but through her melody I have been able to attune myself to it. I should be able to follow her anywhere now."

"We need to head north then," I stated, and the others simply nodded and waited for my orders. It was something they had been doing for centuries now, expecting me to lead whenever trouble struck. I hadn't planned to set myself up for any leadership role, it had just happened. Admonae's comment last night about how they saw me as the strongest of them worried me a little, but I couldn't quite articulate why.

"Beatrice, contact Lennox and Adelita and let them know what's been happening. Tell Adelita to get us a four-wheel drive of some kind, with United Nations papers. Damien, contact Médecins sans Frontières and find out what centers they have set up between here and Egypt, we can stop in at them as an excuse to be travelling. Find out what supplies they might need and pick them up."

"Egypt?" Damien queried. "Do you really think she got that far?"

"I don't know, Damien," I shrugged, "but I'd rather have a plausible reason for travelling, no matter how far we have to go."

"What should I do?" Orfael asked eagerly. Yesterday she was scared enough that we had to delay leaving, today it seemed she was determined to make up for that.

"You and I, Orfael, need to go shopping. Food, water, medicine, camping gear, everything we will need to head north. I'll pick up a rifle, but I want you to keep an eye out for small but hard to get items that we could use as bribes. I get the feeling that we're going to be crossing a few borders."

"I don't like guns." Orfael frowned at me, but I was not in the mood to coddle her this morning.

"That's okay, you're not getting one," I said firmly.

Beatrice sniggered quietly at Orfael's guppy impersonation, but Damien stepped in before an argument could start. "Right then, lots to do. We'll meet back here at midday. That should be enough time."

"Midday," I agreed, and Admonae guided Orfael away under the guise of catching a taxi for the three of us to share to the city center. Smiling at Damien, I leaned in close and whispered, "Ever the peacemaker."

He actually bowed, the cheeky sod. "I am what I am. How are you this morning though, Joan? No ill effects from whatever hit you yesterday?"

"None at all, I feel fine." Surprisingly, I did. Damien peered at me for a moment but seemed to detect my honesty.

"Feel like talking about it?" He enquired.

"Nope."

Damien nodded once, turned, and started to walk towards the street. "As you wish. Call me if you need me."

A few hours later Beatrice pulled up to the church carpark in a bright blue UN hummer, complete with flags, just as I was finishing up a phone call with Margaret. "Okay, sorry again that I'm going to be away longer than I thought. Cuddle Noah for me. Thank-you. Bye!"

Beatrice and Damien jumped out of the Humvee to start loading the many bags and boxes of supplies Orfael and I had gathered. Orfael pointed out what was in each box as I held the long sports bag holding the less than legal items I had managed to collect.

Damien was in a particularly good mood as he bent to pick up the first of the boxes. "How is Noah? I haven't seen the old guy in years."

"As ornery as ever. He's getting completely spoiled by my neighbour at the moment. Being treated like a King."

"Noah?" Orfael's tone made it clear that she thought we might have been playing a trick on her.

I nodded. "My cat."

"Oh." Orfael seemed saddened at the simple explanation. "I don't like cats."

"I know, that's why I've never introduced you. Your realm is all flying creatures Orfael, it's no wonder you're not keen on cats."

Orfael looked thoughtful for a moment before accepting the point. "Why did you call him Noah, anyway?"

I smiled. "He doesn't like water either."

Before she could make her mind up about whether I was trying to make fun of her or telling the truth, Beatrice loaded two boxes into her arms and shooed Orfael away in the direction of the car.

Once we were all loaded up Beatrice hopped into the driver's seat and gunned the engine. She explained that she would have to do all the driving until we were out of the city at least, as Adelita had set her up with the official UN representative identification. Silje would ride next to her in the middle front seat, to better direct our journey following Kateri's trail. I called 'shotgun', causing Orfael to startle and flatten herself against the side of the car, Damien bundling her into the Humvee through the rear door before she could make a scene, and Admonae stepped in after him to claim the other window seat.

"I swear that she gets more like her birds every day," I muttered as Beatrice pulled into the traffic and started towards the northern suburbs of the city.

"Think about it," Beatrice replied. "Each of us was given our realm for a reason. Does it really surprise you that she's the way she is? Or Damien, or I, or any of us for that matter?"

I shrugged, conceding the point. "No, I guess not. But you and Damien are useful, at least."

"We each have our uses and our strengths, Joan," Beatrice added in an admonishing tone. I glanced into the back seat to see Orfael staring up out the sunroof and up into the sky, her mouth agape. Beatrice followed my gaze and stifled a chuckle. "Some are just well hidden."

I nodded. "*Very* well hidden."

Urban life sped past the windows of the car, smaller buildings replacing skyscrapers, houses replacing businesses, then fields replacing houses. By the time the sun began to set we had left the city far behind us. Damien opened a thermos of tea he had prepared earlier and handed around some snacks. We could, of course, go for days without food or sleep, but they had become a habit that was, while not difficult, at the very least unpleasant to break.

So, when you don't have to stop, why would you? Besides, Damien had excellent taste in tea. Not as good as Gary's of course, but Gary's café was half a world away.

By sharing out the driving between the four of us and only stopping for fuel we made good time towards the border of Zimbabwe, arriving just 14 hours after we had started. The trail still led north, but according to Silje it was slowly becoming stronger, which meant that we were at least travelling a little faster than Kateri had.

Crossing the border, however, took a maddening three hours, and wouldn't have even been that fast if not for the little 'trinkets' Orfael had chosen to bring along. Apparently like her ravens, she is exceptionally good at spotting 'shiny' things. The temptation to simply miracle our way past the border guards was immense, but

Admonae wisely counseled us against using our limited powers unless they were really needed.

We continued north, through Zambia and the Congo, Kateri's trail getting slowly stronger all the time. So much so that I was even happy to stop for a half day at each of the Médecins sans Frontières camps that Damien had mapped out for us. They were certainly pleased to see us; or at least they were pleased to see the supplies of the hard-to-get medicines that Damien had managed to procure.

At Kisangani, the trail turned slightly eastwards, pointing straight at Khartoum in Sudan. I passed this information onto the others as we were finishing what passed for coffee at the fuel station we had just filled up at.

"Well, we know she won't be going to the Dahkla Oasis," Beatrice stated with a finality that would broach no argument. "So be ready for the path to change direction again, probably once we cross the border. She may be trying to throw any pursuit off track."

Beatrice's belief that Kateri would avoid the Dahkla Oasis was practically innate - one of the last orders we were all given by the Archangel Raphael before being dispatched to Earth was to never approach the resting places of the seven trees of creation. That oasis had grown up on one of those sites during the Ancient Egyptian empire and was now the location of a UN sponsored archeological dig. We didn't even know which of the seven trees would be buried there, but his command was ingrained within us; we were not to go there.

I find it weird now that I never asked 'Why?' It would be practically instinctual for me to do so now, but back then, as a very new Angel, I guess I took a lot more on faith.

For now, however, Sudan beckoned.

Chapter Seven

The Humvee crested a hill overlooking the Congo-Sudan border. Down below, barely a kilometer away, stood the border post between the two countries. Two small army bases, side by side and each on their own side of the border, with the only road from Kisangani to Khartoum running straight through the middle of both.

I had expected a certain amount of trouble at this border crossing. The two countries were currently not on the best of terms, and I assumed that in a best-case scenario we would just lose most of our bribe items and medicines. Worst case, we would be forced to miracle our way through in order to keep travelling.

What I didn't expect was the place to be empty.

You know those noises that let you know immediately that something is very wrong? It turns out that silence can be worse.

A lot worse.

As we approached what should have been a closed boom-gate across the road we were able to see army vehicles randomly stopped all over the compound. There were no obvious signs that there had been a battle; no smoke, no scorch marks or craters from rockets or artillery; but equally there were no people. Or bodies.

Beatrice was driving again, as we had expected we would need to show her UN credentials to the guards. As we crossed under the open boom-gate both Damien and Silje spoke up simultaneously.

Damien's somber, "They're all dead," clashed jarringly with Silje's petulant, "I'm hungry."

The five of us all turned to stare at Silje, but any snarky remark remained unsaid. Her eyes were opened wide but the pupils like mere pinpricks. Silje spoke again, and a shudder went up my spine. "The light hurts us, but we are so hungry. So hungry."

"Okay," Damien said softly. "That's not creepy at all."

We needed answers, so I needed to get the group moving. "Beatrice," I started, "Kill the engine and lock the doors once we're out. Damien, make sure Silje is secure and stay with her in the car. The rest of us, we need to check this out."

Beatrice baulked at the order. "Do you really think we should leave her behind like this?"

I nodded emphatically. "Yes, Beatrice. She'll only get hurt if we take her out, and Damien will be staying with her. Think of her like our coal mine canary, she's warned us there is something wrong, now leave her in her cage and let us find out what is going on."

Luckily Silje showed no signs of wanting to do anything other than bury her face in her arms, almost as if she was trying to hide from the light.

A quick walk to the actual border crossing allowed us to see that whatever had happened to the army base on this side of the border had also occurred over on the Sudan side. It was as eerily quiet on their side of the chain link fence as it was here. The only difference was that there was a jeep about half a kilometer further up the road lying on its side after running off the road.

"Someone tried to escape whatever happened here," I said, pointing to the derelict jeep.

"They didn't get too far though," Admonae observed.

Beatrice called to us from the door to the main administration building. "Joan! Admonae! Come check this out. This door has been barricaded from the inside."

Orfael volunteered to run up the road to check the overturned jeep for survivors, and Admonae and I went to join Beatrice. Sure enough, a glance through the windows showed that the soldiers had pushed desks on their sides and stacked them against all the exterior doors, and even moved some cupboards to try to block interior ones. Strangely though, the outside of the building was showing no signs of someone trying to get in, and all the barricades still stood unmoved.

"Okay, the three of us should be able to push this door open. Hopefully, we'll find some answers inside." I opened the flimsy flyscreen door and set my shoulder against the main door.

"So long as we don't get shot trying," Beatrice commented, still peering in through one of the windows.

I turned to our resident seeker. "Admonae, anyone alive inside?"

She closed her eyes for a moment, and I saw her face pale. "No life."

I nodded. "Right then, so no one is going to shoot us."

Admonae was shaking her head, and there was a sadness in her eyes. "No Joan, not just no people, no life. Not a single fly, ant, cockroach or mite is alive in there."

"Jeepers," Beatrice breathed.

Admonae turned to look at her. "Jeepers? Really?"

Beatrice shrugged. "Scooby Doo reruns are kind of a thing at the moment."

"Can we concentrate here, people?" They both snapped their heads around to look at me. "Silje's warning had two parts. Whatever did this is still here and hungry, but it doesn't like the light. I personally do not want to be here at sundown, and that's only about an hour away."

They both joined me at the door, and we pushed. It took a few moments but eventually we felt the makeshift barricade behind it give way and the door opened, the smell of cordite hitting me as soon as it did. This was where all the fighting had happened. Once past the barricade and through the entranceway into the building proper we were witness to a rather grisly sight. Skeletons, still in their army fatigues but picked clean to the bone, were lying crouched in corners and up on desks. Every weapon they possessed had been fired, their magazines completely emptied, and from the looks of it every shot had been aimed at the floor.

Almost every shot. In the commandant's office we found his skeleton still in his chair, a tell-tale bullet hole in his left temple.

"That's a whole lot of fear," I said quietly, blessing the old soldier as I did so, wishing his soul to rest.

Beatrice was still out in the main office. "But why were they all firing at the floor? It doesn't make any sense."

From where she was standing by a window, Admonae spoke up. "It might, and I think I've discovered the answer. Come, take a look at this."

We headed over to join her and looked out into the compound, still as deathly quiet as when we left it. The sun was still just over three quarters of an hour from setting, but the nearby hills had started to cast long shadows across a far part of the compound. It was into one of these shadows that Admonae was pointing. I squinted, unable at first to see what she might be referring to.

And then it hit me. "Is the sand moving?"

"Not exactly," she answered.

"Something just under the sand is moving?" Beatrice offered.

Admonae nodded. "Lots and lots of somethings."

"Hells Bells," I whispered.

Beatrice turned to look at me. "What?"

I returned her look with a shrug of my own. "You watch Scooby Doo, I read Jim Butcher. So, sue me."

Beatrice rolled her eyes at me. "Be that as it may, we have to get out of here."

"We can't," I stated, causing both of them to look questioningly at me. "Remember what my realm is, guys? When the HQ's of these two bases don't hear from them, they'll send a squad or three to investigate. And when they don't report back, they'll send a brigade. A lot of soldiers will die, and whatever this is will spread. We can't let that happen."

Admonae nodded. "It can't be just a coincidence that Kateri came through here. This is another one of those twisted miracle-things, isn't it? Like all those simultaneous accidents back in Johannesburg."

Both Beatrice and I agreed. "A plague of insects. Suitably biblical don't you think?" Pulling out the little walky-talky connected back to the Humvee, I thumbed the transmit button. "Damien, we're staying for a bit. Join us, will you?"

We met Damien at the door to the administration building, showed him what we had found, and brought him up to speed. "So... bugs. What type do you think, Damien?"

After crouching down to examine a skeleton, Damien replied, "Based on the condition of the skeletons and where we are, something from the family Scarabaeidae, the common scarab beetle, I'd say."

"I doubt there's anything 'common' about these things, but you're probably right. They've just been miraculously enhanced," Admonae said. "So, what do we do about it?"

The ominous click of the hammer on a pistol being drawn back interrupted our planning, and its wielder standing in the open doorway spoke in a rather authoritative tone: "You are not going to be doing anything other than answering my questions. Arrest these people!"

They wore the fatigues and patches of the Sudanese army and spoke Arabic, but when you have been on this planet as long as we have, languages are something you've had plenty of time to learn. The fact that they had been able to sneak into the building behind Damien without me noticing, however, was not something the others would let me forget in a hurry.

The soldier with the gun pointed at us had identified himself as Captain Kariem. He quickly got us all handcuffed and sitting down in the old Commandant's office. Silje had been collected from the car, but she had apparently tried to bite the soldier who reached in for her, so she was gagged as well as tied to her chair. She had curled her legs up to her chest and was mumbling constantly into the gag.

Beatrice's UN credentials and the fact that the skeletal bodies of the soldiers made it look like they had died years ago had gone some way to tempering the captain's reaction to us, but he made it clear that we were not to consider ourselves off the hook just yet.

Kariem turned back from looking out the window to face us once again. "Let us try this one more time. You say you are travelling between medical outposts delivering supplies, but we found very few of those in your car. Only one of you has UN papers, and yet you all claim to work for them. This young girl is obviously crazy, and you leave her unguarded and unrestrained."

Damien attempted to break in. "I told you, she is under my care. I'm a doctor and—"

"Then I am glad you are not *my* doctor," Kariem cut him off. "But that is all just window dressing. What you have not yet told me is what happened to my men here!"

I tried to mollify the increasingly agitated officer. "We told you we don't know, we only just arrived before you."

"And I told you," Kariem slammed his fist onto the desk for emphasis, "I do not believe you!" He stood straight again, pausing to regain his temper. "Let me tell you what I do believe. I believe that my men have been killed, and that you, or your people, are responsible. Some experimental chemical weapon, perhaps? Maybe biological? I do not know. What I do know is that you know more than you are admitting. I would bet my life on that fact."

Suddenly Silje stopped rocking and murmuring under the gag, going completely rigid in her chair. Through the window, the last rays of sunlight disappeared.

And then, from outside, the screaming started.

You know what I said earlier about silence being worse? I take it all back.

Chapter Eight

Instinct cut in the moment I heard the gunfire start. Screaming for the others to get down, I pushed off with my legs and launched myself, and my chair, into Silje's, sending both of us sprawling onto the floor. The shattering of the glass in the windows heralded the first of the bullets to tear through the office. Beatrice, Damien and Admonae had followed my command without thinking and were safely on their sides against the thick timber of the floor, and the captain had followed suit, experience moving him to flip the desk up onto its side for extra cover.

His lieutenant and Orfael were not as lucky. A sickening wet thud was followed by the younger man slumping against the wall and sliding down it, a trail of blood left behind to mar the white surface. His falling back had stopped Orfael from getting completely out of the way, and a red stain swelled up on her shirt from the bullet lodged in her shoulder.

"Who is attacking?" Yelled Kariem over the gunfire. "Your people or the Congolese?"

"Neither!" I shouted back. "That's your men shooting. They're being eaten alive by millions of scarabs, and they're panic firing. We can help, just get us out of these handcuffs before we're all dead!"

Kariem shook his head and grabbed his pistol from where it lay on the ground. "No. Not until I check this out. We are under attack, and no fantasy story is going to get you free."

"We don't have time for this!" Beatrice grunted with frustration, and we could all feel her miracle flood the room. Fixing the captain with her gaze, she spoke softly, but her simple words cut through all the turmoil: "Trust us".

Kariem moved like a man possessed, and quickly freed each of us from our restraints. He wasn't actually possessed of course, our miracles don't work like that, he simply just now understood one singular truth better than anything he had ever understood in his life.

We were on his side.

Beatrice and Admonae started to lift the now comatose Silje while Damien moved to place pressure on Orfael's wound. I started to point out buildings through the window to the captain. "Kariem, they're coming up from the ground. Inside the buildings won't be safe enough. Order your men to climb onto the roof, that will buy them a little time."

"We could head for the ATVs?" Kariem countered, pointing out through the darkness to the Sudan base on the other side of the border.

I shook my head. "They'd never make it. Get them up on the roof, now. Damien, you too, with Orfael, they'll smell the blood. Beatrice, leave Silje with Admonae, I'm going to need you outside."

Kariem was already giving the order into his walkie-talkie but stopped as he saw us leaving. "What are we buying time for? What are you going to do?"

Admonae shrugged as she lifted Silje. "Knowing Joan, something foolhardy."

As we headed through the building to the main door, I could hear Kariem's men already obeying his order and scrambling up the sides of the building. "Thank goodness they're well trained enough to listen to him. Beatrice, that push you gave him back in the office didn't drain you, did it?"

She shook her head in reply. "Not even close. Turns out that he wanted to believe us anyway, the rest of his demeanor was just an act to test us and not lose face with his officers."

The scene outside was one of chaos. Soldiers were clambering up whatever building was closest, causing the exterior lights to swing wildly from their cords and giving a surreal edge to the compound. Tell-tale mounds of black scuttling scarab beetles scattered across the base marked where some of their comrades had fallen. At least with everyone concentrating on climbing, the gunfire had paused, but I knew that would not stay true for long.

Beatrice ran up to our Humvee and leapt up onto its bonnet. "Joan! They are all converging on this side of the base. Whatever you are planning on doing, you're going to have to do it quickly or we're going to be knee deep in them."

We were running out of time, and while the four of us could miracle our way out of danger, there was no way I was going to abandon these soldiers.

"Joan!" Damien called out from the roof of the administration building. "Over there! The fuel!"

Trying to see what he was pointing at meant a quick dash across the compound towards the main gate, but sure enough there sat a gravity-fed fuel pump connected to a huge cylindrical tank.

"Beatrice!" I called out, as I started to run towards the pump, "I'll need you for this! Get over there."

Dodging as best we could, the two of us sprinted over to the tank. We had each managed to pick up the odd scarab on our legs as we ran and stood there beating them off each other for a few precious seconds before we turned our attention to the tank.

Beatrice groaned when she recognised the symbols on it "Joan, it's diesel."

I grabbed the nozzle meant to refuel the vehicles and braced myself against the tank wall. "Doesn't matter. Just use your power to pressurize the tank. I'll take care of the rest."

Beatrice had obviously grown more accustomed to doing what I told her to do than I realised, as she turned to the tank and placed both hands upon it even as she continued to explain why it wouldn't work. "But Joan, diesel fuel doesn't catch like petrol. It just won't burn. There's no way to get it alight easily."

I turned to lock eyes with Beatrice and mimicked her earlier statement to the captain, albeit without any miraculous power behind it. "Trust me."

Beatrice turned and poured her essence into the tank, creating a miracle to put its contents under tremendous pressure. Before one of the seals could rupture, I turned the hose towards the swarm of beetles and pulled the trigger.

Despite my preternatural strength, the pressure of the fuel gushing from the hose took all that I had to be able to direct the flow and not be knocked off my feet. Needless to say, I was very glad of the tank wall I had braced myself against. Beatrice must have poured all her remaining power into that miracle to get pressure like this, but it had worked, and the spray was able to cover the entire area of the compound, even splashing a little up against the administration building on the far side. As the fuel spread, I could see Captain Kariem pointing and shouting something to Daniel, probably the same concerns Beatrice had voiced only moments before.

With the pressure Beatrice had introduced it did not take long to empty the tank. The fuel covered the compound and most, if not all, of the scarabs, but it had only slowed them down. She pulled her hands off the tank as it emptied and sagged, the effort draining her physically as well as spiritually. "Joan, what now? We need this to burn. We need fire."

I shook my head, taking two steps closer to the fuel-covered mass of scarabs. "We don't need fire, Beatrice. This is the result of a foul miracle. We need *Holy* Fire."

Every Angel has an emblem, a device that we use to extend and direct our power. These emblems differ depending on who the Angel is, and what job they have been sent to do. I had not had the power I needed to draw my emblem since the war, since we chose not to fight; none of us had. I had tried, too many times to count, and while I could always feel it there, it was always just out of reach, and I could never get it to manifest. Looking back, I have no idea why I decided that today, it would work. Perhaps it was what happened back at the church in Johannesburg. Possibly it was because we were responding to a twisted use of miraculous powers. Quite conceivably, I was simply being deluded.

And maybe, just maybe, that is what faith feels like.

I reached my right hand over my left shoulder and heard Beatrice gasp behind me as she realised what I was about to try. I don't know if I paused or not, but I felt like I was moving in slow motion, as if hours were passing as I stretched, reached, and then finally closed the fingers of my hand.

And I felt it.

With a feeling of indescribable joy, I pulled and drew my emblem out into the world once more. Beatrice whooped behind me, and I could see Admonae over on the roof of the Administration building move to distract the captain while her mouth hung agape in surprise.

Like I said, every Angel has their own emblem, suited to their personality and the job they were given to perform. Damien's was a small clay jar that held an endless supply of a liquid that would heal anything. Beatrice's was a scale she used to identify the truth and guilt in any situation. Admonae had a mirror, but I had no idea what it did. Silje had her flute and would spend hours longingly looking through music store windows at their selection of silvery instruments. I hadn't known Orfael before the war, and so had never seen hers. Afterwards, when we had lost the ability to make them manifest, it was considered too painful a subject to ask about.

Mine, like Michael's, was a sword I could will into flame. Nowhere near as impressive as his was of course, but what can I say, it's a classic for a reason.

One touch from the holy flame on the sword was all it took to have the fuel-soaked sand and scarabs burst into cleansing fire. The squealing, high pitched noise of all those little chitinous bodies exploding in the heat is not something I would care to hear again any time soon, but right then it was the sound of salvation.

The roaring flames that now stood between us and the building meant that my sword was nicely concealed from view by the soldiers, and while I was certainly reticent to put it away again after being without it for so long, the mission and maintaining our anonymity was too important to sacrifice for selfish reasons.

Reluctantly, I took one last longing look at that part of me that had been missing for so long. It felt like I was seeing it for the first time, and I swear I saw details along the blade that I had never noticed before. It was like my emblem had changed and grown during the time I wasn't able to draw it, and I was desperate to keep looking at it. Good sense prevailed, however, and willed it back into the ether. All too easily, it disappeared once more.

Immediately Beatrice's arms were about me, spinning me around and crushing me to her chest. "You did it! You drew your sword! I thought that was your plan, but I never dared to think it would actually work. But you did it! And without falling! Joan… You haven't fallen? No, I know you haven't fallen! So how?"

Gently, I worked my way out of her grip. "Later, please. Let's get these people to safety, then I promise to tell you everything."

If the captain and his men noted that the burning sands kept aflame quite a while longer than the amount of fuel would normally have allowed for, no one thought to mention it. Over the next half hour Damien saw to the various bites and bullet wounds on the soldiers, and Orfael, her own wound miraculously healed, did what she could to move people off the roof and over to the relative safety of the vehicles they arrived in. Damien told me later that Silje had snapped out of her fugue the moment I drew my sword, but he had kept her back from helping to maintain the story with the captain.

Our UN Humvee was a blackened mess from the flames and smoke, but it had withstood the heat and, other than losing its little blue flags that used to sit on the bonnet and roof, had escaped relatively unharmed. I was beginning to understand what people saw in these tank-like vehicles, although I don't think I'll ever get used to seeing them used to do the weekly shopping.

Admonae took over negotiating with the captain while Damien and Orfael finished up with the last of the wounded. It wasn't until Orfael called me over while pointing at my own legs that I looked down and realised my trousers were a tattered, blood-soaked mess.

"It looks worse than it is," I tried to say, as she pulled me over to where Damien was finishing up with the last of the soldiers. "Seriously, it's just blood from the scarab bites."

Damien looked up and motioned me to sit, while casting a glance over to where Captain Kariem was standing next to Admonae and watching us. "And these bugs carry diseases, so the wounds need to be cleaned and disinfected, don't argue."

I sat and submitted to his steady hands cutting away the rest of the trousers and applying the disinfectant solution. He used a bare minimum, as it was just for show; we were immune to illness, disease, and poisons after all. I did notice Kariem relax a little as Damien started his ministrations, however, which gave Admonae another chance to draw him back to what she was saying.

"Orfael," Damien got her attention while he worked, "When Admonae secures our exit we won't want to hang about too long in case Captain Kariem changes his mind. Could you go and get the car ready?"

"Can I drive?" The question was directed at Damien, but I caught her motioning to me with her eyes.

"Sure," Damien replied. "But don't start the engine until Admonae gives you the nod. We don't want to spook anyone."

Orfael practically skipped off towards the car and Damien started to put away his bandages and bottles. "Joan, just to make sure. I actually saw what I think I saw, didn't I?"

I nodded, trying to keep the smile off my face and failing utterly. "Yes, you did."

He continued to pack away his supplies, not quite looking up at me. "Keeping secrets from us, or was that a first?"

"A first. Or at least the first time in a very, very long time." I reached out and laid a hand on his arm, causing him to stiffen. "I haven't fallen, Damien. But something is happening. Something big."

"I know." Of all the responses I thought Damien might come back with, his simple acknowledgement caught me by surprise. Then he moved aside his jacket where it lay on the ground, surrounded by the bandages and bottles from his medical kit, and I saw it. His clay jar. This time the gasp of surprised joy was my own.

"I know," he repeated.

Chapter Nine

At Khartoum, the trail turned north-west, and Damien's face paled. When the Dahkla Oasis came into view five days later, he was practically white.

So far, nothing out of the ordinary had happened since the border post. Khartoum itself had been a quick chance to refuel and restock, and while the rest of the journey through the Sudan allowed Damien to visit three medical centres run by Médecins sans Frontieres, it did little to cheer him up. The Sudan-Egypt border didn't cause us any problems, and from there it was a long straight road for a day and a half to the Dahkla Oasis.

One of the few places on Earth we were forbidden to step foot.

Damien was taking this latest evidence of Kateri's disobedience harder than the rest of us because the Archangel that had given us the command, Raphael, was his Archangel. His domain of healers came directly from Raphael. Orfael, however, seemed to have picked up the new hobby of needling Damien about where we were headed and his refusal to accept that fact. Right now, this consisted of her reading from the Wikipedia page she had brought up on her phone.

"The Dahkla Oasis lies some 800 km south-south-east of Cairo, surrounded by the wastes of the eastern Sahara, centered at 25 degrees 30 minutes North and 29 degrees 7 minutes East. The oasis is some 80 kilometers west to east and 25 kilometers at its widest. The local economy is based in agriculture, and there are no known mineral or other viable resources."

"Yes Orfael, we know where it is," Damien practically growled "It's right in front of us, after all."

Orfael grinned, enjoying herself far too much. "Okay then, how about something more relevant. See the huge camp down there? Lennox emailed us about it. That would be part of the Dahkla Oasis Project which has been conducting a study of..."

"I could always put the bullet back into your shoulder," Damien warned.

Orfael continued unabashed, "... the ruins here since 1978, supported by a number of universities and organizations. Among these have been Monash University, The University of Durham, the University of Toronto, the—"

"Enough!" Damien's shout had all of us turning in surprise. I don't think I had ever seen the gentle Damien this angry before. Things were about to get out of hand.

"Okay folks," I said, using my parade-ground voice to cut through the tension, "It's been a long, hard road. This bickering is not like us, and it needs to stop. *Now*."

Silence descended in the car.

To give her credit, Orfael was the first to speak up. "I'm sorry. Truly Damien, I should not have done that. It is just that you are always so, you know, together, about everything. I guess seeing you less than sure for once made me feel a little better. Because that's the way I feel all the time."

Between her admission and the honest, contrite look on her face, whatever remark Damien had planned died unsaid. He just nodded and pulled Orfael into a hug. Not quite knowing what to expect, she stiffened, but then he whispered something in her ear, and she relaxed against him, returning his hug warmly.

From the front seats, Beatrice, Silje, and I watched them until they pulled apart, and then from the rear bench where she had been typing on her phone Admonae gently brought the subject back up once more. "This last email from Lennox has actually shed some light on why Kateri may have come here. We all know that her realm is the environment—well, it seems that's what this dig is all about too."

"We know," she continued when Damien nodded his acquiescence, "that this place was once a lush land full of life, and not the desert it is now. The Dahkla Oasis Project set up by these universities is less about the archaeological ruins, although that is helping to fund the dig, and more about a long-term study of the interaction between environmental changes and human activity in the Western Desert of Egypt. The study is meant to include all the time since the first incursion of humans in the Middle Pleistocene, perhaps 400,000 years ago, down to the 21st century oasis farmers, and all the human activity and all the changing environmental conditions during that time, including modern global warming."

"Okay," Damien started, "It makes sense she would be interested in this place. But I still don't see that as being enough to push her to go against what we were told. I mean, even the Fallen don't go there."

I reacted without thinking, "I keep telling you she hasn't fa… Hang on. You're right, Damien! The Fallen don't go there. I need you to concentrate, Raphael is your Archangel. What exactly did he say?"

Damien cocked his head to one side as he tried to see where I was going with this. "Exactly?"

I nodded and grinned at him. "*Exactly.*"

Damien closed his eyes, sending his mind back hundreds of thousands of years to the last time he stood in front of his Archangel. Damien's voice, when he eventually spoke, carried an almost wistful quality. "Michael was there, with Raphael. He had just finished saying something to Raphael and was annoyed. He left, and Raphael turned to those of us who looked to him. 'My Angels,' he said, 'When you go to Earth you will each perform the task you were created for. You will face trials, but you will prevail. I ask one more thing of each of you, however. For your own safety, please do not visit the resting places of the Trees of Creation. The Trees no longer need our attentions, and those places are not for us.'"

As he finished, one tear rolled down his cheek. Blinking, he pulled himself back to the present, looking at me with hope I had not seen since the attack at the border post. "For your own safety."

I nodded and repeated his words back to him. "For your own safety. All Michael would tell us was 'Don't go there and don't ask questions'."

"So, we're going to do this then?" Damien asked.

"Kateri did," Silje offered with a shrug.

"And so will we," I stated.

We drove into the town surrounding the dig and parked next to one of the larger public houses. Not knowing how long we would be here, Admonae went in and arranged rooms for us as we unloaded our gear. With our accommodations settled, we took the short walk towards the dig site itself.

Damien had argued that he should be the first to enter the dig site, with the rest of us staying a little further back in case Raphael's warning was still relevant and something dire happened to him. I thought that I was the best one to go in first for exactly the same reason, but he would not be persuaded.

The three of us stood by the last building before the dig area, watching Damien stride across the empty ground, getting closer and closer without anything untoward occurring. He had even started to get a bit of a jauntiness to his step when he suddenly fell, face-first, onto the ground.

With a cry, Orfael was off running to him, ignoring my call for her to wait. Beatrice and I took off after her, but she is damned fast when she had a mind to be. As she pulled up alongside Damien she twisted, and we could see her eyes roll back into her head as she too collapsed onto the dirt.

I put my arm out to stop Beatrice from following Orfael and we both pulled up just before reaching the prone pair. They were both lying on the ground about a meter away, and so far, neither Beatrice nor I were feeling any symptoms of whatever had hit them.

Then Damien moaned.

"He's alive!" Beatrice exclaimed.

Watching the slow rise and fall of his chest, I voiced the only conclusion I could. "He's asleep?"

"Asleep?" Beatrice was incredulous, but crouched down to look at them carefully. After a moment, she fell back on her behind with a shocked look on her face. "Joan, I can't feel them."

"What?" I wasn't sure what she meant at first; she hadn't tried to reach out and touch either of them, so it didn't make any sense, until my own angelic senses also slapped me in the face with what my eyes refused to acknowledge. "You're right, it's as if they're not really there. I can see them, but I can't feel their presence anymore."

Admonae and Silje had cautiously come up to join us at this stage. With her head tilted slightly to one side (as if listening to something no one else could hear; which, let's face it, she was always doing), Silje added her own observation. "I cannot hear their song. It's almost as if they were…"

Admonae finished Silje's sentence for her: "Human."

The implications hit me like a freight train. "Quick, they're dying. We've got to get them out of there!"

"Why do you think they are dying?" Admonae asked, "You said they were asleep."

"We haven't eaten, drunk or slept in at least three days, not since we gave the last of our supplies to the medical outpost in Selima." As I explained, I got down on all fours and got ready to crawl to our collapsed friends. "If they're human, they are suffering from starvation, dehydration, and exhaustion. Hold onto my leg in case I collapse, but I've got to get them out of there."

I inched forward, feeling the comforting grip of Beatrice's strong hands on my ankles. The world was starting to spin as I grabbed Damien's foot, and held on as

Beatrice dragged us both back until my own strength returned. Damien gasped and started coughing as he crossed whatever invisible line surrounded this place, and after rolling him over onto his side, Beatrice and I used the same technique to rescue Orfael.

With their angelic strength returning, Damien and Orfael quickly awoke and took deep breaths, shaking off the pain of hunger and thirst with an effort of will. Then, almost simultaneously they stared at each other and cried out, "Bathroom!"

A short time later, back in our room at the public house, the noises coming from the communal bathroom were, shall we say, less than heavenly.

"Ewwww!" Orfael's high pitched disgust was nearly causing Admonae and I to burst into giggles, but when Damien's deep voice added, "Oh sweet goodness, that's revolting! No wonder humans are always so angry!" to the general milieu, we all lost it.

We had almost calmed ourselves by the time the pair of them emerged from the shared bathroom, but Silje muttered, "For your own safety", in my ear, and we dissolved into laughter once again.

"Ha ha, very funny," Damien said, crossing his arms as he watched us. "If we're going back in there tomorrow, the three of you have to do the same thing you know."

That thought sobered us up very quickly, and the looks on our faces were apparently comical enough to make both Damien and Orfael chuckle appreciatively.

Once we had all calmed down, Damien had us sit so he could outline his plan. "So, it seems that as soon as we step across that threshold, we're human. Orfael and I would have eventually died if you had not pulled us out. The only thing that saved us, strangely, was our Wingless state. The fact that we have had to cope without most of our Angelic powers for all these centuries means that we have gotten used to eating and sleeping. Our habits, in some ways, are already partly mimicking human ones."

Admonae interrupted with a question I admit I had been thinking of as well. "So, if a full Angel, or a Fallen for that matter, entered there they would…?"

Damien nodded. "Cease to be, I expect. 'For your own safety', he told us. But we can prepare for it. We spend the rest of today eating and drinking our fill, deal with the … waste, and get a good night's sleep tonight. That should be enough to reset our physical bodies and allow us to handle the loss of our angelic powers."

Admonae leaned forward in her chair. "What was it like? Being human, I mean, not the other thing."

Damien shrugged. "I don't know if I was awake long enough to really get a good sense of it, I mainly remember feeling weak. Very weak. Of course, I was fainting at the time."

Silje looked up with a slightly sad look on her face. "It will be quiet. Complete silence in my head. No music, nothing."

Admonae nodded. "You heard their songs stop. Not change, like they do when you fall, just stop."

Orfael blinked and asked quickly, "But you can hear us now, right?"

Silje smiled and reached out for her hand; it was shaking slightly, and she squeezed it warmly. "Of course, I can. As bright and loud as ever. After all, you can feel us now, can't you?"

"Yes," Orfael admitted quietly.

"There you are then," I concluded. "Nothing to worry about. We will be human, or at least completely powerless, while we're in there, and we regain our angelic powers when we come back out. Today we will prepare and tomorrow we'll go in and find out just what Kateri was looking for. Now, time to get some food, and lots of water. That's an order." I stood and started to hustle them all out of the room. Admonae grabbed Orfael's hand and headed out towards the street and the various food vendors that would be starting to push their lunchtime wares.

Damien hung back a little, motioning to me that he had one more point to make. "Joan, Silje was right on the money about the silence. There was nothing there at all."

I nodded, understanding where he was going with this. "You're worried about what happens to us if our bodies die while we're in there."

Damien paused uncomfortably, before admitting the point. "Yes. If our bodies die, we can make new ones. We regenerate, although sometimes it can take years. We've all done it before."

"Don't remind me," I said with sigh, "My last death involved being burned at the stake. Nasty way to go, I can tell you."

"But in there," Damien continued, "If we die in *there,* I don't think we'll come back."

"Probably not," I agreed. "I imagine that's what Raphael was trying to warn us about."

"But… then what?" Damien asked. "What happens to us then?"

I couldn't help but smile at the irony of it all. "Damien my friend, that's been the one hundred-thousand-dollar question on every human's lips since Abel had a lunch date with his brother."

Chapter Ten

Getting into the dig site was depressingly easy. With our bodies prepared for the sudden loss of our powers, it felt more like a moment of vertigo than the crushing collapse Damien and Orfael had experienced the day before. Security at the site were not even interested in examining our forged passes, waving us through the moment we arrived at the gate and started to pull them out.

Beatrice explained as we walked towards the tent covered entrance to the ruins, "It's because we're white. They've been conditioned to think that the only thieves in town are the locals, and anyone white is part of the university teams. It's sad, really."

Damien nodded, but added, "Without our powers to fall back on, I'm going to choose to see that as a blessing, however wrong it is."

Silje sighed. "It's depressing, but I've seen worse. Which, now that I think of it, is even *more* depressing."

Orfael was muttering to herself in a disgusted tone, so I assumed that meant she agreed, until she finally exploded with, "But I practiced what you told me to say all morning!"

With any luck, the dig workers mistook the five of us face-palming simultaneously as our group merely walking through a particularly ferocious cloud of sand gnats.

At the main tent, we took the opportunity to grab some of the hard hats stored there and quickly entered the ruin itself before any of the actual archeologists could turn up and put us to work. Several interns painstakingly dusting centuries of compacted dirt and clay from fragments of ceramic pottery looked at us enviously as we passed into the ruin, but no one attempted to stop us.

As I strode confidently through the dig, Orfael hurried up to me and tugged once at my sleeve to get my attention. "It's all about looking as you are supposed to be here, I understand that," Orfael muttered, "But Joan, I don't get how you can so easily do that. Why aren't you scared?"

I smiled back down to the younger Angel. "Because I *am* meant to be here. I was put on this world to protect the humans, and that is exactly what I'm doing. Just because they would not understand the threat doesn't mean that I'm wrong."

Silje nodded in agreement. "Even the ones that make us sad at their selfishness."

We turned a corner around ancient crumbling walls and came to the first of the passageways that led underground. After activating the lamps on our helmets, we descended. The frescos on the walls had been lovingly uncovered and cleaned by the archeologists and were a sight to behold, but what we were after was going to be far deeper in the complex. After about half an hour of exploring, we came to an antechamber long since abandoned by the research teams as being, if the signage left behind was accurate, a mere 'preparation room' for religious services held elsewhere.

The depiction of a tree on one of the walls held our gaze as one.

"Can you feel that?" Silje was the first to speak, breaking the trance we were threatening to slip into.

"Yes," we all replied in unison.

"We may have lost our powers," Beatrice added, "But we are still Angels, after all."

"One of the seven trees of creation lies beyond that wall," Damien said. "Which one do you think?"

I couldn't suppress a chuckle. "Knowing our luck, the most dangerous one."

"Knowledge?" Orfael guessed, her hopeful tone at odds with the gravity of her choice.

I had had enough of waiting. "There's one way to find out. Admonae, if you would be so kind as to do the honours?"

"Me?" she squeaked. "Why not you?"

"You," I nodded. "I'm war. You're truth. Do you really need me to explain it further?"

"No, I guess not," she admitted. Taking a deep breath, she stepped up to the stucco painting on the wall and, after pausing for a moment while each of us placed our hands on her shoulders, pressed her hand to the image of the tree.

And she prayed.

You might think that prayer is something Angels do all the time, but you'd be surprised. We never learned to pray like the humans did. To us, talking to God was just talking, we didn't see it as any more miraculous than a modern person would their mobile phone. When the war started, and God suddenly stopped answering, we were at a loss as to understand why. But even though He may have stopped answering us, when an Angel does pray, and I mean *properly* pray, the Universe listens.

Miraculous power embedded deep within the relief flowed out over us in response to Admonae's prayer. It felt ancient, but warm, and we could not help but close our eyes for a moment. When the feeling dimmed and I opened my eyes once again, the colours of the stucco on the carving were no longer suffering from the effects of centuries of weathering, but were as bright and fresh as the day they were put there by its talented and dedicated artisans.

A slithering noise behind us sent a shiver up my spine and caused me to spin about and drop into a defensive stance. It was immediately apparent that we had somehow been moved by the fresco, and the room we were in now bared no resemblance to the antechamber we had discovered the carving in. The room was circular, lit by torches set into sconces in the walls, and with a darkened corridor directly across from the carving of the tree. It was down this corridor that the slithering noise was quickly disappearing.

"We're not alone," I whispered, motioning to the others to stay quiet.

"Just a snake?" The hopeful tone in Orfael's question betrayed her fear.

I shook my head in response. "Too large".

Damien placed a hand on Orfael's shoulder, causing her to jump a little. "And at the moment, remember that there is no such thing as 'just' a snake for us. We're mortal while we are here, which means a small dose of poison or even an infection from a snake bite would be very bad."

"Right then." Confidently, I stretched my arm back, my hand reaching over my shoulder to grasp at the hilt of my sword. Of course, my hand closed on thin air.

Silje snorted and failed to keep her giggle completely silent. I turned to see Damien facepalming theatrically and

Admonae practically stuffing her fist into her mouth to avoid laughing out loud. "Yeah, yeah. Laugh it up. Force of habit, okay? But point taken, Damien." I reached down to the belt at my waist, moved my long coat aside, and drew out the forty-inch-long machete that was hanging there.

Orfael blinked in surprise. "When did you get that?"

"Joan is always prepared," Beatrice whispered, but I had turned back to face the darkened corridor and missed seeing if there was any sarcasm in the look on her face. I decided to assume that there was none.

"Beatrice," I said without turning around, my eyes already starting to get used to the gloom of the corridor, "Grab one of the torches and walk behind me. I want you to light our way without blinding me."

"Yes, Joan." Beatrice carefully lifted a burning torch from its sconce and our shadows danced about in front of me. "It's just wood!" The surprise in her voice was evident. "How do these keep burning when miracles don't work here?"

"I've been thinking about that," Damien replied. "And I don't think we've 'lost' our power here, it is too integral to what we are. I think this place hijacks and uses our power for its own end. If I am right, the torches only lit when we arrived."

"Which means," Admonae added, "Whatever is here knows we are coming. That's quite a security system."

"Might as well not keep them waiting then," I said, not bothering to whisper any more.

Taking the lead, I strode across the chamber towards the darkened corridor at its other side. My boots on the stone echoed throughout the ruin, but I figured that if stealth was no longer an option, then our approach should at the least sound confident. I only wished that I felt as confident as my footsteps seemed.

My approach had its desired effect, however. The corridor opened into a round room ahead of us, brightly lit from the torches placed along its walls. As we approached, the room's only other inhabitant recoiled back and hissed, hugging the tree in the center of the room.

The tree.

It stood, as resplendent and fertile as when it held pride of place in the creation of the world. The room existed only to hold it, the high domed ceiling above decorated with precious stones, sparkling in the firelight to resemble the view of the milky way galaxy at night, just as it would have looked to the tree all that time ago.

Wrapped around the trunk of the tree was a strange humanoid snake, similar in look to a Naga, or possibly Echidna from the myths of Ancient Greece. Its ancient face was full of pain, and fear. But its eyes held a small glimpse of hope.

In a way, that made the obvious pain the creature was in all the more terrible.

There was the scent of miraculous power on the creature, but the smell was indescribably old and stale. It had been touched by heaven, or perhaps by a Fallen, but not for a very, very long time. Unconsciously, I gripped the hilt of my machete and took up a fighting stance.

It uncoiled from the tree and slithered up to me faster than I would have thought possible for its size, and bent its head to one side, baring the side of its neck to my blade.

"Yess," the sibilating voice said, "It comess to keep her promisse at last."

I took a step back, causing the creature to straighten up with a look of betrayal on its face. "No!" it cried. "Pleasse. You musst!" In despair the creature collapsed to the ground, its long snake tail wrapping around its body and hiding its face.

Damien reached out and touched my arm gently, signaling me to back up a little. The healer crouched down beside it, slowly reaching out to touch despite Orfael's quiet gasp of warning. "Easy friend," Damien spoke softly, his calming voice coming from centuries of caring for the sick and injured, and not from his missing miraculous powers. "We want to help you, but you've mistaken us for someone else. We've never met, we couldn't have promised you anything."

"But sshe promissed!" The creature wailed, the heart-wrenching cry ending in a series of sobs that painfully wracked its body.

Damien turned and looked up at me, but all I could do was shrug. I was not the 'she' the creature was referring to. Turning back to the pitiful thing lying in a heap at his feet, Damien laid his hands gently upon it and stroked soothingly, keeping up a quiet conversation as he did so.

"You're hurt, in pain..." he murmured.

"Yess, sso much pain. Alwayss pain now," it replied, the sobs quietening under Damien's touch.

"I can feel that you were strong once, what happened to you?" Damien asked.

"I wass sstrong, sso very sstrong, sso proud. Sstood tall with ssacred purposse. I wass chossen above all otherss," the creature answered, without lifting its head from under its tail.

"And you did a wonderful job," Damien continued, handling the creature like a shell-shocked veteran, "You stood tall, you did all that you were asked to do. But then what happened?"

"Got old. Sso old now. Purposse wass ssuppossed to end. Wass promissed it would end. It never ended, I sstayed when all otherss left. Now all alone, and sso old. No paradisse for Nahassh."

We all took a step back at the sound of that name. Nahash looked up as he felt Damien's hand lift off his body, scared that we were leaving. "But you are here now, just like sshe promissed Nahassh. You will ssend Nahassh to paradisse? You will end the pain? Pleasse?"

Orfael ran to Admonae, collapsing into her arms with a cry. Silje and Beatrice similarly reached out to one another. Damien and I shared a look as Nahash bared his neck to me once more.

"Nahash," Admonae spoke, not to anyone in particular, but needing to put voice to the thoughts in her head to try to assimilate them. "The serpent of Eden."

I nodded, "Then the 'she' who transformed you into this, who promised paradise to you. Who was she?"

"The tree," Nahash replied, his aged spine straightening ever so slightly in pride as he spoke.

"Oh crap." Admonae's words from behind us neatly summed up my own thoughts.

Damien crouched once again beside Nahash. "I'm sorry you're in pain, and I promise we'll do whatever we can to help. You need to tell us though, what exactly did the tree promise you?"

The promise of relief that Damien held out to Nahash helped him pull himself up into a sitting position, and I could see that once he would have held quite the regal bearing. "When Nahassh touched her, so long ago, Nahassh was just planning on hunting one of the birdss in her branchess. But sshe spoke to Nahassh in hiss head. Sshe told him of her purposse, and the ssacred duty Nahassh wass chossen to perform for her. To grow and change, sspeak the wordss with the oness who lived here, to protect her throughout hiss life, and then, when the final quesstion was assked and answwered, thosse born of paradisse would arrive to end Nahassh'ss duty and grant him peace."

"Final question?" I crouched beside Damien, curiosity overcoming my concern about Nahash. "What makes you think the final question has been asked?"

"For sso long, Nahassh sseess no one. Then one like you, one of paradisse, comess and sspeakss with her. Nahassh waitss for the releasse, but sshe just runss away. Nahassh is alone once more. Then you are here, and Nahassh sseess that you are fighter. Nahassh ... hopess."

I followed his eyes to the machete in my hand as Admonae extracted herself from Orfael's grip and joined us. "That had to be Kateri. She got to the tree and asked it a question. You know what we have to do, Joan."

I nodded. "Nahash, we need to talk to the tree. But we won't leave you like this, I promise." Standing up, I ordered Orfael over to the tree of knowledge. "Orfael, if I remember correctly about how these things tend to work, we will each get a question. You go first."

"But I don't know what to ask!" Orfael exclaimed, as she moved to obey my direction.

"We're going to start by being kind to Nahash. Ask know-it-all there who asks the final question."

"But what if the answer is me and we waste our only question?"

Beatrice spoke up: "Then Nahash gets to rest, and I for one would not consider that a waste of a question."

Orfael nodded and moved to place her hand on the trunk of the tree. She closed her eyes for a moment, communing with the tree of knowledge, and when her eyes opened, she spoke one word. "Joan."

I let out the breath I hadn't realised I was holding and turned to Nahash. "That's me. And I will keep my promise."

"I'll go next, then," Admonae said, stepping up to the tree. "I'll find out exactly what Kateri learned here, it may give us a clue where she went next."

After a moment of communing with the tree Admonae stepped back again, her face suddenly pale with whatever answer she received. Being the closest, Orfael put an arm around her shoulder and led her away from the tree.

Realising that Admonae needed some time to process what she had learned, Silje stood and went to the tree. "I guess it's my turn," she stated, as she pressed her palm to its rough trunk and closed her eyes.

After a moment she stepped back, a look of relief on her face. I caught her glance and nodded towards the tree. "So, what did she say?"

"Nahash will get his reward, the promise she gave is true." Silje smiled down at the ancient Naga, and Nahash sighed deeply in response.

"What, you wasted your only question to ask that?" Orfael demanded.

Silje merely shrugged. "I can't go against my own nature, Orfael. I am what I am."

Damien clapped Silje warmly on her back. "If you hadn't asked that, I was going to. My turn." Like the others, Damien communed with the Tree for a moment before stepping back. "She doesn't know if Kateri can be saved. Apparently when the time comes that decision will be Kateri's. Makes no sense to me, but I never could get the hang of oracles. That was always Gary's forte."

Beatrice stepped up to the massive trunk and placed her hand upon it without ceremony. A moment later, she stepped away with a grimace on her face. "Well, apparently this is not a Fallen plot, although they will have had a hand in it at some point apparently. The mix of tenses is interesting, but frustrating. Joan, it is time. You're up, just be careful in how you phrase your question."

Putting the machete back into its scabbard, I glanced over to Admonae, but she merely shook her head in response. Divulging whatever she had learned apparently had to wait until after I asked my question. I stepped up to the tree like the others had, but knowing that my question was going to be the last one the tree ever answered was not something I had prepared myself for, and the responsibility to get it right weighed heavily on me. As I paused, I saw Nahash's nest on the other side of the tree. Nestled away deep inside it was an Egyptian bronze-age Khopesh sword. It was where he had slept the nights away for millennia.

He had been waiting for this for a very long time.

I placed my hand on the tree and the room faded to black, as the tree's voice spoke in my mind. "I have waited for you child. You hold my last question. Ask."

There were so many things I wanted to know. I was furious at the tree's treatment of its 'protector' and wanted to scream 'How could you?' at the thing. I wanted to know why it convinced the serpent to betray the rules of Eden in the first place, or for that matter why The War had to happen at all. And most of all my heart screamed to know why He wasn't talking to us anymore, and whether he heard us at all. But those questions were traps, and I knew what I had to ask.

Chapter Eleven

"Your time here is at an end." It wasn't my question, just an opening statement, but I felt the tree acquiesce to the truth of it. "And since this is something that was set in motion a long time ago, perhaps from the very beginning itself..." To this the tree stayed silent, but I could feel its attention like a weight upon me. I was close.

"I need to ask - what am I supposed to do? Do I stop this, or do I let it happen?" I hadn't asked what I would need to do to stop it, firstly because I had no idea what 'it' was, and also because I had started to worry that stopping whatever was coming wasn't what I was placed here to do. I knew I wanted to help Kateri, but I also knew that something far bigger was going on, and I couldn't just concentrate on her (no matter how much I wanted to.)

The pause before the tree answered felt like an eternity, but it was probably nothing more than a heartbeat. "Child, my time here is done, but the world will go on without me. As for you, your path is as clear to me now as the day I was created. You must do but one thing: allow yourself to be who you are. Trust in who you have become, who you are becoming, and in what you feel. But I will leave you with something else. You will seek out two more of my sisters—One whose time will never end, and another whose time may be ended for her."

Images flashed into my head of the locations of the other six trees of creation scattered across the globe. Originally all seven trees existed in Eden, but space and time were different then, and when what we knew as creation *unfolded* itself into the Universe of man, the trees became rooted across the surface of the planet. I felt a call from one of the trees in particular, and I knew that it was the next one we needed to seek out.

I just didn't know why.

And then, as quickly as it had come, the sense of communing with the tree faded, and the underground chamber in which we stood swept back into my consciousness. My fellow Wingless and Nahash were looking at me and waiting to hear what had happened.

I took a moment to breathe deeply and steady myself before replying. "I know what we need to do. Well, I have an idea at least. But first, everyone else out of the room, please. I have a promise to keep."

As they started to head out, I walked around to Nahash's nest and withdrew the bronze Khopesh sword that lay there. Carrying it, I came around to where Nahash was already prostrating himself for the blow, but I knelt and placed the hilt of the blade into one of his scaly hands.

Nahash looked up, confusion on his face. "I cannot, not to myself. Forbidden. Pleasse, you ssaid you would keep your promisse."

I nodded, placing one hand under his other arm to help him up. "I will, Nahash. But you are a noble soldier, and you have performed your duty for far too long. Face me with your sword in your hand and be that soldier one more time."

I don't know if a creature like Nahash can cry, but his third eyelid flicked across his eyes so fast that it certainly gave that impression. I really hoped it wasn't just wishful thinking on my part. Painfully, he pulled himself upright and raised his sword in salute. I watched as pride infused his ancient body once again as I saluted back and simply said, "It is an honour."

I made sure that I had completely cleaned my machete before I rejoined the others waiting for me in the antechamber.

Before anyone could say anything, however, the torches along the walls flickered and, one by one, started to go out. It was Damien who worked it out first— "The tree is dying. We have to get out of here."

As each torch extinguished, we could feel a part of our miraculous power return to us. We rushed to the fresco on the wall, each laying a hand on it before pushing our returning power into it.

That feeling of momentary vertigo swept over us again, and we were back in the main ruins. But this time the ground was vibrating beneath our feet.

"I was afraid of this." It was Orfael who spoke, with a confidence we had not heard from her since we lost our power by entering this area. Seeing that she had our attention, she explained, "Even without our power you are a warrior, Joan, and Damien is a healer. My realm is the creatures of the air, and trust me, I know when I'm hundreds of feet underground. I think that's part of why I felt so ill at ease down there, it just didn't feel right to me. With the tree dead and its protector gone, my guess is that the chamber that holds it is succumbing to the ravages of time. It is collapsing."

The floor lurched away underneath us, throwing us to the ground. We started to pick ourselves up again as Orfael continued, "And if it was beneath these ruins, then…"

"Then we need to run!" I finished with a yell. Grabbing at Admonae's hand, I pulled her up and started to sprint from the room. Damien had already grabbed Orfael off the floor and the four of us careened out of the ruins following Beatrice and Silje, dodging falling stones and bouncing off walls and each other as the ground heaved and collapsed under our feet.

By the time we reached the chain-link fence that surrounded the dig, the entire area had sunk a good twenty metres as sand and stone rushed to fill the space so long denied to it. Damien started to head back into the dig to help the archeologists, but Admonae grabbed his arm and held him still.

"We have to run." Admonae's face had regained some of its colour, but was still pretty ashen.

"We have our power back," Damien countered, "I have to help these people."

Admonae shook her head and gripped him tighter. "No, we have to run. We can't let him find us here."

I put my hand on Admonae's shoulder and leant in close. "We're all here, Admonae. We have our power back. We're safe now. What did the tree tell you?"

"None of us are safe," Admonae replied with stone-faced certainty. "Kateri's question. Remember I asked the tree what Kateri had come to it to learn. Well, Kateri knew that something had been done to her, that she was changing somehow. She wanted to find out who it was that had forced this upon her. She asked; 'Who is forcing me to fall, making me fall against my will, and what am I changing into?'"

Orfael, God bless her, gave voice to what we all wanted to say. "What was the tree's answer?"

Admonae blanched once more, swallowed hard, and whispered one word in reply:

"*Michael.*"

Chapter Twelve

Kateri's trail had headed north since her encounter with the Tree of Knowledge, and Silje was certain that Kateri was not only returning to England, she was also using her power up at a greater rate to get there quickly. For us, it was time to see if our friends had managed to turn anything up, and warn them that we were on our way back.

Admonae's little announcement had left us more than a little shell shocked and, as yet, we hadn't let anyone else know. The decision to wait until we could tell them in person had less to do with any paranoia about Michael listening in to our conversation, and far more with us needing time to fully process it ourselves before trying to pass the information on.

Or, and I admit this was far more likely, we simply wanted to avoid the conversation for as long as possible. If he knew, Azazel would have made some snarky comment about procrastination being a sign that we were 'going native'. At this point, I'm not sure I could have disagreed with him.

As usual, it was Orfael who brought up the elephant in the room, or the Air Emirates Boeing 747 in this case. We were flying over France on our way back to London, and I think the silence finally got to her.

"But… he's an Archangel!" Orfael blurting out, yet again, what we were all thinking. She had at least stuck to our decision to avoid saying his name and possibly drawing his attention. "The tree could have been wrong … couldn't it?"

Four of us were seated beside each other in the central aisle of the plane; Beatrice and Silje had taken the two seats by the window. Orfael would have launched herself out of her chair with her exclamation if the seatbelt hadn't stopped her, and now she was holding onto my arm and looking up at me. I hated to crush that tiny spark of hope I saw in her eyes, but ignoring the truth wasn't going to get us anywhere. "The Tree of Knowledge? One of the seven trees of creation? No, somehow I don't think it can be wrong."

Orfael slumped into her chair. "But why?"

Damien, feigning sleep, kept his eyes closed as he added, "A better question might be 'How?'".

As much as I hated to think about it, Damien had a point. Archangels may have more raw power than normal angels, and they towered over the Wingless, but they also had a far smaller scope for where they could employ that power. Humans were the ones given 'free will', and I was beginning to suspect that our wingless state had, over the millennia, allowed us to somehow tap just a little into that curious ability. But Archangels exhibiting free will and acting outside their realms? Such a thing should not be possible.

And yet, here we were.

"Let us leave questions of 'why' and 'how' for the moment." I took Orfael's hand in mine as I addressed my friends. "They are both good questions, but I have a feeling that we don't have the luxury of the time we'd need to explore them fully. First, we stop him. Then we can ask."

"We stop him," Admonae snorted with derision, "That's quite a plan you have there, Joan. He's a blessed

Archangel—no, it is even better than that, he is the Archangel *of War*, and your boss, remember? Just how do you suppose we 'stop him'?"

I shrugged my shoulders. It was obvious that the tone in Admonae's voice stemmed more from fear and despair than any real anger directed at me, and besides, we'd been friends far too long to get snippy over something so small as a misspoken word or emotional reaction. My response, when it came, was calm but firm. At least I hoped it was. "I don't know, Admonae, but I know that we at least have a chance to. The tree would not have directed us to seek out her sisters if there was nothing to be done. "

Damien nodded, but said with a wry smile, "We just need to have faith, hey Joan?"

Before I could come up with a suitably sarcastic reply, the mobile phone on my lap buzzed, and I winked cheekily at Damien as I answered it. "Joan."

As I expected, it was Toby's voice on the other end. We had contacted him once we got to Cairo so he could organise the plane tickets home. "Morning, Joan. How's the flight?"

"Cramped," I replied, while glancing meaningfully at my friends.

Toby chuckled. "Best Lennox could do in such short notice. Listen, we are not going to be able to pick you up when you land, you will need to catch a cab to your hotel. I'll email you the reservation."

Orfael looked at me curiously as she picked up on my pause, before replying, "Err, thanks Toby, but I think I'd rather just go home than share another hotel room with these guys, as nice as they are…"

"Yeah, about that," Toby broke in, "there have been a few problems."

I suspected that he could hear my eyebrow raise over the phone. "What problems exactly?"

Toby started, "Now you'll laugh…"

I snorted. "I sincerely doubt that, but please, do go on."

By the time I hung up on Toby, Orfael had gotten everyone's attention focused squarely on me. "Well?" Damien asked.

I smirked back at him. "That faith you were asking about…"

The pilot announced the beginning of our descent into Heathrow, and I laid out what Toby had related to me over the phone. As we had planned, Toby had been keeping tabs on our homes while we were away, and in the last twenty-four hours a series of events had struck that would have made Edward Murphy proud. It had started with Lennox trying to book a flight home to Holland for Adelita on the off chance that she needed to get back, only to find that all the flights had been completely booked out.

Then the fire alarm and sprinkler system were accidentally tripped in the staff apartments that Damien rented from the teaching hospital where he worked, flooding not only it, but the apartments in the two floors below his as well. Workmen and insurance assessors had closed the building until the cause could be found.

Orfael's home, situated directly beneath the flightpath from Heathrow, had been struck by something that had fallen off one of the hundreds of aircraft that used the world's busiest airport every day, and was closed off as a crime scene by air forensic investigators. This had, naturally, also drawn the attention of the local media, leading to the block being picketed by members of a local action group protesting about the height of planes that flew over the populated area. They'd never know that Orfael bought that house especially because of the flightpath, but even though the damage to the house itself was minimal, there was no way she would be able to go home right now without attracting a lot of attention.

Admonae, Damien, and Orfael listened to me relate all this with looks of increasing incredulity. "Someone," Damien said, "doesn't like us very much."

"Or someone doesn't want us splitting up and going home just yet," Admonae offered.

Orfael, at least, didn't seem to be in a hurry to get away from the rest of us. "Odd, that wasn't going to happen yet anyway, but that's okay, we can stay with Joan. Can't we, Joan?"

"Well, you see," I started to reply, but Damien could see the truth in my eyes.

"Joan, spill. What happened to your place? Is this why I heard laughter coming from the other end of the phone call?" he asked.

"Yeah," I shrugged, "It seems that my apartment building has been compulsory acquired by the government."

"What?" Admonae and Damien said in unison.

I tried to get the rest of the news out in one go. "Apparently someone found a map that suggests an old roman temple is buried beneath it. The entire block has been classified as national trust land until they work out if it is there or not. The tenants have all been moved to a hotel for now. That's where we're headed once we land."

"Floods, objects falling from the heavens, and ancient roman churches," Admonae managed to get out between bursts of laughter. "I didn't realise that omens came in such obvious wrappings these days."

"It does seem a little far-fetched," I admitted.

Far-fetched or not, two hours later we stood in front of the Premier Inn in Brentford as the taxi pulled away. Lennox had managed to get into their booking system to 'adjust' my entry, so that the Inn would register the booking by the government for six adults and not just myself. Apparently there had been one suite left in the hotel that would sleep all of us, our 'one bit of luck', as she called it.

The suite itself consisted of two separate bedrooms with queen-sized beds, a fairly serviceable kitchenette, and two couches that would convert into single beds. I claimed the couch closest to the door and left the others to sort their own sleeping arrangements out as I put the kettle on for a much-needed pot of tea. When we had checked in downstairs, the clerk had handed me a letter from the national trust that detailed the times over the next few days that I would be allowed back into my building to collect any personal items, clothing, or pets. Furniture was not allowed to be moved because of 'possible vibration damage to the ancient ruins beneath the building'. The whole thing read like a bad movie script.

"Is that tea I smell?" Damien pulled up a chair at the small kitchen table, reaching for the steaming pot and pouring himself a cup. When I pushed my own still-empty mug towards him, he got the message and filled it as well. "Engrossing letter?" he asked.

"Bureaucratic garbage mostly," I replied as I tossed the letter across the table to him, "But it seems legit. Someone has gone to a lot of trouble to keep us together."

Damien nodded, sipping at his tea. "Well, we shouldn't disappoint them. Listen, Orfael and I are going to head out and see if there are any fresh clothes we can pick up from our places, but we'll be back for dinner. Admonae wants to go and collect some food to cook up. Beatrice and Silje will 'guard the homestead', so to speak. If we're going to try to use our miraculous power as little as possible to stay under the radar, we'll need to fuel these bodies the old-fashioned way."

"Sounds like a plan," I agreed. "Just stick together and be careful."

"And you'll go with Admonae?" Damien asked.

"I hate shopping," I warned him in response, "But yes. I'll go, just so long as we can stop by where my neighbour is staying."

Damien looked up curiously. "I assumed she would have been moved into this hotel like you were. What happened?"

"This hotel won't take pets,' I explained. "So, to keep Noah from being put in a 'government approved' cattery, she went to stay with her niece instead."

Damien smiled. "That's really quite nice of her."

I nodded in agreement. "Humans. I know we're supposed to love them, but some just make it really easy."

Chapter Thirteen

By the time Damien and Orfael returned, ladened down with bags of clothes, the apartment was full of delicious, mouth-watering smells wafting in from the kitchenette. Admonae, as it turned out, was a canny shopper when it came to preparing food. Specifically, she knew just who to call to do it for us.

Which meant that the first thing we picked up along the way was Gary and Adelita. At the moment, the pair of them were happily humming away to themselves as Adelita diced vegetables, and Gary blended spices. Together they stir-fried a meal that would put most restaurants to shame. I wasn't even sure what half the ingredients were that Gary put into the trolley during our shopping trip, but I was certainly enjoying the aroma they created with them.

I could admire how efficiently Gary moved about the tiny kitchenette, seemingly keeping pots, pans, measuring cups, and mixing bowls in a constant state of motion. It occurred to me that, with as long as we have had to practice and perfect skills like cooking, sculpting, painting, calligraphy, (anything really, for that matter), it may seem strange that every one of us weren't complete experts in absolutely everything.

The simple fact is, we're not. Each of us has some skills that we had perfected, like Gary and his cooking, but none of us were ever interested in learning *everything*. Maybe that lack of drive was part of our make-up, part of what made us who we were, or with the pace of human societal evolution, perhaps we were always too busy playing catch-up. Personally though, I have always thought that life simply had a way of getting in the way of such plans.

No matter how long you have, there never seems to be enough time.

The meal itself was glorious, although I'm not sure that the world at large is ready for the Swiss-Thai fusion that Gary and Adelita served up to us. I honestly couldn't tell you exactly what I ate, but I can say that I'd have it again in a heartbeat. The depth and complexity of the flavours in the meal had a secondary effect, however, and a much needed one. It drew our minds and our dinner conversation away from the trials that were facing us and to spices and sautéing techniques and the simple pleasures of cooking. It gave each of us permission to relax for the evening, to forget why we were here, and to find a measure of peace in our shared companionship.

Which is why, much later that night, I found it so incredibly rude to have our night's rest shattered by loud, terrified screaming. That I was the one doing the screaming just added insult to injury.

We had retired fairly early, planning on making a start with the sunrise in the morning. The combination of the wonderful meal and the bottle of wine Damien had picked up had me asleep almost as soon as my head hit the pillow. Angels and Fallen don't sleep of course, but we Wingless had learned to get used to it, unless we wanted to burn our very limited miraculous power on something as mundane as staying awake. We could go for days without eating and sleeping without concern, but we had been exerting ourselves for quite some time now, and a good night's sleep was going to do us all wonders.

But even the Wingless don't dream when we sleep. Azazel had commented as much the morning he woke me—the morning we felt Kateri fall, or at least thought we did. The fact that I had awoken from something that was more akin to a nightmare than a dream was something that still disturbed me, and I had avoided talking about it.

As concerning as that was, at least that nightmare was mine; it was based on something that had happened to me. Finding yourself in someone else's nightmare however - that, as it turns out, is exponentially worse.

I was small, in the body of a young girl. I have never been a child, but now I could feel the weakness and helplessness through the eyes I was looking out of. The bedroom was unfamiliar to me, and I couldn't shake the uneasy feeling that some things that should have been there were missing, although I had no idea what. It was obvious, however, that the myriad of spider web strands covering the far wall were certainly *not* supposed to be there.

Then the web moved, quickly spreading across the ceiling, walls, and floor to surround the bed that I, as the small girl, was kneeling on. I watched, unable to move, as my (I mean, her) dressing table was covered, and my, no, *our* dolls disappeared under the silky grey strands. Where the webbing was thickest, in the corners of the room, glowing red eyes started to blink open; first a few, and then more and more, moving through the web and coming closer and closer.

We screamed when the first black spider leg, the size of a chair leg, stretched up from under the bed and pawed at the pillow behind us. That scream blended with others and the apartment suddenly exploded into view as a large volume of cold water splashed onto my face.

I was standing on the sofa bed, the room lit by the red-orange glow of the flaming sword in my hand. Orfael had flattened herself against the ground to get out of the way of my wild swings as Gary had thrown a large jug of water over me to wake me up. My scream died as my lungs eventually ran out of oxygen, and I stood there, panting and shaking uncontrollably.

Gary was saying something, but I couldn't hear him over the pounding of my heart. It was as if his voice was coming from another room rather than just in front of me. The far end of the room was out of focus and for a moment I thought I saw webbing appearing along the ceiling. I drew in a deep breath for another scream and started to raise my sword arm towards it when Beatrice stepped into view and slapped me, hard, right across my cheek.

I drew back, dropping my sword as I went to cover my face with my hands. The sword disappeared before it hit the bed, and Beatrice wrapped me in her arms, cooing and gently rocking me back and forth like a mother with a child.

I don't know how much time passed, but eventually I could make out what my friends were saying as they talked.

"I've never seen her look like that before." It was Beatrice speaking, while she still held me.

"Me neither. She was honestly scared, and I've never known her to show fear." Gary's voice.

"She wasn't scared." It was Adelita now. "She was terrified. The type of terrified only a child can manage. I could see it in her eyes. I don't think she could see us, not properly anyway. I'm so glad we decided to stay, Gary."

Gary nodded. "When Damien got called in to the hospital, I could see how exhausted you all were. I figured we could stay here to keep an eye on everything."

I slowly raised my hand up to hold Beatrice's arm and the conversation stopped, as did Beatrice's gentle rocking. I raised my head up off her chest and saw the large damp patch I had left on her top. Had I been crying?

"I'm okay now, I think. It's passed." My voice cracked as I spoke, and I felt my vocal cords complain at the abuse I had visited upon them.

"What happened, Joan?" I was worried that Gary's direct question would bring it all flooding back, but there was a surprising lack of emotion there, almost as if it was something I had watched on television rather than experienced myself.

I shrugged in reply. "I had a nightmare."

"Joan," Admonae spoke quietly, still not quite ready to let go of me, "We don't dream."

"Joan does," Gary interrupted, his voice firm, but not accusatory. "Remember back in the observatory? Azazel said that he'd woken Joan from a nightmare."

"Not like this." For some reason I still didn't want to talk to the others about my dreaming, so I tried to steer the conversation back to what had just happened. "I was stuck in someone else's nightmare. A young girl. It wasn't me; at least, it wasn't me when the nightmare began. But as it went on, I was *becoming* her, almost as if I went from watching it to sharing the experience."

"This is too weird," Silje commented, apparently unaware of the irony of an immortal angel saying something like that. "I know we said we wouldn't use our powers, but we need to check for influences."

I nodded my agreement. "Do it."

We sat quietly as Silje carefully extended her perceptions, using a small amount of miraculous power to search the room for anything that could have invaded my sleep. Almost immediately, a glow started to come from beneath the fold-out mattress of the sofa bed I had been sleeping on. Beatrice and I were still sitting on the sofa bed, and as one we leapt to our feet and danced about, madly brushing our hands down our legs.

"What is it?" Called Gary, "What's wrong?"

"Spiders!" We both yelled in unison. Silje dropped her concentration and the sensation of being crawled over by dozens of the eight-legged creatures immediately left us.

Beatrice and I looked at each other in confusion. "But we're..." she started.

"Not afraid of spiders," Gary finished for her. "None of us are. There isn't a single one of His creatures that would scare us like that."

"Not us," I replied, starting to understand, "But they do scare that girl. Time to find out just what is hiding under the bed."

As we folded the sofa bed mattress up from the metal frame, Adelita spotted a folded piece of good quality drawing paper caught in one of the springs of the frame. There was no glow now, but I still decided to use a pair of tongs from the kitchen to grab and pull the paper out.

Folding it open on the kitchen table, the paper showed a simple child's drawing—of the very nightmare scene I had experienced. The bedroom, the dressing table, the webs and the red eyes, all were exactly as I remembered them, and seeing the drawing sent an involuntary shudder up my spine.

Chapter Fourteen

Gary must have noticed my twitching hand, because he quickly covered the drawing with a napkin and gently placed his hands on my shoulders, drawing my attention to him instead.

"Okay..." Gary started, as he directed us all back into the lounge area, "So it seems that we have a child's drawing that can draw miraculous power from an angel and project its image into said angel's head. That about sum it up?"

Admonae hummed, unsure. "But we've been sitting on that couch all afternoon with no ill effects."

Gary nodded. "True, but perhaps proximity isn't enough. Joan was asleep..."

"And dreaming," Orfael added. I growled slightly in response.

"No, Joan." Beatrice, who had yet to leave my side, placed her hand on my arm to quiet me. "It may be important."

I shook my head. "It felt different, I could tell that it wasn't my dream; at least, at first it wasn't. Then the distinction between the girl and I kind of ... blurred."

"Then we need to find this girl," Adelita stated firmly. "So that means it's my turn to see what this drawing holds."

"Be careful."

Adelita acknowledged my warning with a soft smile and stood up from the couch, walking back to the kitchen table where the drawing still lay, covered by Gary's napkin.

Adelita looked back over her shoulder before reaching out to pick up the paper. "Catch me if I fall, Joan."

I nodded. "Always."

Adelita extended her power and the room suddenly felt peaceful. Adelita's realm was innocence, and because of that she did most of her work with children. She was definitely the most suited of us to try to track the girl down through her drawing.

I found myself glancing back into the corners of the room, unconsciously checking for spiderwebs, but thankfully none appeared. I was so preoccupied with this, however, that I failed to realise that a minute had already gone by, and Adelita was practically groaning with effort, the muscles of her arms, across her back, and up her neck tense with strain.

Nightmare or no nightmare, my friend needed me. I went over to her, breaking her concentration by taking one of her clenched fists in my hand and quietly speaking into her ear. "Ease up Ade, let it go now."

She let out her breath with a gasp and collapsed backwards into my arms. She was fine, but momentarily exhausted by the strain. "What did you get?" I asked.

"Absolutely nothing!" The shock in Adelita's voice was apparent.

"A child with no innocence?" Admonae blurted out, "But the Fallen don't go for children!"

"Was something blocking you?" Asked Gary.

Adelita shook her head to both comments, struggling to put into words what she had felt. I scowled at both of them until they quieted down and then helped Adelita to a chair. "Take your time, Ade."

"You haven't called me that in a long time, Joan," Adelita chuckled to herself, but then took a deep breath. I could sense her center herself. "No, I wasn't blocked, and there was no Fallen taint. But there was also no girl. Not really. I mean, it wasn't as if there was no innocence there; I kept feeling something at least akin to innocence, which is why I kept pushing. It was more as if the innocence I was feeling wasn't coming from a human."

"Not human?" Beatrice asked.

Adelita shrugged. "I'm sorry, I know it doesn't make any sense, but that's all I've got. Either way, I can't track her. You'll need to do this the old-fashioned way."

"It can wait until morning, then," I stated. "Rest up everyone, dawn will be here before we know it."

The next morning, we decided not to all land on the hotel reception clerk as a group; Gary had argued successfully that he and Adelita posing as medical professionals would have a greater chance of getting information out of the manager without freaking them out. The rest of us waited outside while they questioned the clerk behind the desk, with Adelita flashing her credentials in order to be shown inside the manager's office. For us, all that was left to do was wait.

I don't know if I mentioned this before or not, but I *hate* waiting.

The smile on their faces as they came striding out into the foyer made it worthwhile, however. We fell into step behind them as they headed out onto the street. Once outside, Gary handed me a piece of paper with a name and address on it.

"So, what's the story?" I poked Gary in his side to encourage him to answer.

"Well," he began, "First, the clerk practically jumped back when I showed him the drawing, almost as if he was expecting it to bite him. After that, any chance he had of feigning ignorance collapsed immediately."

"If that wasn't enough, his exclamation of 'Not another one!' certainly sealed it," Adelita added in a pleased tone.

Gary nodded his agreement. "Indeed. So, once he'd backed himself into a corner, we offered him a way out by asking to speak to his manager, and he jumped at it."

Adelita took up the narrative once again. "She was harder to crack. Gary was bringing out all sorts of child psychology phrases to try to convince her that whoever drew this needed professional help, but she was stonewalling like a professional. Then I asked about the clerk's comment of 'not another one'…"

Inside Erma Lillybottle's office, the unexpected meeting with a doctor and a representative of UNESCO was not going well. "He didn't say that! I mean, wh-why would he say something like that?" Erma spluttered, her hand falling away from the knob on the door to her office, where she was about to usher her two unwelcome early morning interruptions out.

Gary simply pulled his smartphone out of his jacket pocket and, thumbing a few buttons, flooded the small room with the clerk's voice uttering those exact words.

"It's illegal to record someone without their knowledge," the manager attempted to offer as defense.

"Yes, it is," Adelita admitted, "But so is ignoring your mandatory reporting responsibilities to this child. You have already seen our credentials, you know we are exactly the people you are supposed to report this sort of thing to, so why dissemble now? What are you hiding, Mrs. Lillybottle?"

Erma's shoulders slumped in visible defeat. "Okay, look, if I give you the information you want will you at least keep the name of this hotel out of the media? Times are tough, and we really don't need this kind of publicity."

Gary stood, extending his hand to the manager to shake on the deal. "Trust me Mrs. Lillybottle, if there is one thing I will guarantee you, it is that you will hear nothing of this matter reported in the media."

"Cheeky sod."

Gary shrugged at my good-natured rebuke. "Sorry, couldn't resist. Anyway, what we were able to learn was that the lovely little family of Tracey, Edmund, and their daughter Hattie Newman, won the hotel room and theatre package in a local raffle. Apparently, they are the 'never won anything before' type and wouldn't be able to afford anything like this on their own. They stayed for three nights, and the hotel cleaners refused to go into their suite after the first night. The manager didn't know about this later because the family never complained, but apparently the cleaners were just too scared to step inside."

"Makes sense. What about after they left?" I queried.

"Erma had a video of that on her computer," Gary replied.

"Erma?" Orfael asked.

"The manager," Adelita replied, smoothly taking over for Gary once again. "The cleaners were so shocked that they asked her to record the room before they went in."

"There was that much damage?" asked Beatrice.

Adelita shook her head. "No damage at all. But apparently every wall, window, door, and flat surface in the room was covered in children's drawings, blu-tacked up so that they covered the place. Want to guess what they were drawings of?"

"Not really, no." I shuddered at the thought of that many spiders.

"Nightmares," Gary said anyway. "Not just spiders like the one we found. But just about every shadowy what-goes-bump-in-the-night creature you can think of; or in this case, that a small child can think of. It took a full day to clear them all away apparently, and they burned them in the boiler room. It seems they missed one, however."

"Which I found," I commented without enthusiasm. "Yay, me."

Admonae put a comforting hand on my shoulder. "You were meant to. Think about it—The family winning the raffle. Our own homes suddenly all becoming off limits. This room being the only one left."

"Careful, Admonae," Gary said. "It's been so long, and raising hopes like that…"

I shook my head and used the moment to brush away a small tear before the others could see it. "No, not hope, Gary. *Faith*."

"Just as dangerous," Gary dismissed my rebuttal. "The point to focus on is that we have a name and address. We need to go and meet this family."

"But what about Kateri?" Orfael demanded. "Isn't she and whatever Michael is doing our priority? What if all this is just a plot by him to keep us off the trail?"

Gary put on his best bedside-manner voice. "You could be right, Orfael, but this girl has the power to affect one of us."

"To affect *Joan*," Beatrice interjected, as she saw Orfael purse her lips to argue. Orfael clamped her jaw shut at the comment.

"Gee thanks guys," I joked. "It's nice that you're finally seeing the light."

Gary took a playful swing at my shoulder. "Get over yourself, Joan. You may be the strongest fighter, but fighting isn't everything."

I grinned my best maniacal grin and started to draw back my fist, but the glare from a couple of older ladies walking past, trailing their wheeled baskets behind them, made me pause. Yes, what was happening with Kateri was very personal to us, but that wasn't what we were here for. We were put here for them.

"We go to the girl's home and check this out," I said with a finality that ended any other argument. Without hesitation, my friends fell into step behind me as I headed to the subway station. They were right about one thing, after all; from the Wingless that were left, I was the fighter, and that's what I was ready for.

Chapter Fifteen

I've always liked travelling by the subway system in London. It is its own strange little world, complete with unique culture and societal rules. I've never been able to work them all out, actually, and so in a world where I have lived just about everywhere at some point in history, it is one of the few places where I still get to feel like a visitor, a tourist. Here's a tip to remember - as you move through this world, never begrudge feeling that sense of wonder and newness when visiting a place for the first time. Sure, you may be uncomfortable and dubious about the experience, but trust me, knowing absolutely everywhere on the planet so well that you never get to feel that way again is nothing to write home about either.

Days with football matches were the best ones, as far as I was concerned. All the colour of the team's supporters ebbing and flowing between the platforms as if the subway was its own tidal river. Shouts of celebrations, groans of consolation, camaraderie and ... family.

Today, however, I was too aware of our destination to properly enjoy the journey. The idea that awaited me was a young girl with the power to instill such terror in, of all people, me - that's not something one rushes headlong towards unless they have to. And certainly not something one does without a lot of detailed information and a rock-solid plan.

Except now, apparently, as I had neither.

Adelita had been called on her mobile before we reached the train station. Like Damien last night, an emergency in her 'human' life called her away. When someone in our realm needs our help, we don't ignore them; that is what we were put here to do, after all. She had also convinced Orfael to go with her. She had coped the least well of all of us with what happened in Africa, and Adelita quietly told me she thought Orfael needed a break.

West London swept by us in a blur of stations, Berrylands, Wimbledon, Putney Bridge, until we finally arrived at Fulham Broadway Station. The sun was high in the sky by the time we got to the Riley Street tower of the World's End Estate in Chelsea, and we looked up at the series of towering walls of sand orange and red brick apartments.

"World's End Estate?" Spluttered Gary. "Is this someone's idea of a joke?"

I shrugged. "The universe loves a pun. Doesn't quite look like the birthplace of ultimate terror, does it?"

"It does to me," Silje replied, looking a little pale. "Look around. There are no birds on any of the buildings. No neighbourhood cats looking through garbage hoppers. I doubt there is even any mice in the area."

Gary extended his senses for a moment before nodding." She's got a point. Anything that can move on from here, has. If we were to check police records, I wouldn't be at all surprised to see a marked drop in nighttime muggings around this estate as well."

"Safety, thy name is fear?" Enquired Admonae, with a wry smile.

Gary shook his head. "I'm not feeling anything malicious, at a guess it's just a side-effect."

I stood quietly for a few minutes and watched my friends, four celestial beings whom I have seen face Fallen

Angels, monsters, and all the terrors mankind can create, shuffle their feet and fidget as they discussed the social pros and cons of fear as a motivator to good behaviour. Whether they realised it or not, they were delaying going any further. There was no other way to describe it; we were spooked.

When they started meandering back towards the station as they talked, I knew I needed to do something to break them out of the loop they had gotten themselves stuck in. I raised my voice a little as I spoke: "Okay, they'll be time enough to discuss this all later. We're here to do a job, we might as well get it done."

Gary blinked and looked at how far he had moved. "That's interesting. I don't remember deciding to leave."

Beatrice frowned. "Another one of those side-effects, I imagine. Lead on, Joan, I promise we'll keep it together this time."

Taking a deep breath, we marched as one towards Northbridge Tower, the name for the middle of the blocks that made up the estate. The address we had gotten from the hotel manager pointed us to apartment 14C, about halfway up the tower, but even without the actual apartment number I could tell where we needed to go as soon as we stepped from the staircase and onto the 14th floor.

Yes, the staircase. All fourteen floors. We had started climbing the stairs without so much as a comment to each other. It was as if taking the elevator had never even occurred to us. Somehow, being enclosed in a small metal box hanging a hundred or so feet above the ground by unseen cables was not the most appealing of ideas just then.

Silje looked over the railing as we walked slowly along the open corridor that wound its way around the side of the building. "Does this floor seem awfully high to anyone else, or is it just me?"

Gary took a quick look over before moving back to walk alongside the wall of the building. "Nope, it's high," he managed to squeak.

"Said the immortal Angel who should be used to flying with his own wings," came a voice from behind us.

As one, we spun around. Standing there, trying, and failing, to look like she was completely unaffected by whatever power pervaded this area, was Kateri.

"You followed us?" asked Beatrice, hands already balling into fists and readying for a fight.

"No, sorry. Got here about an hour ago. Only managed to pull together the courage to come up from the floor below when I saw the five of you pass by. Which begs the question, Joan, how did you, of all Angels, not see me?"

I did my best to cover my own surprise at seeing her, although I'm not at all sure that I was in any way successful. "I was … preoccupied, I guess. It's this place. Anyway, you've fallen, Kateri, you know the deal. Full power, black wings, smug attitude; the whole shebang."

Kateri shook her head. "No, Joan. I'm not Fallen. Not quite yet, anyway."

"Bullshit," I spat back. "The types of miracles you were throwing around in Africa…"

Kateri pleaded with her eyes, the pain in them quite obvious. "I did what I had to do, what I was *forced* to do.

But I'm not Fallen yet. Falling? Perhaps, but somehow, I haven't quite landed … There is a lot I need to tell you, but not here. I do believe, however, that someone here is central to it all."

"A girl," Silje offered, before Gary could shush her.

Kateri jumped on the admission. "You know who it is, then. Care to share?"

There were so many questions I wanted to ask. What was she? Why had she left us? How did she know to come here? What were her plans now she had found the girl? But part of me just got angry instead. Angry that we always seemed to be on the back foot in all of this. Angry that yet again, I had been caught unawares. And angry that I still felt that running from here as fast as I could was the better part of valour. So instead of answering Kateri directly, I turned and, steeling myself, started to march with a resoluteness I didn't really feel for the door to the apartment at 14C.

"If you want to know, come and find out for yourself," I barked through gritted teeth. I had reached the point where I did not care whether they followed or not. I was going to get some answers.

I found myself pounding hard on the door to apartment 14C hard enough to rattle the door in its frame, as Gary's hand lightly touched my shoulder. "Ease up, Joan," he whispered.

'Do not be afraid'. Ever wonder why Angels throughout history tended to start conversations like that? When we're in full flight, we can be quite terrifying. I took Gary's meaning to heart and calmed myself before the door opened.

When someone pounds on your door like that, especially in inner London, one might quite reasonably expect to have the door answered by someone holding a softball bat or rolling pin raised in defense. The small woman who opened the door, however, was simply drying her hands on a tea towel, without a single crease of worry or concern on her face. Regardless of what was on her doorstep, this woman felt completely safe within her home. Gary and I exchanged a glance, and I could see that he had noticed all this as well.

"Yes?" The woman stepped forward to the threshold of the door and looked around the assembled group.

Gary stepped forward from behind me to take point on the conversation. He knew I was a terrible liar. "Mrs. Newman, my name is Dr. Gary Caff. I'm from St. Mary's Children's Hospital, and we'd like to talk to you about your daughter." I nodded at his flawless delivery and felt the small amount of miraculous power flow out from him saying 'you can trust me'.

Which meant the response he got came as quite the surprise: "No."

The flat denial did not leave us very many places to go. Kateri, on the other hand, obviously felt that she wasn't nearly as restricted in her actions. Stepping forward, she allowed her power to flow, and we could all feel the strange, almost oily texture to her miracle, the same feeling from the trail we had followed all across Africa. It wasn't the type of miracle we used, but neither was it the full black miracle of a Fallen. Could she have been telling the truth?

Regardless, I wasn't about to let her do whatever it was she had planned. Before I could react, however, a small girl wandered out from her bedroom and into the view of the front door. With nothing more than a small smile, she managed to stop Kateri in her tracks.

A small 'eep' escaped Kateri's lips, and she jumped back against the wall and out of sight of the doorway, a look of pure terror on her face. Whatever terrified her seemed to pass just as quickly, but it left her quite shaken.

"You're funny," the little girl chuckled to herself. "It's okay, Mum, these are my friends. You can let them in."

Tracey Newman's reaction was telling. The woman turned back to look at me… no, it would be more accurate to say she looked right *through* me, and her eyes narrowed threateningly. Her voice stayed calm and soft, but it struck through me like a sword. From the reactions of my companions, I wasn't the only one who felt it. "Listen, Angel, you can come in, but you behave, or you'll find out just what Humans can do."

If this was a scene in a movie I was directing, I would have every Angel standing in that doorway silently blink in unison. To be honest, I'm not sure we didn't.

"I'm sorry?" I managed to stutter.

The stamp of a tiny foot and exasperated call of "Mu-*um!*" stopped whatever response Tracey had for me. She bent down and kissed her daughter on the forehead before locking eyes meaningfully with me once more as she addressed her daughter. "I will make tea, but I expect your 'friends' to be gone before supper, understood, young lady?"

A smile bloomed on the young girl's face, and she beckoned to us with her dainty hand. "Come along, it's okay. I'm not drawing right now, just playing with my Legos."

The collective sigh from all the Angels at the door made the girl giggle as she headed back towards her bedroom. Gary was the first to vocalise what we were all thinking. "Creepy."

"Very," added Admonae.

"You shouldn't talk about her like that!" Interjected Kateri, with unexpected vehemence.

I turned to face her. "Why not, Kateri?"

"I … I don't know." Her brow furrowed as she tried to make sense of what she was feeling. "It just doesn't seem right, you know?"

From the looks passing between Admonae and Silje, I could tell that they, like myself, certainly didn't feel there was anything inaccurate or inappropriate in Gary's classification of the girl. Beatrice, however, had stepped slightly closer to Kateri, and the puzzled look on her face seemed to suggest she agreed with her. When I questioned this with a raised eyebrow, all Beatrice could do was shrug her shoulders.

I've always found in these situations that pragmatism at least provided a way forward. I turned back to the still-open door. "I'd rather not have Mrs. Newman make tea for nothing, people. Let's go in."

The moment I stepped inside, a feeling of complete safety came over me. I turned to see how the others were reacting and saw for the first time that the walls, ceiling, and windows of the little apartment were completely covered in various pencil drawings of creepy, frightening scenes or creatures. Above the door itself was the very image that had caused me to scream in the hotel - but here I felt nothing but peace and overwhelming safety. I just knew that nothing could hurt me while I was in this apartment.

Gary had a beatific smile on his face. Admonae and Beatrice were more at ease than I had seen them for decades. And Kateri's shoulders slumped with a sigh that spoke volumes. "I may never leave here," she added. Only Silje looked unaffected by the peace within the room. She simply looked curiously about her, as if searching for something.

We were still standing in the loungeroom when the whistling of a kettle in the kitchen broke us from our reverie. Had we really spent that long just stepping over the threshold of the apartment?

Chapter Sixteen

To say that we had to be directed to sit and partake in tea by the young girl like a group of simpletons would be unkind. Accurate, sure, but unkind, nevertheless. Regardless, we soon found ourselves sipping tea across from this miniscule enigma, while her equally confusing mother busied herself in the kitchen.

Kateri gathered herself quicker than the rest of us, possibly due to whatever else she was going through, and started the conversation we had come to have in earnest. "Okay, love, fancy drawings and weird presence aside, who are you?"

The girl giggled delightfully before answering. "I'm Hattie."

"All right then," I interrupted, not ready to hand control over to a possible fallen, or falling, Angel. "What are you?"

"I'm one of you," she answered, in that tone children exclusively use when explaining the complete obvious to clueless adults.

I looked down at the mismatched teacups laid out on the table between us, and then up to my companions. Beatrice was sitting a little back from the table and keeping more of an eye on Kateri than the child. Kateri, for her part, was doing her best to ignore the attention.

Gary and Admonae looked as puzzled as I felt and were whispering something to each other while they watched our exchange. Silje, however, regarded the girl with a laser-like focus, and a look of concentration on her face that was completely out of character. When she spoke, the friendly, lilting tone her voice usually carried was gone. She didn't sound angry or upset, just … detached.

"One of us," Silje stated firmly.

"Yes, more than you realise." Hattie's voice had taken on the same tonal resonation as Silje's.

Silje leaned forward, her hands on the table. "Let me hear you, then."

"That would not be safe," Hattie replied.

"But you will let me do it anyway." Our heads had been going back and forth during this exchange as if we were all watching some tiny tennis match. It was only when I stopped watching them and looked at the rest of the room that I noticed it had gotten quite dark.

"Err," I started to interject, "Has anyone else noticed…"

"As you wish," interrupted Hattie, and she sat back from the table, crossing her arms in a way that would look quite intimidating if it wasn't coming from an 11-year-old girl.

Silje reached out to hold my hand on one side and Beatrice on the other and closed her eyes. Suddenly, I could hear the music that Silje heard all the time, and I imagine Beatrice could as well. From Beatrice's lack of reaction, I discerned that this was not the first time she had experienced this little trick of Silje's.

The music was awe-inspiringly beautiful, but before I could get caught up and carried away by it, the focus seemed to shift – it was like someone was zooming in on the sound of just one instrument in an orchestra, the same way someone with a telescope could focus on just one person in a crowd. The notes clarified, and somehow, I understood that I was hearing Hattie. Whether through some kind of highlighting by Silje or just an innate understanding, I realised that what I was listening to was indeed a Wingless, just like us, and one whose realm was that of Fear.

A new Wingless. But that was impossible, surely?

With an almost inaudible "*Eeep*," Silje jumped back in her chair and let go of our hands, dropping the connection. Kateri had also taken in a breath with a shocked gulp.

"Silje?" Beatrice reached out for her old friend, but Silje backed away a little more. She glanced from Beatrice to me, but all I could offer was a shrug. While I could tell that Hattie's realm was fear, there was nothing innately frightening about that knowledge, almost as if the power we felt from the drawings just wasn't switched on at the moment. I couldn't understand what had spooked Silje.

"Silje, sweetheart?" Beatrice was still trying to reach the stunned angel. "It's all right, there is nothing here to be concerned about."

"No." Silje's voice was so soft I almost missed what she was saying. "No, it's not that. You don't understand. She's …"

Whatever Silje intended to say was drowned out by a discordant chime that slammed into our senses as if we were sitting in the front row of a taiko concert. An Archangel not only forcefully manifesting just outside in the courtyard between the towers, but one that had arrived loaded for bear.

Michael.

A heartbeat later two smaller tones also chimed into existence outside. I couldn't recognise who they were specifically, but the oily texture to the sound only meant one thing. I jumped to my feet, knocking the little chair back out from under me. "Fallen!"

As one, we rushed to the door of the little apartment and out onto the balcony, passing a furious looking Tracey as she ran into the bedroom to her daughter. Her hand gripped my shoulder as she passed, and she growled into my ear, "Swear you'll keep her safe!" I looked straight into those mother-bear's eyes and did so.

Once outside, I leaned over the balcony. Down below on the ground stood Michael, in all his blazing glory, and two Fallen had taken up a position between him and the building we were in.

Michael's sword hung loose and unlit in his hand, almost as if he saw the two fallen angels before him as little more than gnats. The swagger in his movements as he practically sauntered his way toward them telegraphed that he was looking forward to fighting the Fallen a lot more than he should have. To him, this battle was more than just his job.

"I give you one chance to depart, graceless ones. I come here for someone other than you." We watched as the two fallen angels glanced at one another and stood their ground. One stepped forward to face the Archangel, but I saw the shoulders on the other drop for a moment. His compatriot had raised his own sword and stood pointing it at Michael. "No, *you* leave, you overstuffed peacock! We're here to destroy the abomination!" The fallen glanced back over his shoulder and up at us on the balcony, before looking back to Michael. "Leave now!"

Michael's eyes glowered at the insult, but confusion warred on his face. "But... no. It is of no matter. You will die by my hand, and then I'll do what I came here to do."

Silje stepped back toward the door. "They mean to kill Hattie!"

For her part, Admonae couldn't take her eyes off the Fallen who had spoken, "But ... that was a lie. He lied?"

Gary was watching the second Fallen. "I could have sworn that one waved us away behind his back a moment ago."

It was Beatrice that put it all together. "When his friend was saying 'leave'! That was for us!"

"But why?" I couldn't see why a Fallen would go toe to toe with Michael just to give us a chance to run.

As I paused, Michael stepped forward with preternatural speed and simply decapitated the Fallen before him without so much as a comment. His friend attempted to step up and protect him, but only managed to trade a handful of blows with the archangel of war before he was slammed to the ground and run through.

With a visceral cry of victory that sickened me to my stomach, Michael turned his gaze up at the apartment we were in, extended his wings, and jumped.

I was worried that in delaying our escape I had trapped us, when a sickening feeling of vertigo swept over me. A billowing black shape swept past us from inside the apartment and dove, screaming, at Michael.

It was Kateri, and just before she met him midway up the building, her wings extended in their full glory—but black, as we all felt her make the final choice to Fall.

The explosion of power hit the unsuspecting and unprepared Archangel as a millennium of unused miracles exploded in fury above him. The pair went down, crashing onto the ground in a concrete-splitting crunch. But where

Kateri had spent all her power in one push to stop him, Michael had barely been hurt by the encounter.

Michael practically leapt to his feet with the chance to dispatch another Fallen, his eyes only seeing his next victim lying prone on the ground. The bright silver sword swung high and came crashing down towards Kateri's neck, only to be glanced aside at the last moment by a second, pitch black sword.

Confused, Michael looked up to be face-to-face with a smiling Azazel.

"Trying to do me out of a job, bro?" Azazel stated with brazen impudence. "You know I'm supposed to catch these fine folks when they Fall."

Michael roared in mindless fury and rage at the interruption, but Azazel used the distraction to wingbeat the Archangel and stagger him back with the power of a miracle he had been quietly building up. Azazel stooped to sweep the still stunned Kateri into his arms and leapt into the air, with Michael just a few heartbeats behind them. The trio quickly disappeared into the distance, and I let go of the breath I hadn't realised I had been holding.

We all practically fell back into the apartment, Gary closing and locking the door behind us. With the door closed, however, that previous feeling of safety flowed over me once again, and I finally understood.

"You can't be reached in here, can you, Hattie?" I turned to face the strangely unperturbed little girl, safe in the arms of her mother standing behind her. "That's why the drawings. That's why you had to put them up in the hotel you stayed at. It's how you protect yourself."

"For now," she answered with an impish smile. "I am still very young, you know."

With his back still against the door, Gary muttered, "Yay?"

Silje had broken into tears and stood being held by Beatrice, quietly sobbing into her chest. Losing Kateri, after all we went through to try to find her, was going to be difficult for all of us, but I hadn't reckoned on it hitting Silje quite so hard.

To be honest, I wasn't coping with it very well either. Every step of the way it felt like we had been just a little too late, a little too uninformed. And I hated losing, especially when it meant losing a friend. Feeling the need to lash out at something, I turned my anger and grief towards my old punching bag. "Azazel! Was this his plan all along? Trick us here, send his cronies to kill the girl, and just wait until Kateri fell to protect her? When I see that slimy, manipulative bastard, I'm going to…"

Gary stepped away from the door and grabbed my arm, gently folding his hand over my balled-up fist. "No, Joan, calm down. I don't think they were here to kill Hattie. I think they laid down their lives to protect her. Admonae could tell they were lying about harming her. I saw one try to wave us off."

"Don't be ridiculous, Gary," I snapped back, "They would have to know that they wouldn't have a chance against Michael by themselves, they would have to…" The image of those slumping shoulders came rushing back to me. That was the stance of a soldier being ordered to die. "Oh my god. They *did* know. They knew, Gary, they knew they had no hope."

Beatrice spoke softly over Silje's head "And they did it anyway. But why?"

"Hattie doesn't have a note." Silje's voice was muffled by Beatrice's hugging, so she pushed herself back from the embrace of her friend. "We all have a single note that defines us. She doesn't."

While that may have made perfect sense to Silje, it was obvious from the looks on our faces that it left the rest of us none the wiser. Admonae reached out for Silje's hand and held it gently as she asked, "That's good to know, Silje, but you seemed to be able to still hear her. What does she have, then?"

"She's a melody of sorts, a superposition of three distinct notes. One of those notes is human." Silje pulled Admonae closer. "One is Kateri."

"Wingless don't have children." I spoke before I could stop myself, not quite believing what I was hearing. Silje, however, seemed prepared for this, and she waited for silence before continuing.

"And the third note is Beatrice."

Chapter Seventeen

"**W**hat?"

I don't quite know what tone my voice implied in that one word, but from the way Silje shrunk back into Beatrice's arms, I doubt it was particularly friendly.

Silje's normally soft voice was barely audible. "I'm sorry, that's what I heard."

"Then you were mistaken!" I barked. Gary placed his hand on my shoulder, but I shook it and any attempt to calm me down off.

Silje's eyes blazed at the implication, however, the earlier confidence she displayed when talking to Hattie was back with a vengeance. "No, Joan, I am not! I may be young, you may think I'm 'silly' most of the time, but I *know* the music. I know what I heard and you're just going to have to accept it."

I took a quick step towards the younger angel. Silje had straightened her back; her arms were rigid by her sides and her fists were clenched. The muscles about her jaw tightened at my approach and my soldier's instinct told me she had prepared herself for a blow she knew she couldn't stop.

Just like the Fallen outside had.

I'd scared her – at the point when we should all be pulling together more than ever, I had made Silje afraid of me. And I had done it with just five words. Not for the first time, I wondered just what my friends truly thought of me, and my heart broke a little.

I continued forwards and swept Silje into my arms, holding her tightly. I dipped my head to bring my lips near her ear and spoke as gently as I could. "I'm so sorry. Of course, you heard it correctly, Silje, there is no way *you* couldn't. I should not have doubted you or gotten angry. I'm just so confused. Nothing's simple anymore. We need you – *I* need you. Please forgive me."

Silje's rigid body slowly softened in my arms, and I felt her nod against my cheek. I released the hug but kept one arm around her shoulders, not wanting the contact to end too soon. Coolness stung my cheek where her tears had started to evaporate off my skin. Turning, I saw the rest of my friends starting to relax, and Hattie smiling up at Beatrice.

"Whatever is going on here," I started, surprising myself a little at the calmness I heard in my own voice, "We need to stick together. We may not be all powerful Angels, but we do have each other." I felt Silje's arm snake around my waist and felt immensely grateful for the gesture.

Admonae, bless her, stepped up to fill the silence. "Kateri falling, or completing her fall, or whatever it was she just did, is going to affect the rest of us as well. We need to regroup, check with Azazel on how Kateri is doing, and let the rest know what we've found. And I think we need to do that in person. I'll contact Toby and Lennox and set up a meeting at the usual place."

Gary nodded, quickly falling in behind Admonae's sensible analysis of the situation. "I'll step outside and contact Azazel. What about Hattie?"

Admonae shook her head. "No. She's safe here, aren't you sweetheart?"

Looking away from Beatrice for a moment, she nodded, "Yes, Admonael."

A slight eye-twitch was all the indication that Admonae gave to her discomfort at hearing her full name come from the little girl. "Then we leave her here. It would probably be best if we limit our contact with Hattie—for a while, anyway."

Beatrice pulled her own gaze away from the little face that was looking up at her. "I'm not sure I want to leave, but if you think it's for the best?"

Before Admonae could reply, Hattie reached up and took Beatrice's hand in hers. "It is, Mum. For now."

The silence that followed her use of the parental title was so complete that a passing dust mote was suddenly surprised to find itself embarrassed at the tremendous amount of noise it was making.

"Ooookay..." Gary moved between Beatrice and Hattie, gently taking Beatrice's hand away from the little girl, "Are you okay with this, Tracey? Would you like one of us to stay?"

At the sound of her name, Tracey turned away from looking at Beatrice, her face the image of someone who had just solved a puzzle that had been troubling them for years. "No, thank you, Gary. We will be fine. All of you, however, are welcome back. Although preferably without the additional 'drop-in' guests."

"Tracey, I have to know," I said, "How did you know who we are?"

Tracey shrugged and hugged her daughter closer. "I don't know, not really. I do know that ever since I became pregnant with Hattie, I could see your kind and recognise them for what they were whenever we passed in the street. It didn't happen often though, there seems to be very few of you."

I swallowed hard at that. "I know," I said quietly.

Gary spoke up to pull the attention off me. "Good. Well then, Beatrice, if you could give me a hand outside on the balcony, we'll contact Azazel." Gary steered his friend out the front door and closed it behind them, but not quick enough for them to miss a certain girl's voice happily chirp, "See you later, Mum!"

As sad as I was at Tracey's observation, it was hard not to chuckle at the involuntary flinch in Beatrice's shoulders as she disappeared behind the closing door. Admonae obviously felt similarly as she raised an eyebrow at Hattie. "You did that on purpose, didn't you?"

The glint of amusement in her eyes betrayed the innocent smile Hattie made in reply, before she skipped back to the kitchen, hand in hand with her human mother and asking for cookies.

Still with my arm about her, Silje shook her head in disbelief. "Oh boy."

Outside on the balcony, Gary closed the door and pulled out his mobile phone. Keying 'A', he activated speaker mode and dialed.

Beatrice looked at him curiously. "You have Azazel's number?"

Gary nodded. "Yep, he pops by the café every now and then for a chat."

"Then why did you make Joan call him earlier?" Beatrice asked.

Glancing back at the closed door to the apartment, Gary leant close to Beatrice and answered in a whisper. "Trust me, in situations like these, it's best to make sure Joan has something to do."

The screen on Gary's mobile phone switched to green as the call was answered. "Azazel, great! Listen, mind if we check up on Kateri?"

The speaker whistled, sounding like the other phone was in the middle of a high wind.

"Azazel?" Gary queried, leaning closer to the microphone, "Can you hear me?"

The loud, sharp clash of steel on steel made him jump back, and Azazel's strained voice came through in staccato bursts. "Little...busy! …" He grunted. "... Call … later …"

The line went dead.

"I guess he's still engaged with you-know-who "Gary said, a little sheepishly. "We should leave it for a while."

Beatrice nodded in agreement. "I'm sure we'll get a better reception later."

Gary blinked, looking at the emotionless face of his usually stoic companion. "Better reception? Did you just make a joke?"

"What do you think?" Beatrice replied in a deadpan voice.

"I think I'd be wanting to ask for a second opinion." Gary turned back to the door.

I opened the front door of the apartment onto Beatrice thumping Gary on the shoulder.

With an exasperated sigh, I stalked out of the apartment. "Gary!"

Gary was rubbing his shoulder in obvious pain. "What? She hit me!"

"Yeah, well you probably deserved it," I said. "Let's get out of here."

Chapter Eighteen

Unbeknownst to us, while all this was happening with Hattie and her family, Lennox and Adelita were carrying out their own investigation...

The haunting melody of Michael Nyman's *The Departure* floated across the foyer of the Clarion House Gentleman's Club before Lennox hurriedly mashed the power key to shut her phone down.

Beside her, Adelita cringed at the sound. "Really?"

"I'm not used to going out in the field, okay?" The two of them rushed to hide behind the large bronze statue as private security stomped into the foyer, looking for the source of the music.

"This whole thing was your idea!" Hissed Adelita.

It had been.

After the return of Joan and the others from Africa, and everyone's subsequent strangely coincidental displacement from their homes, Lennox had decided to start digging through the digital world in search of answers. If anyone had 'arranged' this, it turned out they were better at hiding their tracks than Lennox was at finding them. And Lennox was very good indeed. Some of the Wingless even joked that if she were to get her wings back, instead of feathers she would have a series of ones and zeros.

What she *had* found, however, was an old friend. Or at least the tell-tale gap where an old friend should be.

Jehoel, or Joel, as he went by now, was the forgotten Wingless in many ways. After Joan had effectively told him he was no longer welcome, Lennox was the only one to keep a covert eye out for the wayward Angel. It started back around the time of the Industrial Revolution, when Joel had first decided to experiment with experiencing life as a human. *Really* experiencing it.

At dawn, each day when their powers would renew, Joel would immediately use a miracle to rid himself of them, living the next 24 hours completely powerless, completely human. When Joan originally discovered this, she had flipped out, upset at the danger he was putting himself in, and furious that he would remove his capability, however limited it was, to help the humans he had been tasked with protecting.

In the ensuing fallout from their argument, she effectively banished him from her sight, and the rest of the Wingless seemed to feel that meant theirs as well. But Lennox could never bring herself to completely abandon her old friend, and she would continue to check in on him.

With all the trouble surrounding Kateri, Joel had slipped off Lennox's radar, until a text message appeared on her phone the day Joan and the others returned from Africa. It simply stated: *'Now is the time for family. You need to check on your wayward brother. Can't say anything more. A.'* The message had apparently originated from the burner phone to end all burner phones, because all attempts at tracing it ended up with coordinates that placed the call as coming from the middle of the Sun.

Lennox had smirked when she finally confirmed that to her satisfaction. "I guess no one said Fallen had to be subtle."

Long ago, Lennox had developed algorithms that now infested the net, designed to notice applications of miraculous power. In most areas of the world, they would gather only the most peripheral of data, although everything was useful.

In London however, a city with more CCTV and other surveillance coverage than most other places in the world, they truly came into their own. Lennox had even designed the programs to be self-learning, so they continued to get better at what they were designed to do when they were left alone.

One in particular, "Sid," had been told to monitor for Joel, and Lennox sent a command for it to report.

"Ma'am," chimed the smartwatch on Lennox's arm.

"Yes, Sid, what do you have for me?" Lennox replied.

"Well, ma'am, either the creation of a dozen new aspects of Joel, or humans with miraculous power," the program said.

Even though Azazel's text had clued Lennox into the fact that something was amiss, the reply startled her. "Err… Sid? Have you blown a few circuits?" Lennox knew that Sid was more than just lines of code, after all she had used her own miraculous power to lend it abilities akin to the Artificial Intelligence of science fiction, but this report was still not making any sense.

"If I may," Sid continued, "New data awaits you at your terminal."

Curiosity getting the better of her, Lennox switched screens from trying to get a flight for Adelita back to Geneva. Her current failure to book a simple flight for the Angel was a puzzle she was still trying to solve. For the moment, she put that to one side and instead brought up her own command console.

When Adelita returned from getting coffee fifteen minutes later, Lennox was still glued to the screen. "Hey girl, any luck with getting me a flight home?"

"Adelita!" Lennox spun around in her chair, having forgotten all about the mystery of the flights. "You've got to come with me. I think Joel is in trouble!"

"What are you talking about? Are you still in contact with Joel? And since when do you want to go out and work with anything other than these machines?" Adelita was still holding the unclaimed cup of coffee out to her caffeine-addicted friend, and the fact that it had not yet been taken was starting to help her realise whatever had spooked Lennox was something important.

"I'm referring to our brother, Johoel. I'm not in contact with him, not really anyway." Lennox had started to mechanically answer each of Adelita's questions in turn, a sure sign that the technologically attuned angel was stressed. Adelita started to interrupt her friend, but held her tongue. By doing so, she would only slow the agitated Lennox even further.

"I have several programs in the CCTV and other networks that try to keep tabs on him, since Joan forbade us from contacting him directly. They have detected an anomaly that leads me to believe he is in trouble." Lennox omitted mentioning the tip off from Azazel.

Despite herself, Adelita protested, "Be fair, Joan didn't *forbid* us from seeing him. It was more that she wanted to shock him out of doing what he was … doing to himself."

"Possibly true," Lennox conceded, "But ultimately irrelevant."

Adelita held up her hands in supplication. "Okay, okay, not important right now. What makes you think he is in danger, Lennox? Just the expedited version, please."

Lennox nodded, and motioned to the computer screen where she brought up a series of video recordings of London streets, small parks, and shopfronts. "This is Soho, one of Joel's favourite haunts recently. I can usually see him here every day, sometimes begging, sometimes busking, but usually just sitting somewhere and watching the people go by."

Adelita scanned the six different camera feeds on the screen but could see nothing out of the ordinary herself. "And he's not here now? He could have just moved on, you know—gotten bored with Soho and decided to find new people to watch?"

"A good first assumption, but there is more. While my programs have failed to discern where in the city he is, and while that may mean he has left London altogether, they have data patterns that suggest he is at multiple places, sometimes simultaneously." A few clicks of the mouse and Lennox brought up an overlay map that had several golden flashes appear upon it.

"There are the humans in the videos," Lennox went on to explain, "Who look to be casting minor miracles, usually on other humans but sometimes on Automatic Teller Machines."

"In Soho?" Adelita asked.

"In Soho," Lennox confirmed.

An hour later, the two Angels had alighted from the train and were walking the streets of Soho. Seeing as most of the 'miracles' that were recorded being used on people were being used on young women, Adelita had taken the time to weave a miracle from her realm of innocence about herself and Lennox: To any passing human they would appear as completely innocent and inexperienced young women. Effectively, the perfect targets.

Whether it was an unfortunate, although possibly accurate, comment on humanity, or the skill with which Adelita had weaved her obfuscating miracle, only twenty minutes had gone by before a man in his late thirties sidled up to the two 'young' women.

"Ladies! How wonderful to see you again! It's been so long, how are you?" The patter was hardly convincing, but both the Angels felt the flow of an extremely small miracle emanate from the man and wash over them. 'We're old friends,' it said. 'You can trust me, you feel safe with me, you like me'.

It was all Lennox could do to stop herself retching at the greasy feel of it. There was no chance a miracle so weak was going to work on the Wingless, but the lecherous undercurrents in the effort the man was putting behind it made her feel physically ill. On a human, however, his trick would have worked, for a while anyway.

Adelita had a very different reaction.

In a flash, her hands snapped out and grabbed the man's head, fingers at his temples. Feeling how many innocents this man had taken advantage of for his own desires fueled her fury, and her will drove into the man's psyche, exposing all his nasty little secrets to her.

Adelita's vengeance acted at the speed of thought, and with a cry the man collapsed in a sobbing heap on the ground. Before anyone around them could react, Adelita strode off, pulling Lennox along with her and disappearing into the lunch time crowd.

After they had gone about a block from the scene, Lennox turned her still angry friend to face her. "Ade, stop! What did you do? You didn't hurt him, did you? We're not supposed to hurt them."

Adelita breathed deeply, once, twice, and a third time, attempting to calm herself before answering cryptically. "I didn't do anything to him, he did it all to himself."

Lennox frowned, obviously not appeased by the answer. "That sounds like Beatrice talking, not you. What did you do?"

With a self-satisfied smirk, Adelita turned her gaze back the way they had come, to where a small crowd was forming around the crying man. "I found out how he was doing his disgusting little trick, and where he got his power from. I'd guess that is where we will find Joel."

"And..." Lennox poked her impatiently.

"And I reversed all his memories of using the power. Every disgusting little thing he did to someone else, he is now experiencing instead."

Lennox backed away a step. "But that's..."

"Innocence, Lennox," Adelita said firmly. "My realm. He stole it from those girls. They now have it back. Those events never happened to them, and so they will never remember them. They all happened to him now." Adelita paused, and slowly her look lost its hard edge, her features softening. "Only I may have gone too far in my anger."

"What do you mean?" Lennox asked softly.

"I didn't just want to erase the girl's memories of the events, that seemed as much of a violation as what he did.

I erased the events themselves. They never happened. They never met him; he never actually laid a hand on them. It's just that I had to use all my power to do that for all of them; I'm useless to you now, and Joel, until tomorrow." Adelita looked back to Lennox apologetically.

Lennox moved closer once again and placed a hand on Adelita's arm comfortingly. "You did the right thing, Ade; it is your realm, after all. And powerless or not, you're never useless. We will manage. Now, you said you could see where he got that power from?"

Adelita nodded, her smile slowly starting to return. "Yes, the Clarion House Gentleman's Club, just down the road from here."

Chapter Nineteen

Finding the 'Gentleman's Club' was easy enough. Following the images Adelita had gleaned from the erstwhile abuser's mind, the pair quickly found the otherwise non-descript entrance down a side alley near the center of Soho. Adelita punched the 4-digit code into the electronic security panel and the door unlatched with a delicate 'click'.

The elegance of the entrance foyer belied the blandness of the club's exterior. Marble floors, wood-paneled walls, and a gilded sweeping curved staircase immediately impressed on the Angels that this club was a remnant of a time when the aristocracy ruled unchallenged.

Small pillars along the walls near the entrance held various bronze and marble busts of the Presidents of the club throughout its long history. Titles such as Lord, Baron, and Duke adorned the various pillars, the noble features of the commanding faces sculpted to demand respect from the viewer.

The last bust showed that the previous President passed away only a year ago, and where the current President's visage should be there was – a life sized, complete bronze statue of a man.

On a horse.

The two Wingless looked up at the towering statue dominating the entrance before turning to look at each other. As one, they both started to giggle.

And then Lennox's phone rang.

The haunting melody of Michael Nyman's *The Departure* floated across the foyer of the Clarion House Gentleman's

Club, before she hurriedly mashed the power key to shut her phone down.

Beside her, Adelita cringed at the noise. "Really?"

"I'm not used to going out in the field, okay?" The two of them rushed to hide behind the large bronze statue as a private security guard stomped into the foyer, looking for the source of the music.

"This whole thing was your idea!" Hissed Adelita.

Crouched down, the pair quietly crab-walked around the base of the statue, avoiding the guard. At one point, they passed a large brass plate screwed into the base. Without any noble title, the plaque simply stated: "Waylon Dalton - President."

The guard walked up to the main door, rattling its handle and assuring himself that it was indeed locked. Then, after a perfunctory look about the expansive foyer, he slouched back into the side room he'd appeared from.

Adelita and Lennox slowly uncurled themselves and stood. Thumbing her phone back on and into 'silent' mode, Lennox whispered to her more experienced companion, "That wasn't so bad. Is it always that easy?"

Adelita shook her head emphatically. "No. That was odd. He's either a really poor guard, which I doubt, because my guess is this place can afford the best, or he's extremely confident in their security."

Lennox nodded. "Makes sense, there would be few burglars that could read the entrance code directly from one of their member's minds, after all."

Adelita frowned at the sloppy job the guard was doing, but had to agree with Lennox. "You're probably right. Still..."

Lennox's phone vibrated quietly in her hand, and she quickly texted a reply while Adelita's frown deepened. "You didn't have to turn it back on straight away, you know. We're kind of in the middle of a thing here."

Without looking up from the screen as she typed, Lennox whispered, "It would have been messy if I didn't, my programs would have gotten worried."

"Your programs," Adelita deadpanned.

Lennox nodded. "Uh-huh."

"Would have gotten worried," Adelita continued.

"Yup," Lennox replied, still typing.

"Oh boy," Adelita sighed, as she grabbed Lennox's arm and hauled her up the marble staircase. "You and I are going to have a long talk after this. Creating life is a definite no-no."

"They're not 'alive', not really," protested Lennox, as she struggled to get her feet under her again.

Adelita locked eyes with Lennox and pulled her close. "Then you need to convince me of that, or would you rather explain it all to Joan?"

With a gulp, Lennox quickly put her phone back into her trouser pocket. "So, a talk. You and me. After this. Sounds perfect. I'll make tea."

The top of the staircase opened out into a long balcony with an ornate set of double doors in the middle of the wall. The large brass handles adorning the doors seemed like they were created for a giant when compared to Lennox's small hand. "Ready?"

Adelita nodded silently.

With a deep breath, Lennox tried the handle, and finding it smoothly turning without the restraint of a lock, opened the large door enough to peek through into the room beyond.

What she saw took her breath away. Adelita watched as her friend's face changed from shock, to disgust, before finally settling on anger. Adelita reached out her hand to steady Lennox – the last thing they needed today was a second Wingless burning through all their power in a single act of fury, however justified it might be.

Lennox reached up and patted the hand on her shoulder, before crouching and slipping through the door. As she followed, Adelita saw what was so infuriating.

The room could have once been a large dining space, or a noble's ballroom. The doors opened onto a balcony that circumnavigated the room a good fifteen feet above the floor below, and an exquisite crystal chandelier hung from the ceiling ten feet above even the high balcony upon which the Wingless stood. The sheer space of the room was designed to impress.

Surrounding the room were all manner of occult paraphernalia. Candelabras adorned with black candles, wreaths of various poisonous plants, and a goat's head mounted on one wall. Occult symbols were painted in red on nearly every surface, and there was an absolute plethora of pentagrams.

Stairs led down from the balcony on either side of the long room, and a guard armed with an automatic rifle stood at the base of each staircase. They hadn't spotted the two Wingless because they were both watching the middle of the room, and not the entrances.

In the middle of the room, where a long dining table might have once stood, there was now one large pentagram painted on the wooden floor, and in the middle of that was a single hospital bed. The patient in it was wired up to several quietly beeping machines and IV drips. There was also a single narrow tube slowly filling a bottle with bright red blood.

It only took a second for the Wingless to recognise their missing brother, even though his face had the pale, sunken visage of someone comatose and suffering from malnutrition.

Adelita pulled Lennox close so she could make as little sound as possible. "What the *fuck?*"

Lennox tore her eyes away from the grisly scene below to look at her friend. "I didn't know you swore! I've seen this sort of equipment before. He's being kept alive, but barely. Given the symbology in here, I'm guessing they're using his blood and gaining some of his power that way; I imagine it works because when his miraculous power returns each morning, it is dedicating itself to trying to keep him alive."

"But all these Satanic symbols..." murmured Adelita.

"I know," nodded Lennox.

In her shock, Adelita couldn't stop herself from continuing, "They don't *do* anything! They're all bogus. They don't call Lightbringer or any of the Fallen. The only thing they do is really piss Lightbringer off."

"*I know,*" repeated Lennox. She remembered the text she received earlier today; Azazel must have been hoping that she would find Joel before any of his people did. "Can you imagine what one of them would do if they did turn up and found Joel like that?"

Adelita shuddered at the thought. "An angel brought low by humans? Even if it is a Wingless? Soho would resemble a crater within minutes. Maybe all of London, if one of the higher-ups stumbled across this. We are talking a real Old Testament style smiting. Do you think the humans realise who they have here?"

Lennox took a moment to properly take in all the runes and symbols before slowly shaking her head. "No... not really. Look at the runes they have painted around the bed. It's a horrible hodge-podge of ancient Sumerian, Egyptian, Celtic, Norse, but they all basically say the same thing."

"They're all symbols for innocence!" Adelita realised with a start.

"Yes," affirmed Lennox. "They think they've captured a totally innocent soul, and corrupting it is giving them power."

"From Satan?" Adelita's incredulous tone almost made Lennox chuckle.

Lennox sighed. "Yeah, they *really* don't have a clue."

The two friends paused for a moment, each considering their next move. Adelita pointed out how the guards were mostly keeping an eye on Joel, and not checking the stairways as much as they were probably supposed to. "We could sneak down there, and each take one of them out. Grab Joel and make a run for it?"

Lennox shook her head. "I doubt he's in much of a state to run, and besides, I want whoever is doing this to him. I've got an idea. Mucking about with the medical machinery they've got him hooked up to is going to be child's play for me. I can get them to start the process of weaning him off whatever is keeping him asleep, and at the same time, start to send signals declaring an emergency. I'd bet my last feather that whoever is in charge of this nightmare will have those machines monitored from his phone and will come running."

Lennox saw her friend smile at the plan, and then a look of pure mischief crossed Adelita's face. "When they do," she said, "Follow my lead. I may be out of miracles, but no one can look more innocent than I can." Adelita whispered the rest of her plan into Lennox's ear as the pair slowly stood. They kept their heads downcast, and hands held behind their back, as Lennox reached out with her power and set the machinery surrounding Joel into motion.

The effect was almost immediate. Joel's eyelids started to flutter as his unused miraculous power rushed to heal him, now that it was no longer having to fight the continual onslaught from medical science. The various machines around the bed all started to trill, beep, or flash as their sensors picked up on Lennox's fabricated alerts. The guards rushed over to the bed, getting as close as they could without crossing the blood red circle painted on the floor, but completely missing the two women standing at the balcony rails.

The doors at the back of the room burst open as the man the Angels recognised from the statue in the entrance foyer flew into the room and towards the bed. Gone was the military style outfit he wore for the statue, replaced instead by a flowing black robe complete with silver runes embroidered around the hem and along the various seams. Before he reached the bed, Lennox cancelled all the alarms and made the readouts all declare that the only thing amiss was that the battery backup system needed charging.

Waylon Dalton ran a practiced eye over the readouts and connections, assuring himself that all was as it should be once again. Watching him, Lennox realised that while he seemed to know what each piece of equipment was supposed to do, the one piece of the equation he paid no attention to was the patient lying in the bed. To Lennox, that spoke volumes about the man.

Satisfied, Waylon looked up from the screens and straight at the two women standing on the balcony above him. The passive stance they held and meek demeanor stopped him from ordering the guards to immediately open fire. "You there!" he called out, "Who are you? What are you doing here?"

When Adelita answered, her voice was pitched such that it radiated pure, untouched, delicate innocence. "We are gifts, my Lord. For the great Waylon Dalton."

Lennox kept her eyes downcast, but from the balcony she could see Waylon practically begin to salivate as Adelita's words and tone fed his lust and need to corrupt in equal measure.

Waylon motioned for the guards to bring the two women to him, and gave the order to check them for weapons. "And who has provided me with such a gift?"

Remembering the name pulled from the mind of the man who had accosted them outside the train station, Adelita answered, "The most unworthy Ronan Morris, my Lord."

"Ahh, Ronan." Waylon rubbed his hands together as the guards ushered Adelita and Lennox down the stairs. "And to think, I was about to evict him from our coven for his disrespectful attitude. Perhaps he does have the ability to learn, after all."

Adelita approached and dropped to her knees in front of the gleeful President. Lennox quickly followed suit and had to suppress a shudder of disgust as he patted her possessively on the head.

"Look up at me." The command brought immediate obedience from the two Angels, and Waylon smiled lecherously back. "Disrobe."

"My Lord," Adelita replied, before Lennox could move, "Our orders were for us to be for your pleasure alone."

Waylon looked up at the two men standing behind his latest acquisitions. Also affected by Adelita's performance, the wanting they showed on their faces could not be mistaken. Adelita, however, had correctly taken Waylon's measure; he was not a man who shared.

"Quite right too," Waylon stated, before facing the guards and barking, "You two, stop gawking like teenagers and leave us! Take up posts in the foyer and allow none to interrupt me. That's an order!"

Lennox and Adelita felt the power of a corrupted miracle impact the guards as Waylon ensured that he would not be disobeyed. Their boots echoed off the parquetry floor as the guards retreated from the room, followed by the door closing and the click of a lock sliding into place.

"Now," announced Waylon, "Who to play with first?"

"Please, sir," Lennox replied in her best breathless voice. She may not have been as good as Adelita in projecting seduction in tone alone, but she was still an Angel with over a millennium of experience on Earth. "Please, may I be first?"

Waylon grinned evilly. "Of course, my chi..."

Before Waylon could finish, Lennox leapt upwards, the heel of her palm collecting Waylon's chin and snapping his head backwards as her knee buried itself in his groin. The pain overload to his nervous system had him unconscious before he hit the floor.

"I'm so glad he told us to look up," Adelita commented, as she slowly rose. "I so would have hated to have missed that."

"He did say I could go first," Lennox smirked. "Do you want a go now?"

Adelita looked down at the unconscious man. "No point, really, I doubt I could add much to your most eloquent rebuttal."

A groan from the bed spun the women around, moving as one to their friend. The groan was followed by his eyes slowly opening, and Joel's lips twisted into a grimace of pain and fury. His eyes darkened as muscles clenched and strained against the straps holding him to the bed. To the Angels, it was if the room itself had started to darken, and they could feel that Joel was beginning to Fall.

"No!" Lennox and Adelita cried out in unison. Adelita started to tear and pull at the straps holding Joel down, desperate to release him. Lennox leapt up and wrapped his head in her arms, pouring her own essence into him. She could feel that Joel's falling was out of his control, that the pain, anguish at being used, and the sheer internal damage his body had suffered had combined to push him into falling, just to be able to recover the power he needed to survive. Instead, Lennox fed the dying Wingless all the miraculous power she had left, repairing his body as her whispers of love and friendship attempted to repair his mind.

By the time Adelita managed to undo the last of the straps from his legs, Lennox had pulled Joel up into a sitting position, and he was sobbing quietly in her arms.

"Is he okay?" Adelita asked softly, worried about her brother, but not wanting to disrupt the embrace.

Lennox shook her head sadly as she continued to stroke Joel's hair and comfort him. "No, not really. He won't fall now unless he chooses to, but I think it will be quite some time before he is okay again."

Adelita looked around the locked ballroom. "How do we get out of here? You've used all your power."

Lennox nodded to her phone, sitting on the mattress. "I've instructed Sid to activate the government's biological infection protocol on this building and alert Damien. He'll turn up with the police and take us to 'quarantine'. We just need to wait."

"What do you want me to do until then?" asked Adelita.

Joel slowly snaked one arm out from Lennox's hug and timidly stretched it towards Adelita.

Lennox moved a little over on the bed to accommodate her sister. "That should answer your question, Ade. Come help me hug this big lugnut."

Chapter Twenty

The mood on the train ride back to the observatory was hard to define. Kateri finally falling hit all of us, but in an odd way the emotion was muted; after all, we had already started to mourn her 'decision' a few weeks ago, when we first thought we had lost her.

Having travelled the length of Africa trying to find her and working so hard to save her, part of me kept wanting to feel that her final decision was a betrayal. It would certainly be easier. But I couldn't. I knew we had done our best, and while I felt that her choice to fall in order to protect Hattie was regrettable, I couldn't fault her for it.

Listen to me. Maybe I'm mellowing with age.

And then, to add to the mix, there was Hattie herself. A new Wingless. Impossible, but undeniable. It ended up taking some time to convince Beatrice to leave the estate and the impossible girl she was already referring to as her 'daughter'. I had to lay the facts on the line that her presence would increase the chance that Michael would return before she finally saw the wisdom in leaving.

Hattie and her family were safer if they stayed where they were, and we stayed away.

I had Gary send texts to the rest of the Wingless, letting them know we were heading to the Observatory and that we had news on Kateri. They would have all felt her fall in the end and would be needing to know what happened. I just wasn't sure how we were going to tell them. With Gary handling all the communication and me being deep in thought over the meeting to come, I completely missed a message on my phone from Lennox.

Because of that, I was taken by surprise to find the door to the observatory locked to us when we arrived.

I let go of the unyielding handle as Adelita's voice called out from inside: "Joan? Is that you?"

My heart immediately started to race. It had only been just over an hour since we encountered Michael in his full glory, and I quickly fell into "flight or fight" mode. And for me, that is always going to be "fight".

"Ade!" I took a step back and readied myself to shoulder charge my way through the door. "I'm coming!"

"No!" Adelita called through the door. "Gary, stop her!"

I stopped dead, turning to look at my brother. "Gary?"

Gary was looking at me with an equally incredulous look. He just shrugged in response.

I didn't mean to be rude, but the adrenaline was pumping, and I couldn't stop myself. "Just how are *you* going to stop *me*?"

Gary looked from me, to the door, and back to me again before answering. "I reckon I could be a pretty dangerous tripping hazard."

If Gary was practiced at anything, it was in taking the wind out of my sails. He just shrugged again, trying hard not to grin.

The door opened and Adelita quickly slipped out, closing it behind her. "Joan?"

By this stage I was too confused to be angry. "What's going on, Ade?"

"Your phone," Adelita replied, glancing down to where my phone sat in my jeans pocket. "Lennox tried to warn you. Joel's here."

I felt my shoulders slump. "Of course, he is. I was wondering how this day was going to manage to get any worse. Still, he needs to hear what we have to say as much as the rest do. It may even wake him up."

Silje had been quietly standing behind us all, head tilted in that way she had when she was 'listening'. Her soft, singsong voice interrupted whatever Adelita was going to say next. "He's hurt."

"What?" This time I moved far too quickly for any of my compatriots to stop me. Performing a quick side-step around Adelita had me to the door before she could react. The metal of the lock crunched and shattered as I twisted the handle without thought to maintaining any semblance of normal human strength, and I was through into the Observatory itself before any of them could draw breath to call out.

Joel looked like death warmed up. He had been laid out on one of the old couches that Toby insisted on decorating the place with. His bare arms were covered in needle track marks, and he looked like a human who hadn't eaten in a month.

I was across the room and kneeling next to him before Lennox and Toby could react. "Joel! Brother! What happened?" His eyes fluttered open, and his head turned slowly to gaze at me.

"Joan..." Behind me, Lennox was trying to get my attention. "He's going to be okay, we found him in time."

I turned my head and nodded a thank-you to her before returning my attention to Joel. "Who did this to you? I'll make sure they rue the day they ever..."

His pitifully weak hand reached up and stroked my cheek. I think I was as surprised as he was that it came away damp with tears. When he spoke, his voice was quiet, but didn't falter. "It's been done, Joan. Lennox and Adelita sorted them out, and Damien is shutting down their organisation. I'm safe now."

"Why didn't you call?" My hands ran over his body as I spoke, automatically checking for wounds, dislocated joints, and signs of internal damage.

"He couldn't." Lennox replied for Joel as he slumped back on the couch and allowed me to continue my physical investigation of him. "They had him drained and all his power was going into keeping him alive."

I stood and turned to face Lennox, noting that the rest had entered the Observatory and had taken up positions behind her. My eyes flitted from Lennox to Adelita as my voice took on a steel-like edge. "So why didn't *you* call me when you knew he was in trouble?"

Lennox probably hadn't meant her reply to sound like an 'I told you so' comment to a naughty sibling, but it ended up coming across like that anyway. "Well, Joan, *you* ordered him from your sight and—"

"HE IS MY BROTHER!" Something inside me snapped. All my pent-up anger exploded from me, and I felt my sword burst into flame as it appeared in my clenched fist, without me even needing to move my arm up to draw it. As one, the rest of my family recoiled from me, but this time I had had enough.

"NO! You all stand right there. This has got to stop, NOW. Don't you get it? We are *family*. All we have left in this world is each other. I would *never* do anything to hurt any of you, and you *have* to Stop. Being. Afraid. Of. Me!"

The irony of having an Angel of War in a combat-ready stance armed with a flaming sword and screaming that she cared about them was not lost on Admonae. In her best impersonation of Gabriel, she intoned, "Do not be afraid." To be honest, the impression really wasn't all that good, but it had the desired effect.

The flame on my sword extinguished. "We're family," I repeated, my voice softer now, and the tears flowing freely down my face. "We can argue, we can disagree, we can bump heads and annoy the hell out of each other, but nothing changes the fact that you are my brothers and sisters. I love you. You have to know that."

I felt Joel take my hand from the couch behind me. I doubt any of the others heard his whispered apology from where they stood, and I squeezed his hand in recognition without turning away from the rest of my family. "Just concentrate on getting well, you idiot," I shot back at him.

I'm not sure who moved first, but very soon I found myself surrounded by bodies. The hugs lasted for quite some time before eventually giving way to a myriad of little conversations between all of us. We shared our stories and, thanks to Lennox, some much needed tea. I don't believe there was a single point over the next hour when each of us didn't have at least one hand resting on another person, the physical contact affirming the connections and love between us all. Slowly, we became that family I spoke of once more.

As Joel started to fade from all the hugs and attention he was getting, Lennox shooed us away to let him rest. It occurred to me that, in Damien's absence, Gary or Adelita might have tried to put themselves in charge of looking after Joel, but everyone just accepted that Lennox had taken that role.

Over yet more tea, Lennox and Adelita told us the story of how they found Joel, and in return we went over the events surrounding Hattie, Michael, and Kateri's decision to fall. Finally, Gary relayed his phone call to Azazel, and the sounds of obvious battle he and Beatrice had heard.

"I have to admit I'm impressed," I commented. "Holding his own against Michael, even if he was running away at the time. I didn't know Azazel had it in him."

"And while protecting Kateri," Beatrice pointed out.

I nodded. "Very true. That little asshole has some hidden talents, it seems."

"You'd have to expect," added Admonae, "That there had to be a reason he was the one tasked with collecting us when we fell."

Silje smiled through the steam from her teacup. "He always preferred the term 'catching us' when we fell. I think he's a bit of a romantic."

I had never hidden my disdain for the Fallen, or Azazel in particular, but listening to my friends talk about him around me without, for once, feeling the need to walk on eggshells, was nice. I allowed myself to wallow for a moment in quiet regret for lost years and was about to pull myself out of it when Gary noticed.

He leaned over and asked, "Shekel for your thoughts?"

"Azazel," I admitted. "I think I may have done more to pull us apart than he ever did."

"Enough of that, Joan." Beatrice's hand clasped my shoulder as she came around the table. "We're all to blame for that. Or did you forget that we're all Angels as well, hmm? We're just as powerful as you are, in different ways."

I chuckled. "Yeah, but I can still kick all of your asses."

"No, you can't, we're *family*," Silje stated with a cheeky wink.

The moment of crisis had truly passed, and we had come out stronger because of it. "Very true, sister." I toasted Silje with my cup of tea. "So, who wants to be in charge now?"

I watched, curiously, as all the others glanced quickly between themselves and then back to me. "You can be so dense sometimes, Joan." It was Admonae who spoke for them. "You don't lead us because of your martial prowess, you lead us because we grant you the power to do so. Because we need you too. What Beatrice said is very true, we all have our powers, our strengths; and yours is to lead."

Lennox stepped in from the little kitchenette where she had been brewing more tea. Instead of the teapot, however, she held her ever-present phone in her hand. The worried look on her face caught everyone's attention as she spoke. "And if what I am reading here is right, Joan, we're going to need that leadership now more than ever."

Chapter Twenty-One

The room fell silent as we all turned to give Lennox our undivided attention.

"A passenger plane leaving the Beijing Capital International Airport just encountered mid-air turbulence," Lennox read from her phone screen. That was hardly anything for us to worry about, but we all knew our sister. If she thought this was important, it was, but she needed to be left alone to tell it her way. Interrupting her would only draw this out longer.

"The crew are reporting some minor bumps and bruises affecting the passengers, and one of their hostesses is missing. No breach of the aircraft occurred, so they are conducting a search, but according to one of the stewards, she simply vanished." Lennox looked up, the light from the phone screen still illuminating her face. I had a sneaking suspicion that she was reading a real time transcript from the cockpit radio, courtesy of one of her little programs, and I shuddered to think about just how many international laws she was violating to do so.

Then came the sentence that brought us all to our feet. "According to my data, that hostess was Orfael."

I took a moment to cradle my face in my hands. "Merde," I whispered into my palms.

Ever since the humans developed flight, Orfael would spend as much time as she could in planes. She would use her power to get onto flights as one of the flight crew whenever she was bored or stressed. She always said she preferred that than just being a passenger.

The usually quiet Toby spoke up. "I should have known. I offered her a place to stay, or a couch here at the observatory when she couldn't get into her house, but she said she'd rather stretch her wings instead."

"Lennox, I thought you couldn't get me a flight out?" Adelita asked.

Lennox nodded. "I couldn't, but I was trying to do it the normal, human way since I knew you'd need your passport stamped for your position at the UN. I imagine Orfael just miracled herself on board."

A small hint of hope was present in Silje's voice as she spoke. "And off again?"

"Doubtful." I was going to add something about us not being that lucky when all of our phones started ringing simultaneously. I didn't need to look at mine to know who was behind that little trick, and from the looks the others were giving me they had come to the same conclusion.

I forestalled any attempt from my friends to convince me to answer by just calling out to the room. "Yes, Azazel, you're welcome here. Please join us."

Silje physically flinched as we all heard the discordant chime of Azazel manifesting just outside. The door opened and he hastily entered, the usual swagger missing from his movements.

"Sorry for the loud entrance; I'm in a rush." His apology was pointedly made towards Silje as he closed the door behind him.

"Thank you for doing it outside, at least," Silje replied.

Azazel paused long enough to execute a small bow in Silje's direction; even when he was in a hurry, the Fallen

Angel was a showman at heart. He quickly turned back to look at me, however, his face was nothing but serious.

"Now Joan, I know what you're going to say, but—" he started.

I shook my head and interrupted him. "We need your help, Azazel."

"—you need my help, and you have to listen to..." Azazel's tongue stumbled over the end of his sentence as my words started to catch up with him. "Hold on. What did you say?"

"We need your help," I repeated. "I need your help. Just no gloating, please?"

"I, no! I mean yes!" Azazel stammered in reply. "No, I mean, help, I'm here too. Help, that is."

I had to admit I was enjoying watching Azazel being the one completely off-kilter for a change, but I needed to know what he knew. "Good, then you can start by telling us what got you calling all our phones at the same time."

Azazel nodded and started to uncharacteristically pace the length of the room as he spoke. "One of my people has been destroyed. Now I know that is nothing new, casualty of the war and all that..."

Adelita gasped slightly as he spoke. "That's surprisingly cold, even for you."

Azazel nodded but didn't look admonished by her sentiment. "I'll grieve later, I assure you. What's important now is that it was Gaap who was ended, and for some God-forsaken reason his brother Samael has gotten it into his fool head that it was one of you who did it! I think he's taken Orfael to try to enact some sort of revenge."

"But that's ridiculous!" Azazel's accusation was so absurd I couldn't help blurting out the obvious. "All of us working together wouldn't have enough power to even scratch one of you, never mind 'end' you! And if Orfael fell to get that power, all of us, you included, would have heard it!"

"I know!" Azazel exclaimed. "I don't understand any of this, I just feel that she is in danger. And besides, Orfael? I mean, really? What is she supposed to have done, confused Gaap to death?"

Silje interrupted us, speaking up with alarm. "Incoming!"

The note that sounded as a second black-winged figure appeared in the room was less powerful than Azazel's, but somehow sharper, more strident. The figure stood, wings slowly opening up, unwrapping from around her body and folding in behind her back as Kateri stepped up to the group.

Azazel spun, his eyes blazing red. "I told you to stay put! Don't force me to make sure you stay away, Kateri."

"Just try it, sunshine," Kateri growled right back at him, "My family needs me."

Azazel looked from the disobedient newest Fallen to my smirking face and back again before throwing his arms up in defeat. "Fine! But if you draw the big 'M' to us, you're fighting him on your own this time, my shoulder still hurts." Azazel turned to the rest of the Wingless, making a big show of rubbing the offending joint.

"Wuss," I snorted.

The mock-pained expression Azazel wore put a grin on my face. "Joan, how could you?"

"Oh, come on." I strode towards Lennox, hitting Azazel on his shoulder with a solid open slap of my palm as I went past. At the sound of his pained grunt, I was unable to stop the chuckle that had been threatening to erupt since Kateri referred to him as 'Sunshine'."

"How soon after take-off did this all happen?" Admonae was already looking over Lennox's shoulder at her phone as I got up to them.

"Just a few minutes, apparently," Lennox read off her screen.

I nodded to Admonae. "Good question. And that means they were still over the city. We're going to have to start our search in Beijing. What else do we know?"

Lennox scrolled a few pages, her finger deftly manoeuvring several pop-up windows on the tiny screen faster than I could even see what they contained. "It looks like she arrived on a British Airways flight, BA4027, and was only on the ground for a few hours before boarding an Air China flight for the return trip. Looks like it was what she told Toby, she was just stretching her wings and getting away from the stress for a bit."

Beatrice spoke up from near the door. After Azazel, and then Kateri's arrival, she had assigned herself the job of lookout. "Well, that doesn't look like it went to plan. So, no long stay and no hotel bookings to chase up. She probably didn't even leave the airport if I know her."

Silje, meanwhile, had been in a quick whispered conversation with Kateri. As the conversation fell silent, she spoke up. "If Kateri can take me there, I'll probably be able to 'hear' where she is, or where she went to. Just like when we were tracking Kateri through Africa."

"No!" Both Azazel and I exclaimed in unison. We each gave the other an embarrassed glance at our unexpected consensus before turning back to the conspiratorial pair.

Azazel spoke first. "Kateri, I told you that you need to be careful at first, you haven't used your powers for so long, and to be quite frank, you're rusty!"

I joined in as he stopped for breath. "And as far as we know 'M' is still searching for you. Carrying Silje with you will surely alert him."

Azazel continued, "I know you want to help your family, but right now you're more of a danger to them than you know..."

"And besides, Azazel can get us all there far easier than you can, carrying us one at a time," I finished.

"Yes," Azazel agreed, "Azazel can get you all there far easy..er.. Umm. I can?"

I turned to look at the puzzled look on his face. "Yes, you can. You stood toe to toe with 'M'." I air-quoted the final letter, since that was how we seemed to be referring to Michael now.

"Only for a little while," Azazel sheepishly replied.

"And got away with Kateri in your arms," I added as I crossed my arms and stared back at him.

Azazel blushed at that. "But...I hurt my shoulder?"

"Uh-huh," I nodded, pointedly ignoring his excuse.

The puzzlement on his face only lasted a few moments, however. Soon his eyes returned from their state of wide-eyed confusion to their usual piercing gaze, and he straightened himself back up to his full height and attempted to regain control of the conversation. "Okay,

Joan, what's going on? Why this sudden readiness to accept my help, anyway?"

I shrugged. "You offered."

His half-smile told me he wasn't going to accept that. "Oh no, you don't. I always offer. You always say 'no'." Azazel turned to the others and muttered, sotto voce, "Usually not very politely, either."

I uncrossed my arms and took a deep breath. "Call it temporary insanity if you have to. I have recently been made aware that I may have been a little too, shall we say, rigid, in my opinions of late."

"Rigid." Azazel repeated the word with a sarcastic tone of disbelief.

"It's all you're going to get Azazel, take it," I replied.

Azazel considered this for a moment before allowing himself a slightly smug grin. "Then take it I shall. Welcome aboard Azazel airlines, partner."

"Don't push your luck," I started, but then added with a wink, "Sunshine."

When the amateur dramatics from Azazel that followed that comment had subsided, we decided that Azazel would, as quietly as he could, transport seven of us to Beijing to start our investigations. Going with me were Silje, Lennox, Beatrice, Admonae, and Gary, with Kateri joining us because leaving her behind was apparently 'not an option'. Then Azazel would make himself scarce once again in case Michael was still on the hunt.

Azazel's wings folded back from around us and we found ourselves across the road from an absolutely arresting sight. The Temple of Heaven Park in central Beijing exuded peace and serenity, making it hard to believe that this had anything to do with our current predicament.

I rubbed my jaw, feeling my teeth painfully resonating from the Fallen miracle that brought us here. Looking around at my compatriots, however, it looked like I was the only one suffering from any aftereffects. Was I really so prejudiced against the Fallen that my mind was creating phantom pains? They certainly felt real enough.

Azazel, of course, noticed my discomfort. "Everything okay, Joan?"

"I didn't get my in-flight peanuts," I pouted.

Azazel's shoulders slumped a little and he displayed his exasperation in his voice. "You know, Joan, one day I may just give up on you," and with a quick nod to the others, he disappeared.

To the space he had just vacated, I quietly said, "No, you won't."

"Feeling the need to get the last word, Joan?" Gary had moved up beside me as the others were taking in their surroundings.

I grinned back at him. "Nope."

Chapter Twenty-Two

In days gone by, a group of foreigners like us would have attracted a lot of attention in Beijing. Last time I was in China I needed to expend some miraculous power and change my appearance just to be able to move around unhampered. One of the nice things about modern times is that now we just looked like your common or garden variety tourist.

If anything, our general gawking and wandering around looking lost added to the illusion. So much so that Gary soon had a gaggle of small children following him, their hands held out for the near endless stream of small sweets he produced from his pockets.

As cute as it was watching my brother turn into some kind of Pied Piper of Beijing, it needed to be stopped before it got out of hand. "Gary, a word?"

The latest brightly wrapped sugary treat quickly disappeared back into his pocket, bringing a scowl to the young boy's face that was aimed directly at me. "Sure, Joan. What do you need?"

I nodded to his gaggle of small people. "Don't you think having all these children around makes us just a little bit obvious?"

Gary nodded enthusiastically. "As gormless tourists, yes. Avenging Angels? No, not so much."

I discovered that I had to agree, but sooner or later we'd need a little privacy. Gary seemed to understand where I was going and just held up one finger. "Trust me, Joan. This is a little trick I picked up from Adelita."

We continued to walk around the circumference of the 260 odd hectare Temple of Heaven Park. The mob of children shrank and swelled like some kind of living tide around Gary as children left to return to their homes as we travelled too far away, and others joined us from the various houses and shops ahead. It had become almost meditative, the serene Confucian Park on our right, bustling inner-city Beijing on our left, and a sea of innocent humanity around us. I could see how Adelita could have been the source of the idea, but not where it was heading.

When Gary tapped me on my shoulder, bringing me out of my reverie, I was surprised to see our group completely alone. "What? Where are all the kids?"

"Drifted away," Gary answered. "This is the one place they simply don't want to be. Even the lure of coloured sugar isn't enough to draw them to us. But if you asked them why, they wouldn't be able to tell you."

"Adelita," I replied, nodding.

"Adelita," Gary agreed. "Silje, if you would be so kind, this might be a good place to start."

Silje closed her eyes, tilting her head in that way of hers. She frowned in concentration, and even started to grit her teeth. I'd never seen Silje need to try so hard to hear what she was listening for. Something had to be blocking her.

I may not be able to hear what she could hear, but I am good at what I do. And that tends to be smashing through obstacles of one kind or another. I gently placed my hand on Silje's arm and allowed my power to flow into her.

Immediately, her eyes snapped open, and she turned to face the park. She took off with a purposeful stride and without hesitation, we followed. After a dozen or so meters however, she slowed, walking as if she was dragging her legs through molasses. Through gritted teeth she groaned, "Joan…" and I placed my hand on her back once again.

I could feel the pressure wave she was struggling against, trying to turn her away. The wall was not something we were going to defeat without expending some real power, and Silje needed to maintain her concentration to aim our efforts.

Which meant me. Reaching down into myself, I drew one of my limited miracles up, formed it, and allowed Silje to direct the power where she needed it. Connected to her as I was, I 'heard' the chime of the miracle go off, and part of me was fascinated to finally learn exactly what I sounded like to Silje.

With a feeling akin to a wave breaking over us, we were through and found ourselves standing on the top of a set of stone stairs leading down into one of the subway stations that ring the park. Just minutes before we'd all been looking straight at the entrance to the station and had not been able to see it.

Lennox whipped out her smartphone, attempting to bring up our position on the map. We heard her growl, "No service."

Beatrice had been scanning the area, looking for anything that might jump out at us, but turned to look askance at her sister. "But you always get reception."

"I know," Lennox nodded. "There is some real power behind this."

"Guys?" Admonae quietly called for our attention and pointed back out to the street where Kateri was standing, looking confused, on the sidewalk. "I don't think she can see us."

"Why didn't she come through with us?" Beatrice asked.

I didn't want to have to be the one to say it, and luckily Lennox came to my rescue. "She's not one of us anymore." She shrugged apologetically, "Sorry, not a value judgement, just a fact. The question is, what do we do about it? Leave her on the street or try to bring her in?"

As one, they turned to me. I'm not sure why I was suddenly so angry at all this, but it was as if Orfael going missing had lit a fire within me that I hadn't felt for some time. "Fuck that. She's one of us, and I'm sick of losing people. Silje, get her attention if you would, please."

Silje smiled and stepped beside me. "It's probably going to hurt her."

I nodded. "Understood. She's a big girl, she'll cope."

Silje leaned forward slightly and mouthed something towards the newly fallen angel. I imagine it was Kateri's note, only said in the way Silje hears it, much like the chime I heard and recognised as my miracle when I had my hand on her. We all felt the miracle Silje put behind the word, and Kateri obviously did as well, if the way she suddenly grabbed her head and nearly doubled over in pain was any indication.

Admonae swooped out and wrapped an arm around Kateri even as she started to straighten up from the unexpected attack on her senses. Admonae was careful to keep her eyes on us to maintain her connection and was soon passing the quickly recovering fallen angel to Beatrice and Gary, who got her the first few steps down the staircase before she shook them off.

"Silje!" Kateri barked. "That. Hurt!"

"It was necessary," I reached out and took hold of Kateri's arm. "But noisy. Whoever did this will know we've arrived. Be ready."

Kateri quickly pulled herself together, nodding agreement. "So, where are we?"

"Before I lost signal," Lennox answered, "I had been tracking our progress around the park. We'd just passed West Gate 2, so this subway should be the one that is between the gate and the Natural History Museum."

Beatrice gestured towards the wall of the staircase. "That would explain this." Silvery lines and Hanzi were embedded in the wall. They comprised the end of one long branch of an evolutionary tree, depicting some of the modern plants and flowers. The lines stretched along the wall down into the darkness of the subway below, one part of a detailed and exquisitely rendered phylogeny.

"Well, we're obviously in the right place," Admonae stated with a tone of exasperation, "Only the Fallen are quite so needlessly dramatic. No offense, Kateri."

"None taken. The older ones are pretty weird," Kateri replied.

"Nothing for it then. Down we go." Beatrice pulled out her own phone and activated its little torch, illuminating the stairs below. The two of us started down ahead of the others, with Gary, Admonae, and Silje following, and Kateri, black wings out but closed, covering our rear.

The silvery branches of the phylogeny on the wall grew thicker as we descended, with some smaller extensions reaching up onto the ceiling. Where two branches joined, a small diagram of the plant or animal had been set into the stone of the wall, and these too grew in size as we descended towards the main trunk of the tree, towards the main platform of the darkened station.

Down on the platform, several small fires burning in metal garbage bins provided the only light, and set the scene for the grisly diorama at the base of the tree. The Fallen Angel, Gaap, had been pinned to the wall, crucified in fact, and from the wounds that covered his broken body it was obvious that the kill had not been a clean one. Adding insult to injury, a message had been scrawled along his chest with what was presumably his own blood - "Mind the Gaap".

The entire area was resonating with the immense amount of miraculous power used in the murder. We could all feel Fallen miracles, obviously from Gaap, expended in his defence, and something that felt a lot like Wingless power, but I couldn't recognise whose. Whoever had killed Gaap, it hadn't caught him by surprise, and he hadn't gone down without a fight.

That explained the obfuscating field around the station. You see, since the war began, there have been the Rules of Engagement. Any encounter between Angel and Fallen in the realms beyond Earth were complete free-for-alls, but trapped on Earth since the war started, I'd never witnessed one of those battles.

On Earth, however, it has always been strictly forbidden to fight where any mortal could witness the battle. It is also forbidden to use the mortals as tools in the war. And, for some reason I had never discovered, it is forbidden for either side to take direct action against a Wingless.

With his manipulation of Kateri, it was one rule Michael seemed to have come very close to breaking.

No one quite knows where the rules came from, which means we all suspect we know Who they came from; however, they have always been inherently known by all the participants, and they have never, ever, been broken, not even by Lightbringer himself.

There don't seem to have ever been any rules about what we Wingless are or are not allowed to do to an Angel or a Fallen. There barely seemed any point, as the relative power levels between the Wingless and the Fallen or Angels would make any attack on our part ludicrously pathetic. With Samael taking Orfael prisoner, presumably because of what happened to his brother, the Rules of Engagement had been broken.

And I had a feeling that all Hell was about to break loose.

Chapter Twenty-Three

Condensation dripped off the ornate architrave over the platform, the noise of the droplets striking the puddle below echoed around the darkened station.

Kateri shivered before extending her wings to their fullest. "This is freaking me out, sorry. We need some proper light." With a minor effort of will, the station was bathed in a cool white light, emanating from everywhere and nowhere at the same time. "That's better," she sighed.

Being able to see the murder scene clearly did absolutely nothing to calm my nerves.

"Okay," I started, a plan beginning to form in my mind as I talked. "We probably don't have much time and we need answers. I'm sorry folks, but this is going to be unpleasant, and I will need all of you."

There may have been the barest of nervous hesitation from my friends, but one by one they turned to me, ready to act.

"We need to work out exactly what happened, and that's going to mean diving into the event. It'll be gruesome, but it's necessary." Falling back into old habits, I started to assign my troops their missions. "Kateri, I'd like you near the stairs and ready to drape this place with your power. With any luck your fallen note will cover up the noise we're about to make."

Kateri nodded and squared her shoulders, which had the additional unintended effect of flexing all her wing muscles. My back responded with a deep ache of desire, and I found I had to look away.

I turned to Gary. "Gary. Silje isn't going to be able to hear a thing with all the noise Kateri is going to be making, so I need you to keep a hand on her and be her shield. It means you'll cop it all, but you'll be able to stand up to it better than she would."

"No worries, Joan. One impervious wall coming up," Gary nodded.

Beatrice chuckled softly. "Looks like your thick skull is going to be of some use after all, Gary." Gary smiled back, tapping his head with one knuckle as he moved over to stand by Silje.

"Silje..." The look on my sister's face stole the rest of my sentence from my mouth.

"You want me to listen to him die, don't you, Joan?" Silje's soft voice shook with emotion.

"Yes, dear one, but don't hold onto it. It would break you; I know. This is going to be hard, but I need you to be holding onto Lennox. Listen, but channel all you hear straight to her. Don't try to hold it, don't try to understand it. Just let it all go. Can you do that for me?"

Silje's reply was a small, silent nod and she immediately reached out to grab Lennox's hand.

Lennox, for her part, looked more confused than scared. "Uhh, Joan? Not that I'm questioning you, but wouldn't Admonae be better at discovering the truth behind what happened? That's not really my area of expertise."

"No, you're right, it isn't," I agreed, catching both her and Admonae's eyes as I did so. "But you are much better at breaking cyphers and puzzles, Lennox. Whatever happened here was convoluted enough to have completely convinced Samael, Gaap's closest sibling, that Orfael somehow did this. I need you to separate every different signal, note, colour, or whatever it is you'll be getting from Silje and pass them individually to Admonae. And hopefully that will be enough for her to give us some answers."

Admonae stepped up and took Lennox's free hand, putting Lennox between herself and Silje, who was still holding her other hand with the determination of a drowning swimmer gripping a lifesaver.

Beatrice took a small step forward. "And what do you need me to do, Joan?"

I smiled softly, knowing that Beatrice had already figured out her part in the plan. This was not the first time that we had faced something together.

"You're my back, Beatrice." I tilted my head to the others, knowing this was more for them to hear than Beatrice. "While they get the icky jobs, we just get the dangerous one. I don't believe for a second that we'll get through this without being discovered, although hopefully Kateri's masking will give us enough time to get some answers. When Samael does show up, we stop him."

There was a sharp intake of breath from Gary preparing to argue the point, but I reached my hand over my shoulder and gripped, feeling the warm hilt of my sword come into being against the palm of my hand. It ignited with glorious orange flame as I drew it free.

Beatrice smirked at me and muttered, "I'll have to get myself one of those one day," before expending one of her limited miracles to materialise her own blade. It was almost workmanlike, a long, broad affair, probably better wielded two-handed than one. If you've ever seen a statue of 'Lady

Justice' you'll know just what it looked like. After all, Beatrice had modelled for Hans Gieng when he sculpted it.

I touched my sword to hers and it, too, ignited, although we both knew that the fire on Beatrice's would only last one blow. She turned and placed her back to mine, and between us we could see the entire station.

Silje and Gary, trailing Lennox and Admonae with them, slowly walked up to Gaap's body. Silje raised her free hand to touch his wing. With a tentative nod from her, I called out, "Kateri...now!"

Kateri was obviously gaining more control over her returned power as I felt her miracle blanketing us and then building up. It felt more like someone gently piling blanket after blanket over you than the crashing wave of power I had expected she would produce. Silje grimaced for a moment before Gary took the brunt of it for her, his own face taking on the rather comical look of someone who can feel a fly crawling over their nose, but there being something in the way stopping him from brushing it away.

I knew the feeling from a different experience. Bugs inside motorcycle helmets. Just say no.

Silje, Lennox, and Admonae then all closed their eyes and bowed their heads in unison, concentrating. It was now or never.

Admonae couldn't know the swirling madness of interwoven and entangled images and sounds Silje and Lennox were dealing with, inside Admonae's mind she received a fairly coherent sequence of images from Gaap's perspective.

Samael and Gaap in a tavern as they feel the plane carrying Orfael fly over the city towards the airport.

Gaap in a subway, travelling in the tunnels beside the tracks. Moving furtively…hunting something? Eluding something? Too hard to tell.

The image swam again and Gaap is at this station, the place where he was killed. He is panting, hard, wings extended in full glory. Blood drips from the many shallow wounds all over his body, wounds caused more to weaken than kill. He knows his adversary can best him, but he can't understand how, or why.

A noise behind him. He turns and sees his attacker leaping towards him once more. The littlest Wingless, Orfael, rushes forward, and, grinning madly, thrusts her sword through his chest.

As if from a great distance, Admonae hears Silje call out in pain, but forces herself to concentrate on the scene before her, squeezing Lennox's hand hard enough to cause Lennox to gasp, and the connection to waver.

"Lennox!" Admonae exclaimed, "Quickly, before we lose it. That last scene, I can feel that it's not right. Dig! Come on, I know you can do it!"

"But Orfael is there, I can hear her," Lennox whimpered.

"No," Admonae begged. "Please, Lennox, please try."

Lennox clenched her jaw hard and opened the connection to Silje to its fullest. The pain of being impaled passed to her as well and she screamed in unison with Silje, but with that came the last piece of the puzzle. The last two entangled notes finally split.

As one, Silje, Lennox, and Admonae let out one last gasp and collapsed to the ground. Almost immediately, Kateri came flying bodily backwards from the stairwell, hitting the ground and sliding all the way back to the wall, a sickening crunch resonating through the station as her head impacted the wall.

In a blur, Samael flew past and around me, bringing his sword down as if to sever the wings I no longer had. Behind me, Beatrice raised her sword just in time to block his blow. Her sword screeched with the impact, the fire I had lent it flaring and burning itself out in defence of its wielder, and saving both of our lives.

With a roar, Samael spun, collecting Beatrice across her jaw with his elbow and sending her sprawling to the ground. None of us are a match for a Fallen, but Beatrice had bought me the time I needed to spin and face our preternaturally fast assailant.

When Angels fight, they go for the wings. Remove the wings, remove most of your opponent's power. It's almost hardwired, which is why Samael had tried to use that tactic against me even in my wingless state. It was natural for him to expect me to do the same, but he made two miscalculations.

One, I wasn't trying to kill him.

And two, I'd spent far too many centuries around human soldiers.

As he drew his wings backwards to protect them, I quickly stepped forward, brought my sword up to connect with his and dragged it out of the way, and with all the strength I possessed, slammed my head upwards into his jaw.

My sword flared and I heard the scream of the metal being sliced in two and then falling to the concrete floor as

I stepped back, momentarily dazed by the blow I had inflicted. Samael was on his back on the ground, similarly disoriented. I knew I would never get a second chance, that kind of trick is the sort of thing that would only work once, so I stumbled forward on shaky legs and bent over in order to place the end of my broken, shortened sword at the Fallen's neck.

"Joan, stop!" Beatrice's scream made me pause and blink, forcing my eyes to come back into focus. The sharp point at the end of my still flaming and intact sword had just penetrated the skin of Samael's neck, drawing blood. Confused, I drew back a little and looked to the ground beside me. There, in two pieces, was the sword I heard break.

It was Samael's sword.

"How?" I asked, my voice shaking.

"That's what I want to know, Trazael." Samael practically spat out the words from where he lay. "And why? My brother would never have attacked your little murderer. Lightbringer may have forbidden any action against you...disappointments, but I don't care anymore. I'll destroy this entire city and all of you with it to repay you for what you've done!"

Kateri came awake with a start, rolling forward and holding her head in pain before starting to get up once more. A blow like that would have taken any of us out for good, but there are benefits to having your wings back, Fallen or otherwise. A snarl spread its way across her features, and she started to move towards Samael.

"Wait!" Admonae painfully picked herself up from the ground where she had been lying. Beside her, Gary was doing his best to try to revive Lennox, after propping Silje up against the wall, who was just starting to come around. "Wait, I've seen what happened," Admonae repeated.

"So have I, Admonael." Samael replied. "Gaap showed me as he died. The murderer identified by her own victim."

"Orfael didn't kill Gaap," Admonae started, but Samael interrupted her.

"What do you want to call it? Gaap couldn't fight back! He would never cross Lightbringer. He actually believed in him! It was murder, nothing less."

Admonae shook her head, clearing the last of the ringing from her head. "No," she replied, her voice softening. "It was murder, Samael, it just wasn't Orfael." Admonae called on the last of her power to reveal truth, and we were all able to witness the moment of Gaap's death, replayed for us on the station platform.

Samael whispered a pained "No..." As he was forced to watch his brother's killing once more, but this time, as Orfael was about to strike, the image blurred and froze.

There, in Orfael's place, was Michael. In one hand was the sword he used to kill Gaap, frozen just before the moment of impact. And in other he clutched a single, long white feather.

A feather from an Angel's wing.

Orfael's wing.

Chapter Twenty-Four

"Admonael, please..." Samael's pained request was answered by an understanding nod by Admonae, and the image of Gaap faded from the scene before us. Michael, however, remained visible.

Each of us stared at the ghostly, transparent form of the Archangel. It was almost impossible to pull your eyes away, in fact. I heard Silje comment from where she sat against the wall that the feather definitely bore Orfael's note, but there was still something not quite right about what I was seeing.

I moved around the figure, trying to work out what was niggling at me. The stance was correct, I had definitely seen Michael move like that in a fight, especially when going in for a killing blow. So, what was it that seemed wrong?

Lennox could see my agitation and painfully got to her feet, levering herself up the wall before limping over to me. Gary tried to tell her to sit back down, but he was too busy helping Beatrice by this point to actually stop her.

Lennox had that look on her face that spoke of a million tiny calculations going on in the background, so I waved a hand to shush Gary and stepped back a little to give her room. Lennox's eyes kept flitting between Samael, me, and the image of Michael, the frown on her face deepening with each sweep of her head. She reached the spot where Gaap had been standing and paused for a moment, Michael's blade excruciatingly close to her chest, before straightening her back and allowing a curious little smirk to form on her lips.

"It's definitely Michael," I spoke up, breaking the silence that had enclosed around us. "I've seen him fight too many times to think it was anyone else. So, tell me, Lennox, just what is it about this that's bugging me so much?"

Lennox nodded over to where Samael was just now getting to his feet. "That was a good move, Joan."

"That it was," Samael nodded in agreement, "but..."

Lennox interrupted the Fallen Angel. "You broke his sword in two."

Samael stopped and looked down at his cleanly snapped weapon. "More like clove it in two. How did you manage that, by the way?"

I followed Samael's eyes to the weapon on the ground and saw the clean cut that had divided his blade. A sick feeling started to form in my gut, and when Lennox spoke next it solidified into a hard, cold rock.

"Michael's sword isn't aflame," Lennox stated plainly.

There it was.

Standing out in plain sight. Michael was driving forward with his sword, the original flaming sword charged with guarding the very gates of heaven itself. No Angel could mistake it for anything else.

Except here the blade was just cold, bare steel.

"Maybe he had it like this on purpose?" I practically stammered, not wanting to believe what it might mean. "You know, to mess with the evidence? I mean, remember the fight at the apartment block in London, it wasn't alight then either."

Samael and Kateri shook their heads in unison. "That sword can't be used like that. It doesn't have an 'off' setting," Samael replied. "Besides, I know the two who sacrificed themselves that day. They were not of Gaap's standing, he would need his sword aflame to battle my brother."

"I didn't realise it at the time," Kateri added, "But when he was chasing Azazel and I after I fell, he had to will the flame into existence when he went to attack Azazel. I felt him need to do it after every blow, but it didn't register at the time."

"That didn't register?" Samael asked.

Kateri shrugged. "There was an awful lot of running happening."

Samael nodded. "He would need its full power to go after Azazel, that's true."

With a nod and an extension of concentration, Admonae allowed the scene to move forward in slow motion from where she had frozen it. Lennox sheepishly stepped out of the way as the sword point drove towards her heart, and right before the moment of contact we all saw Michael will his sword into holy flame, but we could also feel that he had to expend a miracle to do it. The sword never lit itself, Michael had to light it.

Admonae dropped her miracle, allowing the image of Michael to disappear. Gary decided to draw our attention back to me. "But what has that got to do with Joan breaking Samael's sword?"

I could have strangled him.

"If I'm wrong," Lennox answered, "And Joan is just that good a swordswoman, then Samael will be able to reform his sword with a miracle."

Even though I had never known it to have happened, I couldn't help myself quietly praying, "Please be wrong, Lennox."

Samael extended his wings, held out his hand, and drew forth his power. It flowed over the pieces of broken sword lying on the ground.

And absolutely nothing happened.

Silje coughed, the noise of the fallen miracle causing her to gag slightly. "That, is one broken sword."

Then everyone turned to look at me. There was no point in denying the evidence. For Samael's miracle to fail it had to be going up against the action of something more powerful. Like the sword of an Archangel. And not just any Archangel, at that.

I raised the flaming sword still in my hand. I hadn't sheathed it during Admonae's demonstration in case Samael had a change of heart and attacked again. Silently, I willed the fire be extinguished, and I swear the flames actually sneered at me before continuing to lick merrily up and down the sword blade.

"Oookay..." I drew a deep breath and turned to Samael. "I'm not even going to pretend to understand, how, or why, or even when this happened, but apparently I now wield the sword of heaven."

Privately, I had my suspicions that it was actually the sword wielding me, but that was a problem for another time. A soldier always makes use of what is at hand. "With that in mind, Samael, would you care to explain exactly what you have done with Orfael?" I didn't move to get any closer to the Fallen angel, but I did raise the point of the sword suggestively in his direction.

I heard Gary gasp at my audacity and Beatrice release a quiet, almost evil chuckle, as Samael involuntarily took a small step backwards. Before his anger could ignite, however, Kateri stepped up and put an arm around his waist. His head whipped around to look directly at her as she smiled disarmingly. "We're all on the same side here, Samael. Michael's the enemy, not us."

"Us?" Samael queried with one raised eyebrow.

Kateri nodded, releasing him, but not stepping back. "Us."

Beatrice, meanwhile, had quietly moved to take her position behind me, should she be needed, and now gently placed one hand on my shoulder. Quietly, she whispered, "It's going to be okay, Joan, show him. Sheath your sword."

I winced at her emphasis on the ownership of the weapon but took my sister's advice and swung the sword around to its resting place between where my wings would be. As it came to rest in its spot it faded from sight, but I could still feel its warmth running down my spine.

The movement had drawn Samael's attention, and as the sword disappeared, he let go of his breath in a sigh that spoke of deep sadness, but also of acceptance. His wings extended once more and curled about him as he started to crouch. After a brief pause, he stood again, and the curled form of Orfael lay on the ground before him. "She is unhurt, even in my rage I could not strike at her. She will awaken in a moment."

Seeing her safe drained the remaining tension from my body. "You were able to strike at me readily enough."

Samael twitched that expressive eyebrow of his again. "You were armed, Tra... Joan. I just didn't realise what with."

"You're not the only one, apparently," Gary commented as he moved to sit by Orfael. She started to wake as if from a very deep sleep and stretched her arms out, cat-like, to cuddle Gary.

"Just a few more minutes," Orfael muttered sleepily.

"Yeah, she's fine," chuckled Gary.

Kateri bent down and placed a forefinger gently on Orfael's forehead, miraculously putting her back into a deep sleep. Looking up at her curiously, Gary reached for her wrist. "Kateri? What are you doing?"

Ignoring him, Kateri turned to Beatrice and me. "Joan, let Samael keep Orfael for the moment." As Beatrice stiffened, Kateri held a placating hand up. "Give me a chance to explain, Beatrice. If we leave Orfael with Samael, it will let Michael think that his plan is working, whatever the hell it is he's up to, and Samael will keep her safe."

Beatrice wasn't so easily mollified. "I'm not sure leaving her alone is such a good idea."

"She won't be alone," Kateri replied. "Samael will stay with her, and he can call Azazel for help if he needs to."

Samael nodded in agreement with Kateri. "I couldn't bring myself to hurt her when I thought she was guilty, I'm certainly not about to let anything happen to her now."

I looked deep into Samael's eyes as he spoke. Everything I saw told me he was telling the truth, and yet every fibre of my being was screaming against leaving Orfael with the Fallen.

"No." The single word from Lennox cut across the silence that had descended.

Kateri spun around to face her. "Lennox? You don't trust me?"

Lennox shook her head, "It's not that, Kateri. I honestly believe you and Samael will protect her. But falling changes you, Kateri, whether you want to believe that or not."

Kateri looked hurt by Lennox's statement, looking first to me and then Samael for support before turning back to her. "I'm still me. I haven't changed. I'm your sister."

Lennox nodded, but crossed her arms. "My sister wouldn't be suggesting we keep Orfael unconscious without her consent."

A look of honest puzzlement crossed Kateri's features, but I could see Admonae behind her silently agreeing with Lennox. "But it will keep her safe? Michael won't be able to find her. It just makes sense, it's the simplest way. It's …"

"Expedient? Efficient?" Lennox interrupted.

Kateri drew breath to agree before the realisation hit her. "Oh." Her shoulders slumped, wingtips drooping sadly to touch the floor.

Admonae stepped closer and gently took one of Kateri's hands in hers. "You are still you, sister. The power you have regained just tends to make you think of solutions, not people. Just hold on to that, to us."

In a soft, quiet voice, Kateri added, "I didn't even think…"

With a gasp, Orfael awoke once again, sitting up in Gary's arms. Seeing Samael crouched in front of her, she let out a little exclamation and tried to burrow herself into Gary's chest to get away from him.

Beatrice's ire rose once again. "I thought you said you didn't hurt her."

Samael scuttled back, hands raised. "I didn't. I probably scared her quite a bit, but nothing more."

With arms wrapped securely around Orfael, Gary slowly got up, helping her stand with him and moving her over towards Lennox. Silje joined the three of them and together they quietly told Orfael everything that had transpired. I noticed that Gary had moved her so her view of Gaap was blocked by one of the station platforms pillars, and when the group got to that part of the narrative Orfael craned her neck in an attempt to see past it before the others drew her back to the story once again.

I caught Samael's attention and nodded to where Gaap's body was still hanging. Together, we, Beatrice, and Kateri walked over to him and started to lift him down as gently as we could. It took a few minutes, but we wrapped him in a bolt of linen Kateri created, and when he was prepared, Samael bent to lift his brother's body.

As he slipped his arms underneath Gaap's swaddled form, Orfael appeared on the opposite side of the body and lifted with him. Face to face, over the body of their departed brother, Wingless and Fallen shared a silent moment. Without looking away from Samael's face, Orfael spoke, "Samael and I will take care of Gaap from here on."

With all that had happened, I placed one hand on Orfael's shoulder to get her attention. I had to be sure. "You realise this means you'll have to stay with him until Michael is stopped?"

Orfael nodded, turning her face to me. A single tear had left a track in the dust down her face, but whether it was for us or for Gaap I had no idea. "Go save the world, Joan," she said. "It's what you do."

Chapter Twenty-Five

Leaving with his brother's body and carrying Orfael wasn't beyond Samael's power, but in order to do it as quietly as possible, and avoid leaving a trail to follow, he timed dropping the obfuscation miracle that still sat around the subway station with their dematerialisation.

Almost at once, the sounds of the city above came flooding back into the previously silent station, and in a very short time, a crowd of footsteps could be heard descending the stairs from the street.

I looked around at my companions and took a deep breath. I was happy to be leaving this place. "Well, time we were going. We've still got…Silje? What are you doing?"

Silje was up on point, like a ballerina, with her arms stretched out high and a beatific smile on her face. Her back was ramrod straight, but her arms were bent, at the shoulders, elbows and wrists at different angles. All ten fingers were splayed wide and almost imperceptibly moving in some unfelt breeze.

Lennox turned to Admonae and asked, "Tree?"

Admonae nodded in return. "Tree."

As we watched, the stiffness in her limbs melted away and she gracefully descended back onto her feet, arms flowing down to her sides. Her smile broadened as her eyes refocused on us.

"Welcome back." I think I kept the sarcasm out of my voice.

"We need to go west, Joan." Silje's eyes were shining with joy. I'm not sure I could handle always experiencing creation the way she does, but I have to admit from time to time I found myself just a little bit jealous. "I know where we need to go next, west to Lhasa. There is a—"

As one Lennox, Gary, Admonae and Beatrice all spoke in unison with Silje, "—Tree waiting for us there."

I tried and failed to contain a snort of laughter at the surprised look on Silje's face. "You heard it too?"

Shaking my head, I reached out to take Silje by the hand, or else we'd never get out of there. "Well, I didn't hear anything Silje, you can tell me what happened while we walk."

As luck, or fate, would have it, the daily train, the Z21 from Beijing to Lhasa in Tibet, hadn't left by the time we reached the terminal. With the stops along the way, the journey would take about 45 hours to travel the nearly 4000 kilometres west and four kilometres up to the famous Tibetan plateau. Lennox had organised tickets over the internet through Toby back in England as we walked to the city's main station, and together, they had managed to secure us a family sleeper cabin.

"If we're going into a Tree's area of influence," explained Lennox, "We're going to need to eat and sleep normally to prepare ourselves."

Beatrice screwed up her face. "On train food?"

The bark of laughter Gary released was heart-warming. "Never fear, Beatrice dear, I shall secure us provisions and prepare them in our cabin. Everything our bodies will need, and tasty to boot, I promise."

"Instead of tasting like a boot?" Admonae countered. At Gary's wounded expression, Admonae laughed and hugged him.

"Okay," I called their attention back to the task at hand, "We've got just under an hour before the train leaves. Gary and Beatrice, grab the meal supplies we need. And some tea please. Silje, Lennox, and Kateri, we'll need warm clothes, jackets, boots. Admonae, you and I will get climbing gear, backpacks, anything else we might need. Forty-five minutes people, that's all you have. Don't haggle, just move fast. Go."

We split into our groups and moved off quickly, old habits sweeping Kateri back into her role as one of us and not simply using her power to create everything we needed. I was glad she didn't argue—I wouldn't be able to properly explain why, but I deep down felt we needed to do this our way.

True to form, forty-five minutes later we were sitting in our cabin, large bags and boxes of supplies stowed on the floor between us. Shortly afterwards, a whistle sounded, and the train slowly pulled away from the station.

We'd have two nights on the train before arriving in Lhasa, so we were able to take our time settling in, trying out and stowing all our gear safely, and arguing good-naturedly over who got the seats by the window. Lennox had her ever-present tablet to surf the web with, and Kateri used a very minor miracle to get us a few good books to help us wile away the hours. It was a pleasant and much needed change of pace for the seven of us. While our wingless bodies had remained unaffected by all the exertion over the past few weeks, the constant stress had taken a toll on our hearts and minds.

I watched Kateri laugh and joke with the others as the countryside rolled past the window. It was like a shadow was slowly lifting from her heart, and with that everyone else's faces shone just that little bit brighter as well. We hadn't really gotten the chance to mourn the loss of our friend, and here she was, just like how we remembered her. I found myself remembering all the Wingless who had chosen to fall, to regain the family that I had so easily cut ties with. For perhaps the first time since the war, I wondered if I had made the right decision in doing so.

Doubt is not something that has ever sat well with me. Once I've made a decision, I rarely revisit it, I just accept what it brings and move forward. This mess with Michael had shaken me more than I realised, and the feelings it was dredging up inside me were not at all welcome.

Whether it was because Silje noticed my silent brooding or simply knew me far better than I thought she did, I soon found her sharing my couch with me, snuggled up against my arm. Her eyes were on Kateri, and she whispered to me such that the others would not be able to hear our conversation.

"She's not the same, Joan," Silje whispered. "She's still Kateri, she'll do what you tell her to do, and I still trust her with my life, but she has changed."

I looked down at Silje's gentle face. There was no ill-judgement in her tone, she was just describing the world as she saw it; or in her case, heard it. Quietly, she continued, "It is all new to her, but falling does change you, and it will change her more as time goes on. She doesn't want that, she doesn't want to lose us any more than we want to lose her, but it is inevitable in the end."

"That sucks," I whispered back.

Silje snuggled in deeper before closing her eyes. "It is what it is. Her falling was different, so it may take longer. It may not affect her the same way as the others, but there will be changes."

"Silje," I asked, "How did you know I was thinking about the other Wingless that fell?"

She snuggled closer as she answered, "It's the only time your eyes are ever sad."

It was late in the second night, with dawn still a few hours away when the train started to brake unexpectedly. We had been slowly travelling up the foothills of the Himalayas for a few hours now, and I knew from the itinerary that there were no more scheduled stops until we reached Lhasa.

Beatrice must have come to the same conclusion I had, as she was busy jostling those around her. "Wake up. Something's wrong."

I followed suit with my side of the cabin, and we had everyone roused by the time the train had come to a complete halt. Our altitude meant that it wasn't pitch black outside, but it was certainly dark enough to see that there were no lights of a town—we had been stopped in the middle of nowhere.

Kateri waggled her shoulders suggestively in the dark cabin. "I could pop out and have a look if you want, Joan?"

As tempting as that was, I had to vote on the side of caution. "No, Kateri, if Michael is the cause of this he'll be listening for any miracle, no matter how small. And he'd hear you a mile away."

The lights in the corridor that ran down one side of the train switched from the dull red of their night setting to full brightness. I could hear the doors at either end of the carriage being opened and booted feet entering the corridor.

Beatrice brought her head back from the curtained window that looked out from our cabin into the corridor and hissed, "Red Army. Border patrol from the looks of it."

Lennox, typing madly away on her tablet in the corner, perked up. "Excellent. Delay them if you can, I have an idea."

"No miracles, Lennox," I warned.

"No miracles, Joan, I promise," she replied.

Sharp arguments in Mandarin were occurring in the cabin next door and one from a cabin down the other end of the carriage. Since they were going cabin to cabin it meant that if the soldiers had been told to look for someone specifically, and the way our luck ran, it was us they were after. They didn't know where we were yet, but that thought didn't give me any great comfort.

Peering through the edge of the curtain, Beatrice gave an update. "They're carrying photos, definitely looking for someone in particular, but I can't see the image properly."

I growled in response. "Damn it. It has to be Michael. He's using them to look for us."

"I thought soldiers were your realm, Joan?" Gary queried.

I nodded. "Individual soldiers are, but armies are his. And the largest police force in the world just happens to be the Chinese Red Army."

"And they're just outside the door," Beatrice added as she let the curtain drop and stepped back from the door.

"Aaaand *now.*" Lennox punctuated her comment with a final firm strike of the enter key on her tablet keyboard.

Almost immediately, the shoulder mounted radios on the soldiers all started to squawk in unison. Excited voices issued curt commands and the sound of running boots reverberated through the carriage as the troops double-timed it off the train.

I slowly turned from the door to look at Lennox sitting in the back of the cabin. "No miracles...so what just happened?"

"Well," Lennox started, "The good news is that they just got a message stating that foreigners matching our descriptions had been spotted at a nearby private airfield."

Gary bit at the dangling line. "And the bad news?"

"I described us fairly accurately, so the fact that they ran off so fast..."

Admonae finished for her: "Means they were definitely looking for us."

As quietly as we could manage, we repacked all our gear for a quick getaway and waited. A nerve-wracking twenty minutes later, however, we felt the train lurch into motion once again, and we breathed a collective sigh of relief.

As much as we needed to be rested before entering the area of the Tree, none of us were able to get back to sleep after that. We chatted softly to one another, conversations roaming from Lennox's obvious skill in cracking the Red

Army communication codes, guessing what Michael's reaction would be when he worked out what we had done, through to wondering which one of the Trees of Creation was awaiting us in Tibet.

By the time the sun rose, bathing the mountain in cold light, we were ready to jump off the train. I'd decided that using Kateri's wings to safely get off before the train reached the station was probably the smartest move under the circumstances. That's why when the train arrived in Lhasa to a Red Army welcome, we were climbing up a yak trail cut into the side of one of the oldest mountains in the world, and silently marvelling at the view.

Chapter Twenty-Six

Fragile flames licked at the bottom of the pot, causing a sweet-smelling steam to waft up from the surface of its contents and drift gently over to where we sat. The great expanse of China laid stretched out below our makeshift camp, and we watched it slowly be covered in a growing shadow as the last rays of sunlight disappeared behind the even larger peaks of the Himalayan mountains behind us.

My body ached with the exertion of the climb, but it felt like a good ache. Following the image planted in my mind from the Tree of Knowledge as to where we needed to go, we climbed over cliffs and ridges with only the occasional wild goat to witness our passing. Sometime during the afternoon, we had passed into the influence of the Tree, making the rest of the climb something of an ordeal for Silje and Lennox. By the time we were able to find the shallow cave that was now serving as our campsite for the night, we were all feeling the strain on our now fully mortal bodies.

"You are going to be disappointed by the tea," Admonae stated, as she poured from the pot into the tin camping mugs we each held out. "We're too high up. The lower atmospheric pressure makes the boiling point of water lower as well."

"I have no doubt you're right, Admonae," I replied, as I brought the mug to my lips for a taste. "But this is hot, at least tea-like, and wonderful."

Gary, however, had the grimace produced by his first sip still plastered on his face. "This is almost as bad as the tea at British Rail."

As Admonae got around to Kateri, she found she had fallen fast asleep with her empty mug still cradled on her lap. "Poor lass. I guess losing all that power hit her harder than she expected. Should I just let her sleep?"

I shook my head. "No, wake her up, just be gentle. If she doesn't get some food and liquid into her before she sleeps, she'll be in a far worse shape tomorrow."

Tucked in beside her, Silje put her arm around Kateri, hugging her, and gently swayed her awake again.

"Mwah?" Groggily, Kateri tried to stand, but Silje held her down until she woke fully.

Admonae held out the pot. "Come on sleepy-head, drink up!"

"Are we there yet?" Kateri mumbled before Silje raised the mug to her lips and Kateri had to concentrate on swallowing.

Sitting on her other side, Beatrice reached out and gently pulled Kateri's long messy hair out from between her lips and the mug. "Not yet, I'm afraid. We're close, but I'm not even sure what direction we go from here."

Silje shuddered a little at Beatrice's comment and let Kateri go in order to hug her arms around herself. "I'm no use with that, the world is silent, just like last time. I don't like it; it freaks me out not to be able to hear everything."

Lennox waved her phone out in front of her with an indifferent air. "And this is useless. I can connect to a satellite easy enough, but what we're looking for isn't exactly going to be highlighted on Google Maps."

Gary turned to me as he finished his tea in one big gulp. "*Eargh*. Well, I for one don't want to spend any more time drinking this stuff than we have to, no offense Admonae. Which way do we go from here, Joan?"

I finished my own tea, stretched, and stood. "Well, we could start a standard search pattern, but the area isn't exactly what you'd call flat." I twisted my chest around, left, then right, limbering up stiffening muscles. "We could always split up, but that seems like a whole lot of unnecessary danger when we could just ask the person who has been keeping an eye on us for the past hour."

In my 'stretching', I had moved close to the edge of the cave, and with my last words I spun and flung my hand out, intent on grabbing the neck of the person hiding just out of sight. A loud crack rang out and fiery pain lanced up from my knuckles to my shoulder. I pulled my arm back just as quickly and stepped away, cradling my throbbing fingers against my chest.

Around the corner, staff clicking on the stone, strode a smiling monk dressed in Tibetan robes. "Your training is impressive, Trazael," he stated, in an almost fatherly tone, "But you still rely too much on your angelic nature."

Any biting comment I may have had lined up died on my lips at the sight of my assailant. "Raphael?"

It seemed wrong somehow, seeing him like this. No wings, a lean, almost wiry body, his face so heavy with wrinkles and age that I hadn't recognised him until he spoke. He just seemed wrong, too unreal.

Too human.

The others hadn't moved, each looking up at the old man with shock on their faces. Kateri's eyes also reflected a little fear, and I felt I needed to move to block the archangel's view of her.

The soft smile he granted us made me realise just how futile that movement had been. Standing where we were, Raphael was as powerless as we were, and yet if he had wanted to harm us, there was nothing we could have done to stop him. The age in his body, the surety with which he held himself, everything pointed to him living here for ages past. Where we had done our best at quite short notice to adapt ourselves to the loss of our powers—he had lived it.

Raphael relaxed his stance, however, and slowly laid his walking staff up against the cave wall. "Apologies for my delay in announcing myself, Trazael. Had you come alone I would have welcomed you earlier, since you choose to come in the company of a Fallen, I felt it prudent to watch a while."

"Uhh, it's 'Joan' now." I hated that my voice sounded like I was embarrassed as I corrected the archangel. I had no problem sounding annoyed when correcting Michael, or being downright rude to Azazel, but in front of Raphael I was suddenly a young, inexperienced angel once again.

His gentle, fatherly smile in response didn't help with that feeling one bit. "And so, I find myself apologising again, Joan."

It was Beatrice who prompted the archangel back to discussing his arrival. "And how do you feel about us now?"

Raphael turned to face Kateri and executed a respectful bow. "Now I can see she comes to be with you, not against me or the Tree I swore to protect. You are all welcome here. When you are ready, I will lead you to what you seek."

The lure of somewhere warm awaiting us soon had us all on our tired and sore feet once more, packing away our makeshift campsite. We chatted with Raphael as pots disappeared into backpacks and bedrolls were retied. Taking his cue from my name, Raphael started by asking each of us to reintroduce ourselves to him. This sensitivity to our sense of identity put us at ease with the archangel quite quickly. From someone else I may have suspected this as the reason behind his question. But from Raphael it just seemed kind.

Silje asked if he was affected the same way we were by being this close to the Tree, effectively being cut off from the rest of the world. Raphael agreed that it did, he was no more immune to the effects of a tree of creation than the rest of us, and it was the reason why he was unaware of our current names.

That admission started an avalanche of questions, which is probably a bad analogy considering the mountain pass we were climbing at the time, but I guess it shows what my mind was concentrating on. Why was he here? How long had he been here? How could he stand the silence for so long? How had he survived without power?

Patiently, Raphael answered each of us in turn, and listening to his calm voice made the arduous climb seem manageable. "When the war started there was a concern that, should it go bad for the rebellion, an attempt would be made to use this Tree as a way of turning the tide in their favour. I personally did not believe that the Lightbringer would do such a thing, but Michael nonetheless insisted that I come here to guard it personally. I acquiesced and have been here ever since."

Kateri spoke up for the first time as his gaze fell upon her. "We're not going to do anything, I promise. We don't even know which tree is here. It called to us, or to Silje, actually. It called us here."

Raphael nodded, turning his head back to the path ahead of us. "I know, child, she told me."

"But that brings me to Silje's question," Raphael continued. "The silence is not something you ever get used to, that is true. But each dawn I commune with the Tree, and through her I hear the song, albeit only her part in it. That touch is also what has sustained me all these millennia, although as you can see, it has not stopped me aging altogether."

Beatrice beat me to the punch with her next question. "Which Tree is she?"

Raphael chuckled, shaking his head slightly. "Sorry my dear, but that is not my story to tell. She will tell you herself when you meet her. Or not."

By this time, we had neared a plateau on the mountain, with one long steep slope left to ascend. Kateri slipped on the ice and stumbled, her exhausted legs giving way beneath her. Before any of us could react, Raphael had jumped back to where she was walking, swooping her up in one arm as the other planted his staff into the snow as an anchor. He pulled her to his chest just before she would have gone over the side.

They stood there, unmoving, on the edge of the precipice. We all had adrenaline from the moment surging through our bodies and were panting as if we had run a mile. Kateri shook against Raphael's chest, and at first, I thought she was reacting as we were, trying to fill our lungs with the rarefied air at this height.

However, when she slowly pulled away from Raphael, I could see the wet patch on his tunic where her head had rested. She had been sobbing like a child as he held her.

I could have kicked myself that it was only then that I remembered. Raphael wasn't just an archangel to Kateri. He was *her* archangel, the one she answered to just as I was under Michael's command. She went to pull away, but he held onto her arm, causing her to look up at him questioningly. With that paternal smile of his, he swept his arm about her waist and guided her up the rest of the slope, taking more and more of her weight as she slowly relaxed into him. It was an act of forgiveness for her falling that none of us expected, especially since we knew that Raphael could have no knowledge of the events that led up to her decision.

At the top of the rise, the plateau was home to a magnificent Tibetan temple complex. It was lit by a thousand small flames, making the entire place look like it was floating in a sea of fireflies. From here we could see the Tree herself, standing strong in the centre of the plateau. It was a truly glorious sight.

Raphael led us to one of the large outer buildings of the complex. Steam from warm baths wafted out the ornate open doors as we approached. "Please, rest, eat, sleep. You will be summoned in the morning," Raphael stated, as he turned to leave us.

"Thank you," Kateri said, as she released her grip on his arm. There was a lot of emotion packed into those two small words, and Kateri's lips shook with the effort of saying them. Raphael simply smiled once more before bending over to whisper something in Kateri's ear. Then he turned and walked back towards the temple.

Chapter Twenty-Seven

The Kunlun Mountains in Tibet are believed to be the fabled paradise of Taoism. Looking out across the temple plateau as the sun rose the next morning, I had a small inkling as to why. The stark beauty and serenity of the landscape was such that the slight noise of my breathing almost seemed like an affront to the perfect stillness before me. As the first rays of sunlight touched the large bronze bell in front of the central building of the complex, a monk struck it, sending a pure, deep note flowing across the compound. I turned and stepped back into our lodge as the others awoke to that beautiful sound.

While we dressed, a young monk delivered a tray to our lodge holding covered bowls filled with a mix of rice, vegetables, and spices. Each was slightly different, which of course meant we ended up trying a little from each of the bowls, sharing them around. Almost without thinking about it, our breakfast transformed from an act of necessity in feeding our bodies into an opportunity to bond and share at the beginning of the day.

"This is lovely, really," Gary commented as we were picking at the last remaining grains of rice at the bottom of the bowls. "But if they had just included the saffron from that dish with the chili in this one, and the soy from Silje's, then they would have the perfect dish."

"But perfection is not the goal." We turned as one at the sound of the old voice at the entrance to our lodge, its playful tone delighting in the trap Gary had fallen in to. "Imperfections should be embraced, not corrected. The little bits of imperfection in a flower, a sunrise, within each of us and within your meal are the elements of chaos that give each life individuality and distinction. This is what we cherish."

Admonae had gotten to her feet as the old man had spoken, bowing deeply as he finished. "Tao-shih, you honour us."

With a smile and a shake of his head, the Tao-shih, the Master of the temple, dismissed Admonae's formal greeting. "Nonsense, child. All are welcome here who come to learn. I am also on a journey of discovery, and I am interested in asking each of you a question."

He motioned Admonae to sit once again and moved into the circle we had formed on the mats during breakfast. The bowls still laid before each of us, and I noticed him quickly scanning each. With a sly smile he took his seat between Lennox and myself, and as he settled, I couldn't help but search for what he saw in the bowls. I could see nothing remarkable in the remains of our meal, but when I looked up again, he was watching me.

The Master nodded to the bowls and asked, "What do you see, child?"

Part of me wanted to laugh at this man of no more than eight decades calling me a 'child', but there was a gentle kindness in his way that made his comment seem appropriate. "I don't know, I see our bowls. I see we have finished all the food and I'm happy we have wasted none of it."

He nodded his head, but I knew that nod was in acceptance of a shortcoming in my reply, not a sign that I had achieved the answer he sought. "That is because you attempt to make sense of what you see. You look for patterns, similarities. It is what we are trained to do from birth, to help make sense of our world. However, try again, but this time look for the differences."

I looked back, confused. I started to treat the room like one of those 'spot the difference' drawings in the London Times. My bowl was right in front of me, centred, the chopsticks placed together perpendicular to where I sat. Beside me, Beatrice and placed hers next to Silje's so that the two were touching. Gary had kept his close to him, Admonae had replaced the lid on her bowl. Little things, but in each I saw an aspect of the person who had eaten from it, a small piece of the friend who had held it last. Unknowingly, we had left our mark on the scene and had told the Master a little about ourselves in the process.

I looked back up at the old man to find him smiling genuinely at me. "Now you begin to understand," he said, before turning to the group, "And with that understanding comes growth."

Beatrice allowed a little annoyance to creep into her voice. "What? But she didn't say anything."

"Not with her voice," the old monk agreed, "That is but one small way we communicate."

The Tao Master folded his hands in his lap and allowed his gaze to take us all in. "You know that your compatriot, Raphael, has been here since the human world began. Our arrival here is but a recent occurrence in his lifetime, but he has been welcoming of our ways and indulgent of our questions. However, there is only so much that the Tao can learn from one who professes to be perfect."

Beside him, Lennox commented, "Nobody's perfect."

Her words earned her a scowl from Kateri, but a nod from the master. "True, my child, but his very nature will not allow him to see otherwise. You and I can see that this rigidity of thought is a flaw, however he is not made like us, and so he cannot. It would be like asking a fish why it cannot run. It is simply not in their nature."

"Us?" Gary queried.

"Indeed, us. I, of course, am far from perfect, for I am human. But Raphael has told me of your original choice, and that you were able to make such a decision shows a level of freedom he does not possess. In truth, while he admits to not understanding why you made the choice you did, more importantly he does not understand how such a choice was open to you at all. With that freedom, I presume, comes individuality. And with that individuality, comes the imperfections the Tao cherish."

Free will was always His gift to the humans. But it couldn't be as simple as that, not really. We had decided not to fight, just as others had decided to side with either Lightbringer or Michael. Lightbringer himself decided to lead a rebellion, and he was His first created, the oldest of all of us. The concept of what is and isn't 'free will' never really sat well with me, and the Tao-shih was not making the idea any easier to come to terms with. Then again, being a Taoist, that was probably his goal all along.

I broke that chain of thought and brought myself back to the conversation. "Let's say we agree with your interpretation for the moment. What is this test you have for us?"

Concern flashed over his features for a brief second before his face relaxed once more. "Test? No child, there is no test. Not everything is a battle one must win. I have a question for each of you, one that I want you to feel free not to answer. This is my opportunity to learn, to grow, but your participation is entirely voluntary."

Admonae had been listening quietly since greeting the master, but now spoke up. "What is your question?"

The Master paused for a moment to take a deep breath before answering. "One that is easy to ask, and difficult to answer, my child. I would like to learn from each of you: what do you consider to be your greatest flaw?"

We each fell silent. It was as if that simple question had released our inner demons; the fears, failures, and doubts that we all work so hard to keep locked away. I could see why, as an archangel, Raphael would have been confused by the mere concept of this question. Why he had been unable to answer it?

He was made to be flawless, and so he was. In his mind, at least.

Silje spoke first. "I still feel that a lot of the world goes over my head, I am one of the youngest of us."

"Youth is not a flaw little one, it is just a state of being. Consider the question a while longer," replied the Tao-shih.

Sitting beside the master, Lennox sat up straight and drew our attention. "You know I love all of you without reservation, and deep in my heart I know you feel the same about me. But in the dark of night, when I am all alone with just the glow of a computer screen to keep me company, I feel alone. And I blame you. Logically I know you care, I know that if I called, you would come, but emotionally, it feels like sometimes you're just not here." Lennox motioned with her clenched fist to her heart.

After a moment she let her arm fall back and continued, "There are so few of us now, and you are all quick to tell me how self-sufficient and competent I am, but sometimes it feels like just an excuse to not bother checking up on me. In the light of day, I know it's ridiculous, that I'm just being silly, but I feel left out. Not wanted. And I get jealous."

We listened in silence. This was not the time for discussion, or platitudes meant to reassure. We were being privileged to share in a rare glimpse into each other's private worlds, and our presence was all that was required or wanted. The impulse to run around to Lennox and hug her was nearly irresistible but a small motion from the master stopped me.

Gary cleared his throat, drawing the attention off Lennox. "Well, for me I think it basically comes down to cowardice. I like to think that I chose not to fight because of the lack of strength in the arguments of either side, or my love for the humans, or my passion for my mission here on Earth. But when I'm alone in my café, I can't help but feel it was really because I was just scared. Scared to choose a side, scared to fight, scared to die. And I hate that."

Next around the circle was Kateri. She looked a little sheepish as she smiled and said with a shrug, "Well, I fell." The Master smiled softly and shook his head almost imperceptibly, and Kateri dropped her head in defeat. "Okay, I know. Doesn't count."

She grimaced to herself and then started again. "I know I finally fell to protect someone, but I was getting really disappointed and fed up with humanity because of the way they treat the world they've been given to live on. At times I've thought of crossing the line, of removing some of the risk to the environment by removing certain humans ... permanently. I'm quite ashamed of that, and I have never acted on those feelings, but sometimes I just get so angry."

Admonae shook her head as Kateri finished, and our attention moved around to her. Her face showed obvious emotional stress, but her lips were held tightly closed. "Sorry. No. I can't. Not now, anyway."

The old monk bowed respectfully towards her. "May you find peace from your pain, my child."

Sitting beside Admonae, Silje moved slightly forward for her turn. "Okay, please don't take this the wrong way, Lennox, but I envy how they see you. I feel like you all see me as the exact opposite to Lennox, unable to look after myself, incompetent, foolish, always needing to be protected or shielded. It really makes me angry sometimes. I'm not silly, I just see things differently to nearly everyone else. I resent it, and it makes me sad."

Beatrice couldn't restrain herself and gave Silje a tight hug in silence before sitting back up and looking around the circle at us all. "I'm a judge. I weigh up all the facts of a situation and make a decision. Once made I see it through to the end, you all know that. Every time, every choice, no second guessing, no doubts."

Beatrice reached out and took Silje's hand in hers. "Except it is all a lie. I doubt all the time. There have been moments when I lose all faith, not only in my decisions, but even in my ability to *make* decisions. I'm not a genius like Lennox, or able to see the truth like Admonae. I don't have Joan's courage or Gary's people skills. But I am the one who has to make the decision, and most of the time I'm afraid I'm just guessing."

And then there was only me left. My memory drifted back over all the events that had happened to us since we started looking for Kateri. All the responsibility for finding her and working out what was happening fell to me. It was a mantle I placed on myself without thinking, it just seemed normal, but then my thoughts drifted back to the memory of watching Kateri wake on the train with that beatific smile–at ease–at peace. I realised how envious I was at how easy everyone was with each other, at the simple comradery they all shared.

My little explosion back at the observatory was just the tip of the problem. Whether they truly were sacred of me or not, the outcome was still the same. I may lead, but I never really belonged.

When I brought my attention back to the group, all their eyes were upon me. And in that moment, all the complicated emotions snapped into clarity.

"My flaw would be that I allow myself to feel betrayed by my friends, sometimes I think I even jump to that conclusion because it's easier than facing the truth. That I push you all away as a way of protecting myself." My eyes lowered to the mat between us. At that moment I couldn't look at their faces. "I betray you before you get the chance to betray me. I push you all away and then blame you for leaving me."

The shuffling around the circle made me look up once again. The tears in the eyes around me told me more than any words ever could. It was heart-warming, but equally it was time to move on.

I turned to the monk who had listened patiently to our stories. "So, what about you? Turnabout is fair play, after all. What is your greatest flaw, Tao-shih?"

The old man chuckled quietly for a moment before answering. "I would have thought you might have worked that out by now, child." He paused, and then with a wink he finished:

"I can be terribly condescending."

Chapter Twenty-Eight

Once the Tao-shih had left we sat in silence, looking at each other for a minute before suddenly collapsing together in a group hug that had us all talking at once. Everyone had something to say to each of the others, and it made the entire morning feel like we had been through some sort of cleansing.

It was Gary who put voice to the idea first. "I bet that old coot planned this from the start. He wanted us all properly purged and restored before we met his precious Tree."

"Probably," echoed Admonae. "Raphael may have clued him in as well; gave him some pointers on how to push our buttons."

"Feels good though, doesn't it?" asked Beatrice.

The smiles that went around the group showed we all felt the same.

Thirty minutes later, we had gathered at the entrance to the Tree's walled courtyard. We could see her beautiful branches stretching up and over the walls, and this close to her Silje wasn't the only one who was able to hear her call.

From within the courtyard, the Tao-shih opened the door for us, letting us enter. Raphael was just removing his hand from the trunk of the tree, and he slowly stood, turned, and walked over to us. There was something...renewed about him this morning. He seemed lighter on his feet than he did when we met yesterday, and I took it to be the effects of his dawn commune with a Tree of creation.

Raphael bowed respectfully to the Tao-shih before addressing us. "She has requested that each of you place a hand on her trunk at the same time." The only reaction from the Tao-shih was the elegant raising of one eyebrow, but Raphael obviously caught the meaning of the movement. "I know this is unusual, Master, but it is her request."

The Tao-shih nodded. "I will leave you all to your meditations, then."

Raphael's next words sounded almost pained. "And I must do so as well."

Kateri reached out and timidly placed one hand on the archangel's arm. "You're not staying here with us?"

Raphael shook his head slowly, almost sadly. "That too is her request. I am to remain outside the courtyard until you leave." He patted Kateri's hand on his arm, lowering it from him before falling into step with the Master, walking out of the courtyard. Two younger monks appeared and closed the doors from the outside, leaving us alone with the Tree.

I took a deep breath and centred myself. "Well folks, no point in wasting any more time. We've come a long way to do this and we're as ready as we'll ever be. Shall we?"

Without waiting for an answer, I strode forward towards the Tree. My friends fanned out around its base and as one we stepped up, each of us raising one hand. I cast a quick glance around to see that we were all ready and placed my hand on the rough trunk,

As my hand touched the bark of the tree, her voice filled my head. Rather than it suddenly appearing, however, it felt like she had always been there, but only now could I hear her.

"Finally, you are ready to begin the journey you have completed," she said.

Before I could even start to try to understand her rather cryptic statement, everything went dark and then something slammed into my face. Part of my mind couldn't help but complain—don't those two things usually happen in the other order?

The sky above me exploded into colour and quickly brought me up off the damp ground and onto my knees. Grass and dirt stuck to my cheek, evidence of my inelegant faceplant into the ground, and my hair tangled about my face like the tentacles of a deranged octopus. The explosion was soon joined by a second, and then a third, before my jumbled brain slowly recognised the expanding balls of light and colour as a fireworks display.

The soldier within me kicked into action—'check your team' it demanded. Tearing my eyes away from the fireworks, I was able to make out the forms of my friends slowly picking themselves up off the ground around me. The intermittent flashes of light from the fireworks revealed that we were in a children's playground on the bank of a river flowing through a modern city.

Gary found his voice first. "Oh, dear heaven, that smell! That's the Thames, no mistaking it! How can we be back in London?"

Recovering faster than all of us, Kateri was already on her feet and helping Silje sit up. Looking around the city skyline across the river, she asked, "It can't be real, can it?"

Admonae shook her head, bringing one hand up to hold her forehead. "It's real, I feel no falsehood or illusion in this."

Another explosion of light assaulted our still recovering senses—this time, however, it was no fireworks high in the sky. This was close, very close, and the chime of the celestial chorus rang in place of exploding gunpowder. As one, our heads snapped around to the children's fort in the middle of the playground, and to the two glowing figures hovering in the air just above it.

"What do they think they are doing!?" Admonae's astonished gasp gave voice to us all. Before us, in all their heavenly glory, were Michael and Azazel, facing off like the pair of veteran combatants they were. Michael's sword was pointed directly at the Fallen's chest, its flame burning brightly in the night. Azazel's own weapon, complete with an azure flame of its own, was held in a guard position, having just successfully warded off Michael's blow.

Beatrice had a look close to panic on her face. "But…but they can't fight here! They could be seen! This is just so wrong!"

Azazel, it seems, had a similar concern. "Nice try, Michael, but enough is enough. We should take this elsewhere, away from the city."

"Defiler!" Michael growled. "Deceiver! You dare lecture me?"

Gary backed away from the awe-inspiring sight before us. "Ahh, folks, I hate to say this, but Michael is starting to lose it. We'd better make sure no one else can see this."

Silje nodded in agreement and moved to join him. "Not starting to, he's lost. Listen to his voice, Michael's snapped."

Too fast for the human eye to see, and almost too fast for ours, Michael and Azazel started to trade blows once again, causing the sky to explode in light and the symphony to resound with the discord they created. Michael had pulled out all stops, fury fuelling the strength in his blows, but Azazel was blocking or dodging each one. Sometimes only just, but he was still untouched.

Despite myself, I felt a growing respect for the fallen angel's martial prowess. Our 'friendly' little neighbourhood Fallen, the one given the menial work of following us about and waiting for us to fall, was standing toe to toe with the Archangel Michael, General of the Army of the Heavenly Hosts, and so far, at least, he was unharmed. Azazel hadn't landed a blow on Michael either, but it was still impressive. What's more, there was a continual flow of miraculous power from Azazel ensuring that the celebratory fireworks high in the sky over London were exploding in time with their combat, masking the worst of their conflict.

There was no such accommodation to maintaining the veil from Michael.

With a clash that I felt reverberate in my bones, Azazel managed to block a blow in such a way that it actually forced Michael back for a moment. Azazel's eyes were burning red, and the scowling look on his face was more serious than I had ever seen him. "Enough, Michael!" Azazel's voice carried a note of steel that I hadn't heard before. "Stop this madness now! Look at yourself, look at what you are becoming!"

I couldn't help but feel that his voice was somehow…older than usual. Silje was looking at the pair with confusion on her face, letting me know it wasn't just me imagining it.

The fight had paused, and I allowed myself to hope for a moment that Michael had come to his senses and was about to take their encounter elsewhere, but then he spoke, and the venom in his voice chilled my blood.

"You…Of course. It had to be you. Drop that insulting façade and face me," Michael spat at Azazel.

Azazel raised his sword back into the guard position and floated a few steps backwards, away from the Archangel. "Now, Michael," Azazel said in his normal voice once more, "We really need to leave here. *Now.*"

In response, Michael let out a howl that could only be described as primal, raised his flaming sword high above his head, and brought it down hard against his opponent's block. We could all feel the raw, untempered miraculous power Michael poured into that blow. As it struck, an exploding wave of force swept out from the pair across the park, knocking all of us back and leaving us sprawled in the dirt and grass. Behind me, I could hear a young woman's voice cry out in pain, and I realised just how terrible that blow must have sounded to Silje.

The echo of the blow was still ringing in my ears when I looked up to see what had become of Azazel. To my surprise he was still standing, but there was an odd shimmering about his body. With a high-pitched noise like glass shattering, a very, very old miracle that was wrapped around Azazel's body collapsed. Azazel's features blurred for a moment as reality reasserted itself and revealed, standing in Azazel's place, the Lightbringer himself. Lucifer. His first Angel, and Michael's only older sibling.

With all possibility of any further obfuscation gone, Lightbringer's shoulders slumped a little, and he sighed deeply. As he did, his magnificent, pure white wings extended out behind him, and he looked at Michael with disappointment on his face.

"Oh, brother," the Lord of the Fallen sighed sadly. He then stepped sideways and in towards Michael in a fashion that didn't completely conform to the laws of geometry or Euclidian space. He easily swept past Michael's now extinguished sword and wrapped Michael in his wings before forcibly shifting both of them out of this plane of existence and to who knows where.

With the immediate danger past, I painfully got to my feet and looked about for my comrades. They were each pulling themselves together in a similar fashion, with Gary helping Silje sit up off the ground. It had hit her hardest of all of us, as I thought it had.

But the cry I had heard came from the other side of the park.

"Oh no." Realisation hit me like a freight train. "There was someone...*aargh!*"

Suddenly, it felt like my wings, folded as they permanently are across my back, burst into flames. I screamed and collapsed. It was as if a white-hot metal bar had just been laid across my spine, but just as quickly as the pain had hit, it stopped. The others gathered around me, showering me with questions and concern, but I was having trouble regaining my breath and my silence just amplified their worry.

I finally managed to point towards where I had earlier heard the cry, causing Beatrice and Kateri to head that way looking for trouble, believing I was pointing at whatever had caused me to cry out. As the others helped me up once again, it almost felt like that hot bar was still there somehow, on my back, although none of my friends were reacting to seeing anything there, and the pain had not returned.

Kateri extended her black wings and was practically snarling as she stalked over towards the children's swings. Beatrice was backing her up, moving around to stop anyone there from escaping towards the road. As Beatrice moved into a shadow from a streetlight, there was a quick intake of breath, and we could hear her call out, "Kateri! Oh no, quick, come help!"

Chapter Twenty-Nine

I was trying, and failing, to brush off the helping hands of my friends as Beatrice called out. The tone in her voice wasn't scared; it was concerned, worried. By concentrating solely on breathing, I was finally able to gasp out, "Let go already! I'm fine, it's passed. Go help Beatrice!" Lennox, thankfully, refused to leave my side. She obviously realised that I was depending more on leaning on her in order to stand than I would care to admit, but the others rushed off to help Beatrice.

By this stage, Beatrice and Kateri were on their knees on the ground, bending over a prostrate figure lying between them. Beatrice looked up from the unconscious woman in front of her and into Kateri's frightened eyes. "She's dying! She must have been caught by Michael's blow. That raw power could strip her soul out–we can't let that happen Kateri, we've got to do something!"

Kateri swallowed her fear and grabbed Beatrice's hand. Ignoring the confused look Beatrice gave her in response, Kateri placed Beatrice's hand directly over the young woman's belly. "It's worse than that, Beatrice, they're *both* dying."

Beatrice gasped. "She's with child!" The tiny life was merely a few weeks old, but it was still perceivable to the wingless angel. Without thinking, she placed her other hand on top of the one Kateri was using to hold hers, and poured all of her miraculous power into the mother and child.

Kateri's eyes went wide, and she tried to pull her own hand back out of Beatrice's grip, but it was too late.

Beatrice's miracle flowed through Kateri's hand, burning the Fallen Angel as it did so. Kateri howled out in pain and her own miraculous power rushed to heal her hand, burning Beatrice in return.

The pair of Angels, Wingless and Fallen, screamed together as they continued to pour life into the human between them. Their cries melded together in the night until it sounded like the cry of a mother giving birth. Beatrice's power, meagre in comparison to a Fallen, gave out first, and the pair released their grips on each other and fell back onto the grass.

A car sped past the park, its horn blaring as we stumbled across the grass to help our friends. Drunken revellers hung out of the car's back windows, loudly proclaiming to the world "Happy New Year!" as the car hurtled around a corner and out of sight.

"That explains the fireworks," Admonae stated, as she got to Beatrice and knelt down by her sister.

Silje ran to Kateri's side, replying as she carefully lifted Kateri's head up onto her lap, "But...it's only just April, isn't it?"

Gary had gotten to the human who Kateri and Beatrice had been trying to save. "Hold on, begin the journey you've completed? You have got to be kidding." Gary summoned a small ball of light over the woman and looked closely at her before sitting back. "Yep, of course it's her. I mean, who else would it be?"

Admonae swatted Gary across the shoulder. "What are you talking about? Is she going to be okay?"

Gary nodded. "Oh, she'll be fine. Her and her daughter. Or should I say 'our' daughter?"

Admonae raised her hand in warning. "Do you want me to smack you again?"

Gary moved the floating globe of light closer to the now-sleeping woman's face. "Look at her, Admonae. You've seen this face before. It was just a decade or so older the last time you looked at it."

Looking down, comprehension dawned on Admonae's features. "She's Tracey Newman?"

"You know she is," Gary replied.

"Then the child..." Admonae looked from Tracey to Kateri and Beatrice, who had turned their heads to look at Tracey when Admonae had spoken her name.

"I'd say we've solved the mystery of how a new Wingless can be born," Gary replied. "*We* happened. That bub has three mothers. Tracey, Beatrice, and Kateri. Not all that romantic as far as conceptions go, but then again we were pushed back through time by a Tree of Creation to do this, so who am I to judge?"

Kateri sat bolt upright, her Fallen constitution recovering from the strain quickly. "I...I have a—?"

Beatrice, lying in Admonae's lap, finished Kateri's sentence, "A daughter. It seems we do."

We all fell silent with the revelation. Other than the obvious biological interplay that went into creating life, none of us really understood how or when humans gained their unique soul. That part of creation was never shared with the hosts of heaven, and the process was as miraculous to us, as our miracles were to humans.

And now, we had been involved, somehow, with the creation of this specific life. It was humbling.

It was terrifying.

Kateri stood, turning left and right, obviously not knowing what to do. "I've got to get back to her!"

"She's right here," Beatrice replied.

"Huh?" Kateri was struggling with the enormity of what had happened. "Not her, the other her. The older her. Dammit, you know what I mean!"

I had been watching all this from the edge of the group, while keeping an eye out for anyone else who might decide that a midnight walk through a riverside park was the perfect way to celebrate the new year. I was also having my own minor crisis. The burning and pain on my back had faded to nothing more than a hazy memory, but the puzzle pieces had been quietly slipping into place in my head.

Michael's sword had no flame in London when he was chasing Kateri or in China when he battled in the underground train station. I watched it go out with the blow against Azazel tonight, a blow that violated the laws of heaven and nearly killed Tracey and her child. The flame of heaven had done more than just go out; it had abandoned him.

And then I felt the fire at my back.

With a confidence I did not know I had, I reached back over my shoulder and gripped the hilt of my sword. It flowed into existence in my hand, and I drew it. My normal, plain sword shimmered into view before me for but a moment before it shifted, lengthened just a little, and then burst into holy flame.

Tracey drew in a huge breath as the light of heaven's flame shone on her face, her eyes flickering open and colour returning to her cheeks. I quickly sheathed the sword and Gary also doused his glowing light, plunging us back into shadow.

The evidence was inescapable. Michael's sword had abandoned him. And for some unknown reason, it had chosen me.

Poor planning was my first guess.

Tracey opened her eyes and lifted one hand to hold her forehead. "What? Who are you? Ohhh, my head."

Silje moved to comfort her. "I'm Susan. I think you fainted, my friends and I found you here. Do you live nearby, can we help you get home?"

When Silje turns on the charm she rarely needs any miraculous power to get people to relax around her, and tonight was no exception. After introductions and a gentle amount of persuasion, Tracey was up and walking us back through the darkened streets to her home.

What Tracey didn't realise, of course, was that while she was walking through what would normally be considered a rather rough area of London at night, she was surrounded by six Angels. Two of them had just discovered they shared a very personal connection to her unborn daughter, and another that she was now the chosen bearer of the Sword of Heaven itself. Right now, Tracey Newman was probably the safest person on the planet.

I hoped, however, that no one was going to be idiotic enough to try to mug us this night, as we were all so on edge with what had occurred that an overreaction on our part was definitely in the cards.

Luckily, the walk was peaceful and filled with pleasant conversation. Some gentle persuasion from Silje for Tracey to see her doctor about her 'fainting' tonight was accepted, and a few knowing smirks were shared that Tracey would soon be finding out about her pregnancy.

Once we got to her building, Tracey got onto the elevator, and we waved her goodbye. Following her up to her apartment would have seemed a little too familiar, and I felt that we had interfered in her life enough for one night. Or for one lifetime for that matter.

"Sooo..." Gary posed, drawing the single syllable out until he had our attention. "Just how do we get back? Are we supposed to hide away somewhere and just wait?"

Silje tipped her head to one side and up to the sky, listening, before shaking her head and looking back at us. "No, this part of the song is coming to an end. It feels like it will be over by sunrise."

"Then all we have to do is wait," Beatrice stated.

Gary put his best 'offended' look on his face, gasping theatrically. "All we have to do? No! Dawn is still a few hours away and we have some serious celebrating to do!"

Everyone started talking at once. Kateri, Admonae, and Lennox questioned the sensibility of interfering too much with the timeline and attracting attention. Silje enthusiastically supported Gary's idea and Beatrice stood there quietly, still wearing a slightly stunned and exhausted look on her face. That at least made sense–where Kateri could regenerate her power the moment she extended her wings, the miracle back in the park had completely drained Beatrice, and she would not get even her limited amount of power back until the sun rose on her.

This felt like a win, however, and we'd had precious few of those recently. When the discussion hit a lull, I spoke up. "Friends, I'm going to have to side with Gary on this one." I held up a hand to quell his over-enthusiastic cheer before continuing. "We'll find a nice, out of the way diner and have a quiet celebration. We can toast the New Year, for the second time for this particular year, and we can be with our new mothers as they get a chance to talk to each other and be a family."

Admonae nodded at that last part. "Family. That's who we are, you too Kateri."

Kateri almost looked like she was on the verge of tears, "That's a lovely thought Admonae, but we all know the truth. I've fallen. I'm no longer part of your family."

"Incorrect." Beatrice's abrupt, sharp interruption brought Kateri up short. "You fell to protect us. You are one of the mothers to our child." Beatrice's face softened and a small smirk grew on her lips, "And besides, at this point in history you haven't fallen yet."

The rest of the evening passed in gentle bonhomie. In the corner of an all-night café, crowded into a booth around steaming mugs of cocoa, we joked, hugged, and talked. Dawn was still about an hour away by the time conversation about the impending joys and responsibilities of motherhood was brought to a close by Gary casually commenting on the irony of a group of Angels cooing over the birth of a child who was already over a decade old.

As Gary was removing the last remains of the soggy, chocolate-soaked marshmallows that he had been pelted with from his hair, Admonae drew a deep breath, and with a pause, addressed the table.

"It has been a momentous night, an amazing and wonderful one, but we should at least acknowledge the other…little bombshell dropped this evening," she hesitatingly said.

"That wasn't just another illusion, then?" Lennox asked hopefully.

Admonae and Kateri answered in unison, "No". After a pause Admonae continued, "It was real. It seems that Azazel is the illusion, and a masterfully woven one at that."

I snorted. "He is known as the master of deception and manipulation after all. He's been playing us since the war."

Gary shook his head, comically sending a final blob of marshmallow onto the table. "Sorry, Joan, I don't buy it." He held up his hand to forestall my comeback and continued, "It's no secret there is no love lost between you and the fallen, present company excepted Kateri, but I honestly think he did it because he cares about us."

"Then why lie to us about who he is?" I spat back.

Lennox placed a hand gently on my shoulder. "Would you have accepted him if he hadn't? Joan, be realistic, you would have fought him before he had the chance to say hello."

Lennox accurately read my silence as agreement with her statement. She squeezed my shoulder before letting go and continuing. "Think about it. He was the first Angel ever created, the Lightbringer, tasked with igniting the suns. He was there at the genesis of each of us, watched us awaken and open our eyes for the first time. He has known us our entire lives, has been our 'big brother' throughout all of time. He may have rebelled against our father, but we are still his family."

We were all quiet for a time after that. I still didn't trust him, but for some reason I couldn't bring myself to voice that thought. It was Kateri who finally broke the silence.

"Well, he'd better behave himself from now on–he's an uncle now, after all."

The first rays of sunrise streamed through the window and with it the smell of the rarefied, cold air of the Himalayan mountains wafted through the café. In the time it took me to blink, we were back in Tibet.

Chapter Thirty

Judging from the angle of the sun, barely any time had passed in the present since we had placed our hands on the tree. I found myself reluctant to remove my hand from the trunk, hesitant to rejoin the world. I felt something press into my palm as I lifted it from the bark, looking down, I saw I was holding an acorn-like seed. From the reactions of the rest of my friends, each of us had one.

In my head, a voice resonated as I looked at the seed. "A gift. A link through time to who you were, will be, and are." A puzzled look passed between each of us, but we all still carefully placed the seeds into our pockets. If a Tree of Creation, especially one that has proven abilities to play with time, gives you a gift, you take it.

There was no sign of Raphael or the Tao-shih outside the courtyard when we cracked open the gate and snuck out. They obviously expected our 'communing' to take a lot longer than it apparently did. We were able to cross the compound back to our lodge and sneak back inside without encountering another soul. I'm not sure why we felt that was important, I think we just needed some time to ourselves before facing the troubles of the world once more.

Kateri and Beatrice shared a final hug before she stepped back and placed her hand on the doorframe. "Sorry Joan, I'm going to leave explaining all this to Raphael in your capable hands. I'm going to take a shortcut back to …" She stumbled over the word until a delighted but shy smile emerged "…To our daughter. I'll keep an eye on her while you do what you have to do." We watched as she practically skipped out of the lodge and across to the edge of the plateau, where the miracle-cancelling effect of the Tree would end. Balanced on the brink of the precipitous drop, she extended her arms and stepped off the edge.

We held our collective breaths as the seconds ticked by. Her fall would soon take her beyond the Tree's influence, but time seemed to stretch in that moment. A blink of the eye later, however, we could see her glorious black wings as she swooped upwards in the distance, showing us she was safe, before activating her power and miraculously transporting herself back to England.

Almost on cue, Raphael emerged from the lodge of the Tao-shih and started to cross the compound towards us. I moved back into our lodge as Raphael arrived, signalling to the Archangel to follow.

Once we were all seated on the cushions that surrounded the small brazier in the floor, Raphael spoke. "Joan, may I enquire if you found the answers you sought?"

His calm voice managed to sound menacing to me, as if hiding a test that I hadn't known we were taking. I shuddered involuntarily and searched his eyes for any hint of duplicitousness. I could find none, but it left me wondering just when I had become so untrusting.

For his part, Raphael sat unmoving, seemingly happy to wait for as long as was required for me to be prepared to answer his query. He'd obviously been taking lessons in inscrutability from the Tao-shih.

Beatrice broke the silence. "We learned a number of things." With a tilt to her head, she added, "Such is the way in journeys of self-discovery, is it not?"

Raphael nodded acquiescence. "It is, yes. Very well, I will pry no further. I will trust you to use your newfound wisdom appropriately. I should leave you to your meditations."

"Actually Raphael," Gary spoke up, putting on his best 'sorry-mate, bar's-closed' grin, "We're going to be heading home. Things to do, you understand."

"I am afraid I do not, no." Raphael replied. "And I would advise against too precipitous a departure. You should take the time to fully embrace and acknowledge the blessing you gained here. It is not something to be taken lightly."

I backed Gary up. "Sorry Raphael, it's just the way it is. Some things just won't wait."

Raphael shook his head and sighed like a disappointed father. "Always in such a hurry. You have spent too long among the humans, Trazael."

"And you've spent too long out of the world, Archangel!" I had seen red at the admonishment and use of my proper name, rising to his bait far too easily.

Sitting beside me, Silje placed her hand on my thigh and pressed down, encouraging me to stay seated. Lennox spoke up, hands up in a placating motion. "Raphael, Joan, everyone. This is not how we should part. Raphael, we all have obligations to the human world we cannot leave for long, and you have your path to tread here. Doesn't the Tao tell us that each of us shines a light on the path we walk? If someone else joins us while we walk and walks with us for a while then we have company, if not, we walk alone, but still we walk. It is time for our path to leave yours once more."

Raphael had the honesty to look admonished by Lennox's words. "You are correct, Lennox, and I am sorry Joan. I have allowed my curiosity to get the better of me. I will leave you to your preparations for travel."

After he had taken his leave, I let out the breath I had been holding. Silje leant over and hugged Lennox. "That was brilliant! I had no idea you knew so much about the Tao."

Lennox hugged her back and then grinned as she brought her phone out from the folds of her coat and waggled it cheekily in front of her. "I don't, I had SID run a quick website search and put something together."

"An Archangel schooled in spirituality by an AI. I love it," chuckled Gary.

Admonae shrugged and grinned. "You have to admit, that's very Tao."

Beatrice, as usual, was the one to name the Himalayan Elephant in the room. "How do we want to get back to England?"

I saw each of them turn to me for an answer. I had one for them, but it was going to cost me a decent amount of humble pie. "I'd like us to get our gear together as quickly as we can and head off the plateau the same way we arrived, so that is all Raphael sees."

A collection of nodding heads agreed with that proposition. "Then, as soon as we're out of the area of influence of the Tree, I call Azazel to take us home." Their nodding froze, and I saw Silje's eyes grow wide. Gary drew breath for a comment, but my fist slammed into his solar plexus before he could start. "Don't, Gary, just don't."

He doubled over, gasping as a squealing Silje jumped across the mat and into my arms. Lennox and Admonae stood and started to roll up our sleeping mats while Beatrice patted Gary on the shoulder, before helping him up.

"Come on, old soldier," Beatrice snickered, "that was barely a love tap. And besides, you were probably about to deserve it."

It didn't take us long to pack our gear back into our backpacks, and Admonae left to pass on our gratitude and farewell to the Tao-shih. By the time she returned with the old monk we were ready to go.

I stepped forward and bowed to the Tao-shih, allowing time for Admonae to slip back into the lodge to pull on her coat and pack. He returned the bow, smiling softly. "I wish you well in your journey. Your visit has done much for Raphael, although I do not believe he yet realises it. With our lives being so condensed compared to yours, dedicating them here has benefit. But Raphael has stagnated, and I believe you have blown on the embers of a long-quieted fire."

I bowed once again, "Goodbye, Master. You have given us much to think about in return."

With that same smile, he leanedt forward and held my hand. "Farewell, not goodbye." Releasing my hand once again, he turned and slowly made his way back across the compound.

I took a deep breath, tightened the straps on my pack, and turned to my friends. Glancing around to each of them, I took the time to pause and search their faces. What I saw lifted me. They were ready for whatever was to come.

We started walking. At the edge of the plateau, I took one last look back at the temple compound before turning and stepping onto the goat trail that led down the mountain. We passed the cave where Raphael had found us and soon after we were out from under the influence of the Tree.

While we were walking down the mountain path, I had been wondering exactly how I would react when the moment came to call Azazel. Would I hesitate? Change my mind? Would I grit my teeth in fury that I needed to rely on him or stand holier-than-thou over him, now I knew his secret?

As we left the Tree's influence, I felt my strength return and my body ceased to struggle with the rarefied air at this altitude. I stopped, enjoying the peace of the moment, before reaching out my hand for Lennox's phone. After all, her phone was the only one that would get reception a short way from a hidden Taoist temple in the middle of the Himalayan mountains.

Lennox activated her screen and placed the phone into my hand without comment. I looked down at the open Contacts list and snorted.

"Cute area code," I observed to no one in particular.

Lennox shrugged. "He put it there, after all."

I nodded. "Advertising much?"

As I went to push the call button, Admonae held her hand up for me to pause. "Joan, what do we tell him? Do we keep what we know a secret?"

"I'm a terrible liar," Silje added.

It was only at that point that I realised I had the answer to the questions I was asking myself since we left the temple. Part of me always felt like Azazel was keeping something from me. Like an annoying itch that never goes away, it had coloured every interaction I had with him, usually without me consciously thinking about it. In my eyes, something about him just never added up correctly. Now, however, everything just made sense. He was the first of us. Our eldest sibling. I felt that had to count for something.

"My friends," I motioned for them to all come close so they could hear the conversation once I called him. "You do and say what you need to. I am not going to ask you to go against your nature. For me, this information is not a weapon, it isn't something I plan to use against him. He's kept this persona running for millennia, and for most of that he even had Michael fooled. I have to believe there was a reason for that beyond just playing games with us. Unless keeping that secret puts us or someone else in danger, I see no reason to speak of it."

I pushed the button.

Chapter Thirty-One

The on-hold sound that leapt from the little phone's speaker was tinny and faint in the thin mountain air, but unmistakable all the same.

The opening lines from *I'm Too Sexy* by Right Said Fred rang out from the phone's speaker. (*click*) "Joan! You called! Everything ok?" Azazel's voice held a touch of concern.

"Really?" I was doing my best to keep the laughter out of my voice and failing. "That's your hold music?"

"Truth in advertising Joan, it never hurts. What can I do for you?" If Azazel was stung by my question, he wasn't about to show it.

I couldn't help but wince slightly as I asked for the favour. Some habits do die hard, and I'd had this particular one for a very long time. "We're standing on a mountain top in Tibet and need to get back to civilisation quickly. Think you could give us a lift?"

"Is this becoming a thing we do?" came the smarmy reply over the phone. "Are you sure it's not just that you miss my smiling face?"

"Yeah, that's it," I answered, while turning to my companions and dramatically rolling my eyes. "I've come all the way to the highest mountain range in the world just to see you again."

Azazel's voice appeared behind me at the same time it came out of the phone. "Oh dear, it is the thin air, she's delirious. Luckily here I am to save the day!"

My retort died in my mouth as a heavy downbeat of wings sucked what little air we had away and then a cacophony of city sounds, traffic, machines, and the hubbub of humanity crashed in on our eardrums. Between blinks we had been transported to an alleyway off a busy London street. It was quite jarring after the silent peace of the Himalayan mountains, and the less said about the smell the better. Somehow, though, I found it comforting.

I could see my friends likewise shifting their emotional gears back to coping with the modern world that now enveloped us. We had been with humanity for their entire journey from cave to metropolis, experiencing the slow crawl of their progress alongside them. I found it interesting, and, if I'm being honest, slightly disturbing that we had integrated so deeply with humanity that we could be affected in the same fashion as they would be by the enforced solitude of a place like a monastery in Tibet.

Azazel was nowhere in sight, and I had my doubts that he came all the way to London with us. Before I could question why he wasn't here milking the situation for everything he could, my gaze fell on Silje standing at the back of our little group. She had her head tilted ever so slightly to the left and a puzzled look on her face.

"Silje?" My question caused everyone else to turn and look at our youngest sibling.

"Something's wrong, Joan. Something's…off-key?" Silje replied, obviously anxious that she couldn't quite describe what it was she was hearing.

That by itself was unusual enough to worry me. I'm not sure why I asked my next question, the words were out of my mouth before I realised it. "Can you hear Michael?"

Silje's voice in reply barely rose above a whisper, and the whitening as the blood drained from her face preempted her simple reply. "No."

I sighed. "Oh bugger."

In the observatory, Toby's eyes quickly skipped from screen to screen across each of the three computers that sat facing him on his desk. Every monitor was flickering, showing random scenes from across the entire history of mankind. Every image was one of battle, bloodshed, war. What's more, Toby instinctively knew that every image was real and not the product of some re-enactment or digital manipulation, even though many of the images came from long before cameras had ever even been imagined.

Close to panic, Toby was punching commands into the three keyboards in front of him. Nothing was changing the scenes playing out on the screen, every command he entered was ignored by the very technology he and Lennox had helped inspire.

On the screens, the violence in the images was becoming more brutal, more visceral with every passing moment. With a horrified look, Toby pushed back from the desk and stood with a suddenness that caused his chair to roll back and tip over behind him. Without thinking beyond his need to stop whatever was happening, he stretched his arms out wide and called on his store of miraculous power for the day, sending his will out towards the computers.

Almost immediately the two-dimensional images stretched out through the air from the computer monitors towards Toby, distorting as they did so before sticking all over his body, tethering him like webs to the screens. Whereever the images got hold of him, Toby's body seemed to be pulled back along the pictures towards the screens. He was slowly but inexorably being pulled into the nightmarish scenes before him.

Toby let out a scream, possibly the first truly terrified scream of his existence, and tried desperately to pull away, to step back, but he was obviously fighting a losing battle against whatever power was pulling him in. In the room behind Toby, Michael stepped out from a shadow, his wings extended in all their full glory.

"My, my, Tobiel, just what kind of mess have you gotten yourself into now?" Michael's voice dripped with false concern, and his face shone with a predatory grin.

"Michael!" cried out Toby. "What's happening? Help me!"

"What is happening?" Michael asked. "Why, that is every war mankind has ever waged on themselves since one of them first picked up an animal's thigh bone in order to beat his neighbour senseless over a nicer cave. I was there for every single one of these battles, you know, and since you care so much for all of these…apes…I'm giving you a gift."

Still struggling, Toby was weakening and slipped a step closer to the desk. "Gift? Michael, what in God's name are you talking about?"

"I'm sending you to live in those moments. All of them. And since I know time is precious, I'm going to let you experience them all at the same time." Michael nudged Toby yet another step closer to the computer screens on the desk with a careless push of one of his wingtips. "I'm sure you'll find it quite a unique educational experience."

"You're insane!" Toby cried out.

"And you are weak. You struggle, but you are slipping. You Wingless cannot hope to stand against a miracle from a true Angel, and I," Michael paused to lean in close to Toby's face, spite dripping off every word he spoke, "...am the Lord's Archangel."

Toby slipped closer and closer to the trap that had been laid for him. Closer into having his consciousness spread over all the violent, horrendous moments of human history. For a gentle, creative angel like Toby, this would be his own personal hell. As Michael watched Toby's strength waning against his miracle, he chuckled viciously, and a single word was spat out as an insult.

"Wingless."

Toby let out a pained scream that slowly transformed into a primal roar of anguish. His eyes flashed red, and a single tear escaped and ran down his cheek. Toby's head dropped in defeat, and black wings unfolded from his back as he gave in and fell.

With the full miraculous power of a Fallen Angel rushing back to him, Toby broke the miracle trap that was drawing him in. Relief at his success washed across his face as Toby drew a cleansing, deep breath. He had barely closed his mouth, however, before that breath exploded from it once more, carrying droplets of blood out with the air. His face contorted in pain, and he looked down to see the point of

Michael's now blood-covered sword pushing out through his chest.

Michael gave the sword a vicious twist, bringing the newly fallen angel to his knees.

"Idiot," Michael chuckled. "You fall, you become my prey, those are the rules." Flames started to spring up from the fatal wound in Toby's body as Michael's laugh rang through the darkening room.

By the time I and the others got to the observatory, it was well ablaze and surrounded by the London Fire Brigade. Four engines and their crew were spraying the heritage building with water, but it was clear the already crumbling building was as good as gone.

For once, I wasn't the one that was being held back from rushing into danger. In fact, it was my hand gripping Lennox's shoulder that was stopping her from running straight into the burning building.

"Toby!" Lennox called out, her voice breaking with emotion and careless of the fact that no one would be able to hear her over the noise of the fire fighters.

"He's gone," Silje stated flatly.

Lennox spun on Silje, "He's not gone! He fell, we all felt that. Where is Azazel? He must have collected Toby, it's his job!"

Lennox was clutching at straws, and I think she knew it. Silje had been very sure when she told us Toby had gone while we were all still running to get here. She had nearly tripped when whatever she heard had hit her. It was just moments after we all felt him fall, and that delay, while small, was significant.

"Lennox," I called her name to pull her attention off Silje and on to me. "You know, deep down, Silje's right. We all do. He's gone."

"But where was Azazel?" Lennox broke down into sobs and I gathered her into my arms, letting her cry on my shoulder. "He's supposed to catch us, isn't he?"

"That," I agreed, "Is a very good question."

Chapter Thirty-Two

As the sun rose and dawn spread its warmth across the city, we were quietly sipping tea in Gary's Soho shop. It had seemed a sensible place to gather since our usual meeting place had been taken from us by the fire. I had been the last to arrive, having chosen to stay back and ensure there was no physical evidence of Toby left behind for Scotland Yard's Coroner to dissect. I hadn't expected any, as we had all felt Toby fall before the end. But something inside me needed to make sure.

Or maybe I just wasn't ready to say goodbye.

I don't know if I really expected Azazel to join me once the others had departed, but he either didn't come, or he kept his presence hidden from me. Knowing who he truly was now, I had no doubt he could keep himself hidden from me if he chose to, and I found myself hoping he was watching from somewhere. I found his absence irksome, even if I had done little to make him feel welcome over the past millennia.

Did I miss him, or was it just that he represented yet one more part of the foundation of our existence that had been stripped from us? He may be a Fallen, hell, we now knew that he is The Fallen, but dammit, he was our Fallen. And he should have been here for us.

Gary had my favourite tea ready for me when I did arrived, pouring a generous cup as the shopkeeper's bell attached to the front door tinkled disturbingly loud in the otherwise quiet and sombre shop.

Looking around the café, my friends were each processing the shock and grief in their own particular ways.

Gary had slipped into his caregiver mode, seeing to everyone else's needs so he didn't have to think too much about his own. Silje had withdrawn into herself, while Beatrice hovered over her like a guardian, well, Angel. Lennox was pacing back and forth along the back wall, muttering to herself as she went over every aspect of the day, looking for any little detail she might have missed that would have warned us about what was to come.

Admonae had taken it upon herself to bring the others up to speed as they arrived. She was currently huddled in a booth with Joel and an exhausted looking Damien, the three of them peering intently at Damien's laptop screen, deep in a Skype conversation with Adelita.

I, then, was the last of us to arrive. I glanced behind me as I closed the door on the slowly wakening city. A streetsweeper was slowly inching its way up the road, a pair of early morning joggers in brightly coloured Lycra stomped past the shop windows, and the streetlights welcomed the sun by blinking once and going out. The city and its teeming horde of human life loomed large on the other side of this fragile glass door, and it made our little group seem all the more inconsequential as a result.

We had lost so many, choosing to fall, since we had been banished to Earth. Some Fallen had been destroyed since the war, but none of ours. They may have chosen to fall, but they all kept their distaste of the war and fighting our brothers and sisters. This was the first time we had felt such a loss.

And then there were ten, I thought to myself.

Gary pressed the steaming mug of tea into my hands and leaned behind me to turn the lock on the door.

I blew gently on the hot liquid and took a sip. "Thank you, Gary. Perfect as always."

Gary's hand gripped my shoulder for a moment before he moved off without a word and started to rather ineffectually clean the coffee machine. It was clear my friends were standing on the brink of despair. Non-combatants in the war, they had just been exposed to the reality of it in a way they had never had to experience before.

They say that new experiences are harder to assimilate when you are older. Try it when you get to our age.

This was not my first encounter with war and death, however. I sometimes questioned why I refused to fight; I did hold the same doubts as my friends as to the whole validity of the war, but I always wondered if my own sense of contrariness played a bigger part in my decision than I realised at the time.

Michael always just had a way of pissing me off. And now he had taken one of ours. I had no proof it was him, of course, but I had learned to trust my gut on Michael a long time ago.

What my gut was telling me now was that our little group was on the verge of shattering. Part of me wanted to let that happen, allow my friends to go their separate ways and have some respite from the struggle. Stronger, though, was the realisation that there was no way I would be able to finish this without them.

The only question was, what could I possibly say at a time like this to bolster them enough for what was coming?

"White," spoke Beatrice.

I slowly blinked. That wasn't quite what I would have picked as an opening line to a stirring speech. I joined everyone else in the café in turning to look at Beatrice.

"They were white," Beatrice elaborated. She had one hand gripping Silje's shoulder as she stood behind her, and was staring somewhat chillingly off into the distance. From the look on Silje's face, Beatrice's grip was anything but gentle, and at her whimper Beatrice seemed to realise what she was doing, and she released her with an apology.

Admonae turned Damien's laptop around on the table to point its webcam at Beatrice, for Adelita's sake. "Beatrice," Adelita's voice came out of the little speaker in the computer, "I realise that British Imperialism led to a large number of ills in this world, but I highly doubt you can seriously lay the blame for this at their feet."

The ridiculous nature of the comment served to snap Beatrice back to the present. "Sorry, forgot you can't hear my thoughts."

Gary opened his mouth to make some snarky comment, but Lennox just reached out and placed her hand over it.

"When we were in the past," Beatrice continued, "When the illusion surrounding Azazel dropped. His wings..."

Collectively, we all finished Beatrice's sentence. "Were white."

"Surely," stated Gary, as he reached up to remove Lennox's hand from his mouth, "That had to be just another layer of illusion?"

Admonae visibly concentrated for a moment, replaying the scene in her memory, feeling it with her realm. "No. There was no further obfuscation. What we saw was real."

"How?" Lennox asked. "When you fall your wings turn black, everyone knows that. How can his not be?"

Adelita's voice emanated from the computer once again. "I'm still having trouble believing what you told me you saw, but think of it this way. Why do they turn black? There is nothing special about the colour, no mystical significance. It could easily simply be because our original wings are white, and so when we fall, we assume our wings will become the opposite. Our wings turn black merely because we expect them to."

Joel nodded in agreement. "Azazel, when we talked, always maintained that when Lightbringer felt he was doing what was right when he started his revolution. He didn't feel it was an evil purpose. I always thought he was just repeating the party line, but perhaps that's why his wings didn't change?"

"Considering what we know now," I added with a wry grin, "That would have been a rather self-serving conversation on Azazel's part."

"It makes sense," Beatrice replied. "Because the only other explanation that comes to mind is that he…"

"…never fell," Silje finished..

The room descended into silence at that point. As problematic as the conversation was, it had served to break my friends out of their grief for a moment. Even though I would have loved to explore the ramifications of this idea further, it was more important to make use of the mental and spiritual momentum the group had regained.

I looked over to Gary and could see that he had reached the same conclusion as I. He smiled and pointed to a container full of spoons on the café bar. I rolled my eyes and shook my head at him, but understood the metaphor he was reaching for.

"As fascinating as all this is," I broke into the silence, "we have a more pressing issue to concern ourselves with."

"Without mentioning any names that certain people might hear," interjected Admonae.

I nodded in agreement, "Exactly." I moved to stand in the middle of the café so I could easily see each of my friends, gauging how they were coping. "Silje, I know you will have been going over and over in your memory what you 'heard' when it was all happening. Can you tell us anything more now?"

Silje looked up from the tabletop she had been staring at and wiped the tears from her damp cheeks before answering. "I think so. I've heard so many of us fall, some from sadness, most from loneliness, a few in anger. I remember Kateri's fall of desperation, doing so to protect the child."

I nodded and smiled, not wanting to interrupt but approving of Silje choosing not to name our newest Wingless.

"But if I had to put a name to this," and Silje's face grimaced as she said the word, "*noise,* then I would have to say that Toby didn't entirely choose to fall, he was pushed."

"By which side?" asked Beatrice.

Silje shook her head. "I'm not sure. It didn't sound like anything I have heard before. But I'll know it if I ever hear it again, that I can guarantee."

Gary snorted. "I certainly know where my money would go in this bet. The big 'M'."

"I have to agree with Gary," I added.

"Twice in one day?" mocked Lennox.

"A sure sign of the end times," chuckled Damien.

Gary smiled ruefully, allowing our friends their joke. Laughing together was important right now, and Gary was happy to lead with his chin to make it happen.

I let the quiet laughter go on a couple of seconds more before speaking again. "The way it looks to me is that our unnamed party decided his previous attempts to deride, taunt, and threaten us into falling weren't working fast enough, and he has taken more direction action."

"But he's more rigid than any of us," said Admonae. "His ability to think outside his impregnable little box of rules is almost non-existent."

"That's true," replied Adelita, "We've all seen how the higher up an Angel is, the less freedom they seem to have. But remember, his entire being is focused on winning that damn war. What if he has come to the conclusion that the reason he can't win, why he can't start some glorious final battle, is because there are non-combatants on the field? Us."

"Logical," agreed Beatrice. "His rules do forbid him from removing us directly..."

Again, Silje completed Beatrice's thought, "But if he could force us to choose a side, then our non-combative status is removed. And there is only one side that is still accepting new members."

"But if all he needs is for us to fall," asked Lennox, choking back a sob, "Why kill Toby once he did?"

I wanted to say, 'out of spite,' but held my tongue. Out of all of us, Lennox was closest to Toby, and she didn't need to hear my malicious reading of the events, despite how accurate they may have been. "I imagine at that stage, with a Fallen in front of him, his, oh what's the word... his 'programming' just took over."

Lennox nodded, the term meaning more to her than to me. "His programming. That makes sense."

Gary put down the teacup he had been drying, the gentle clatter of the fine china against its saucer drawing our attention to him. Looking up, he asked, "The real question now is, what is he going to do next?"

Chapter Thirty-Three

The jingling of keys in the front door lock heralded the arrival of two of Gary's employees, calling a halt to our conversation. As the barista's entered, they were obviously surprised by their boss already serving a group of people inside the locked and darkened café, but after an assuring nod from Gary, they took it in their stride and went about their usual morning start-up duties.

Damien was the first to take his leave after his pager went off, delivering information about yet another emergency back at the hospital. Beatrice expressed her wish to check in on Hattie, and Silje volunteered to go with her, filching a chocolate chip cookie from the counter as they left. Gary just shook his head and reached into his pocket for the coins to pay the register for the cookie.

Lennox wanted to swing by the old observatory to say a prayer and asked Admonae to accompany her. It made sense she wanted to visit the site one more time, but I was equally glad she chose not to go alone, and she wanted someone else other than me to accompany her.

Joel said he wanted to do some more catching up with Adelita and turned the laptop back towards himself before grabbing a breakfast menu, settling in for a longer stay.

"You going to put some hours in, boss?" one of Gary's employees asked, as she turned on the main lights and flipped the 'Closed' sign over on the front window. "It's just that we're getting behind in the books and Sue and I would like to get paid this week."

Gary shrugged as he turned to me. "Looks like the mundane world calls, Joan. I'll keep an eye on Joel. You good?"

I nodded, "I'm good. You see to your people." As I headed to the door, I called out to the two workers behind the counter, "Oh, and if he doesn't pay you on time, let me know and I'll take it out of his hide!"

Their good-natured laughter buoyed me out through the door and onto the pavement. Smiling to myself, I walked a good half a block down the street before it suddenly occurred to me that I had absolutely no idea where I was going.

That realisation stopped me mid-stride, almost causing the person walking behind me to crash into me. Why they walk down busy streets with their noses buried in their mobile phones I have yet to understand. I had long ago stopped berating mankind for these little idiosyncrasies though, as usually after a decade or so I would understand exactly why they did what they did. Human social evolution is just so fast that celestials like me were, more often than not, just left on the sidelines wondering what had just happened. I moved out of the steadily growing stream of morning pedestrians into a small service alleyway between buildings and watched the world move past me.

The early morning joggers were slowly disappearing from the streets, being replaced by delivery vans, businesspeople in suits, children off to school. Everyone moved past me with a purpose. Each of my friends had someone to be with or someone who needed them. All of them would have welcomed me if I had asked to accompany them, but right now none of them needed me.

Yet again, I felt how leadership can create a distance between friends. I had certainly not asked to lead the Wingless, but they said they saw me as doing so. That, however, made me somehow different, placed me a step apart from the rest.

I wondered if this was a small taste of what the Archangels felt when they looked at the rest of the host.

"Or, more likely, I'm just being a self-indulgent, melancholy little idiot..." I muttered to myself.

"I very much doubt that, Joan." The voice in the alley behind me was slow and heavy with emotion. "And I am so very sorry."

I turned to face Azazel. His eyes were downcast, and his usual cocky smile was nowhere to be seen. His shoulders were slumped in defeat, and his wings were completely tucked away. There was a small flinch from him as I stepped forward, but then a startled "Oh!" as I wrapped my arms around him and buried my face in his chest.

Tentatively, he returned the hug, and we stood there silently, the tears I couldn't shed earlier staining his shirt. I only looked up when I felt a droplet fall on my forehead, seeing the trail the tear left down his face. Without letting go of the hug, I blinked away my own tears before indicating his with a nod. "Archangels don't cry, Azazel."

He stiffened slightly at my words. He was the oldest of us all, and nowhere near the fool he played for us. He knew what I meant by my words, but he also recognised that I still used the name he chose to hide behind.

"Very true, Joan," he said slowly, measuring out his words carefully. "But I am no Archangel."

I looked deep into his eyes and unexpectedly saw the truth in his words. "Good enough." Then I added in a low mutter, as I placed my head back onto his chest, "For now at least."

I lingered there a moment longer, although I honestly couldn't tell you whether it was more for my benefit or for his. Slowly disentangling myself from the hug, I took a small step back and a deep breath, centring myself once more as I raised my hand to forestall him. "Please don't go, not yet. Just tell me what happened."

Azazel likewise composed himself and started his characteristic little pacing back and forth across the alleyway as he spoke. "There was some sort of trap set up. Almost as if the room they were in was shifted out of time, slightly." He paused and shook his head for a moment before continuing. "It caught me by surprise. I would have never expected Michael to be able to think of something like that. It won't work again mind you, I know what to look for now, but it delayed me long enough to prove fatal for poor Toby."

"How's Kateri?" I asked.

"Furious," sighed Azazel, running one hand through his hair apprehensively. "I've got some people keeping an eye on her, so she doesn't go and do something stupid, but she wants to throw down with him."

I placed a hand on his upper arm, stopping his pacing. "Thank you. I know you'll look after her."

"You know," Azazel formed a small half smile as he replied, "I could protect you all if you would just..."

"There you go, pushing your luck again." I resisted the urge to waggle my finger at him.

For his part, Azazel just shrugged. "Had to try. The boss would get annoyed if he found out I passed up this opportunity."

I couldn't help but roll my eyes at him, "Of course he would. Let the record show you tried, I threatened to punch you, and we moved on. We wouldn't want to upset your 'boss' after all."

He smiled at that, his head slightly cocked as if about to ask something, his eyes intense. But the moment passed, and he decided to drop whatever question he was going to pursue. Instead, he reached out and gently placed his hand on my arm. "Seriously Joan, this is different. This has become truly dangerous. I don't know what he will do next, and I can't keep you safe while you're Wingless."

I placed my hand on his, squeezing gently so he knew my gratitude for his motives, but then removed his hand from me. "I know, Azazel. Trust me, I know exactly where you are coming from. But this is something I have to see through."

He nodded and took a step back. "Why Joan?" He wasn't pushing the point any more, this time his question came from simple, honest, confusion.

"Because he made this personal. Because I have to stand with my friends. And because I choose to." I chuckled a little to myself as I flippantly threw a question back at him, "After all, why do you do what you do?"

His reply came slowly, almost as if he was hearing the words himself for the first time, "Because I have to? Why does that seem strange to me now?"

"Careful, Azazel," I said as I turned and headed back out to the main road, "I'm beginning to think that hanging around us Wingless can be contagious. You don't want to catch our...peculiarities."

As I hit the end of the alleyway, I heard the downbeat of his wings and felt the miracle vanish, leaving me with a rather self-satisfied grin on my face as I weaved my way back into the moving stream of humanity. My encounter with Azazel had unexpectedly lifted my spirits and, on top of that, now I knew where I needed to go.

This had all started with Kateri. We knew now that her seemingly erratic behaviour was due to her attempts to avoid Michael, but we hadn't satisfactorily explained why he had chosen her for his target. At least not to my satisfaction, at any rate. With Toby's death fracturing us the way it did, I couldn't just accept that she was a random victim. Michael and 'random' simply did not go together.

Toby was not a fighter, not in any sense of the word. He wasn't a great tactician, a brilliant planner or, in reality, any sort of threat to Michael at all. What he was, however, was the central hub of our little family. From the very beginning he kept us all in contact with one another, regardless of how far apart we were or what technology, or lack of it, any particular century handed him. Whenever any one of us couldn't contact another directly, he was always there to pass the message on for us. And he could do it without anyone being able to intercept our communiques.

He was at the centre of our little group. In a sense, he was our heart.

By removing Toby, Michael had separated us from each other, something I was only now just beginning to understand the danger of. Grief has a way of clouding the mind, but the release I had shared with Azazel had allowed me to process some of that. Not all, but enough. Toby had been a lynchpin in allowing us to work as a cohesive group.

And that pin had been removed.

Similarly, there had to be something Kateri knew, something she possessed, or something about her in particular he was after. It was obvious Michael was pushing her to Fall, but there had to be more to it than that. If that was all it was, any one of us would have sufficed, and he would have found an easier target to manipulate among the remaining Wingless than Kateri represented.

With Azazel's people doing their best to stop Kateri going after Michael in a fit of rage, there was only one other place she would go. Hattie.

Earl's Court Station was the closest, so I started off down the street in its direction at a brisk walk. Beatrice and Silje had a good head start on me, but I wasn't looking to catch up with them. I figured that this way they would have some time with the girl before I arrived, and their presence might also act as an additional lure for Kateri in case I was wrong about where she might be planning on going.

As I stepped onto the train carriage and found a seat, I debated whether to phone ahead to Beatrice to let her know I was coming. It would be better not to surprise her, but without Toby our communications would no longer be secure from any celestial eavesdropping. I tried to tell myself that I was probably just being paranoid, but instead of calling I found myself tapping out a quick text message to everyone; 'Careful - Comms no longer secure. Joan.' before putting my phone away again.

Once a soldier...

Chapter Thirty-Four

ousing estates in the middle of the workday are quiet, almost eerie places. The children are in school or community day care, the adults either off working or, more likely, looking for work, and the elderly are camped by their televisions watching the impossibly convoluted lives of their favourite daytime soap opera.

There isn't a complete absence of humanity, of course. Every now and then the silence will be pierced by the demanding cry of a baby, or someone hanging clothes out to dry on the airers that dotted balconies across each side of every building. But the hole left by the missing lifeforce that would normally fill the buildings was a noticeable feature in the atmosphere of the place.

Well, to an Angel at any rate.

I was reassured when I could feel whatever protection Hattie manifested in the estate still active. Where once it tried to dissuade me from entering, however, now I felt a warm welcoming sensation. And damn it felt good to be recognised.

Climbing the steps to the Newman's apartment, I found that I was unconsciously flexing and gripping my hand, shaking my arms and stretching the muscles across my shoulders and neck. I stopped when I realised what I was doing–these were the initial stretches I would make before drawing my sword for battle. Looking, I could see that there was no one back the way I came, and nothing else seemed out of place. If something was setting me off, it wasn't here. At least not yet, anyway.

As I resumed climbing the last flight of stairs before the Newman's floor, Silje came flying around the corner at the top of the stairwell, turning to rush down the stairs and practically bowling me over.

"Joan!" she screamed in my ear as I grabbed us both and twisted until my back slammed into the wall. It knocked the wind out of me momentarily, but it was better than tumbling back down the stairs together. "You're here! I had to go find you, they sent me to find you, but you're here!"

I gripped both of Silje's upper arms and held tightly to move her mouth back away from my ear. A little too tightly, if the grimace she gave me was any indication. "Yes, Silje, I'm here. Now, slow down and tell me what is going on."

As she replied, Silje grabbed my hand and started pulling me back up the stairs to the apartment. In fact, she nearly pulled me off my feet with her urgency. It was a timely reminder that within the small, seemingly frail body and sometimes flighty mind of my friend, there was still the will of an Angel.

"It's Hattie," Silje was saying as she led me quickly along the balcony, "She said you needed to be here, before Kateri arrived."

I stiffened and brought Silje up short, almost giving her whiplash with the sudden stop. "Before Kateri arrives? Is Hattie in danger? Is Kateri going to try to hurt her?" My voice shook with anger at the idea of such a betrayal, even as I was finding it difficult to believe myself.

Silje shook her head violently in response, "No Joan, but there is something wrong. Very wrong. I think she's scared."

"Kateri?" I asked.

Silje shook her head once more, slower this time. "No. Hattie."

The Angel, albeit a very new one, of Fear, was scared. "Fuck," was all I could mutter.

We resumed running, and half a minute later we practically burst through the door to the Newman's apartment. The soldier in me took over as I took stock of the situation. Both of Hattie's parents were obviously absent, probably at work. All of Hattie's protective drawings were in place, and a few new ones had been added, brimming with new power.

Hattie and Beatrice sat cross-legged facing one another in the middle of the loungeroom floor, the coffee table having been moved out of the way, and they seemed to be meditating. Beatrice opened her eyes and looked surprised at our entrance, probably not having expected Silje to return with me so soon, and Hattie's face was scrunched in what looked like pained concentration.

I could feel the building of a miracle from the little girl, our newest Wingless, and even I could sense the discord within it. A quick glance at the look on Silje's face confirmed my suspicions. Hattie was about to empower the very first miracle she had ever created that was outside her realm.

And it was a big one. This was not going to be easy on her.

Silje started to back up towards the door as her sensitivity to the discord Hattie was creating started to overwhelm her senses. Beatrice silently motioned me to sit with them, forming a triangle on the floor, and she reached out for my and Hattie's hand.

As I sat, Hattie too reached out and grasped my other hand, completing the circle. Her voice, when she spoke, was strained but oddly calm. "Beatrice-mother, I call on your essence to connect to Kateri-mother and pull her to us. Joan, I call upon your strength and essence to protect us from what follows."

Beatrice and I were part of the miracle now, lending our power. This wasn't how our miracles usually worked, they tended to be very personal and individually crafted aspects of our celestial will, but then Hattie was no ordinary Wingless. To be honest, I still wasn't sure what she actually was, and I certainly didn't understand how she was doing whatever it was she was about to do.

My speculating was cut short as I felt the miracle build to a crescendo. There was a pulling sensation somewhere in the back of my mind, and suddenly I was looking down a long, dark corridor with a strong wind rushing past me. It reminded me somewhat of the pressure wave you feel in a subway station just before the train arrives.

Then, without warning, the pressure sped past me, and I was thrust into the centre of the corridor in its wake. Instinctively I pulled up my own power, the mental equivalent of drawing my sword, and a wall of holy flame appeared before me. I felt, rather than saw, a pursuing presence bounce off that wall and disappear to who knows where, and then the miracle ended, and I was back in the room once again.

Only now, in the middle of the three of us, lying on her side in the fetal position and barely conscious, was Kateri. She was a mess of cuts, burns, and bruises, but what took my breath away was the sight of the back of her shirt completely soaked in blood, with two rents in the shirt revealing deep gashes down her back where her wings should have been.

It was, perhaps, the most horrendous sight any of us could conceive of, but none of us were the type to scream or panic, not even to this. Instead, Silje's choked gasp, and the pure bitterness in Beatrice's voice as she spat the name "Michael," spoke for all of us. It was obviously his handywork, his 'calling card' if you will. More concerning to me at that moment was that I knew exactly why this was Michael's preferred method of dealing with the Fallen. It was effective, immensely painful, overly cruel, and inevitably fatal.

Hattie just looked down in horror at the damage wrought on one of her mothers. Beatrice looked up at me, her eyes silently asking what could be done for Kateri, those eyes misting over with tears as I slowly shook my head in response.

Kateri's eyes snapped open, and her hand shot out to grasp my arm. "Joan!" she gasped out, her voice reflecting the agony her body was in, "I'm sorry…tried to stop him… didn't realise what he…was after…"

Beatrice placed her shaking hand on Kateri's shoulder, softly saying, "Save your strength, love, it will be alright."

Kateri shook her head, causing her to groan out in pain once again. "No, must talk. No time, must tell…"

"NO."

That single negative carried such weight that it immediately captured all our attention, even that of the fatally wounded Kateri. The word possessed a power of authority I had not heard in a very long time.

And it had come from Silje.

"No more," Silje added. "No more of my friends are going away."

If it wasn't for the unyielding tone in her voice, I might have been forgiven for thinking that our gentlest sister had simply broken in the face of the events of the past twenty-four hours. But I had heard that tone before, spoken by someone pushed to the edge and not only willing to do anything in order to strike back, but who had a plan she was not going to be swayed from.

That time, the voice had come from my own lips.

This time, I simply looked up into Silje's face as she stood above us, and said, "Tell us what you need us to do."

Silje nodded without really looking at me. Her eyes stayed glued to Kateri, and her brow furrowed in concentration. "Her song is broken, it's fading. But her daughter holds a portion of her song."

I turned to look at Hattie. This circumstance was unique, but I couldn't see how it was going to help. Kateri's wounds were physical as well as spiritual.

"There is not much left," Silje continued, as she reached out and pressed a hand to Kateri's back and the other over Hattie's heart. "But there should be just enough to…"

Still bound together by the original miracle that had brought Kateri to us, Beatrice, Hattie, and I all convulsed in unison as we felt the last of our miraculous power pulled from us, through Silje and into Kateri. Quickly drained, we all fell back, breaking the link.

As soon as my head cleared, I shot back upright. Kateri's wounds on her back had healed, leaving two angry, ugly scars visible through the torn shirt. As I reached out to touch her, Beatrice was shaking her head and starting to sit back up, but Hattie and Silje were lying unconscious on their backs. Kateri was warm to the touch, but her chest was still.

Beatrice looked up at me hopefully. "I don't think she's breathing," I said as I moved to roll her over onto her back. As I shifted onto my knees to start to move her, however, the world spun on me, and dizziness forced me unceremoniously onto my backside.

"My turn," Beatrice stated flatly, moving to take over from what I was trying to do. By the time my vision cleared once more, Beatrice had Kateri rolled over and was well into administering CPR. I watched as I concentrated on pulling myself together. Before too long, I knew Beatrice would feel the effects of the miracle as I had, and she would need someone ready to take over. In fact, I could see she was already beginning to flag.

Just as I was starting to move back into a kneeling position, however, Kateri gasped in a huge lungful of air and started to choke, a mix of blood and saliva issuing from her mouth as she did so. Beatrice stopped the compressions on her chest and moved Kateri into the recovery position. Silje and Hattie were also beginning to stir, and I felt my shoulders slump as the tension began to run out of them.

We weren't completely out of the woods yet, so I couldn't help but fall back on my nature, which meant taking stock of what we had. We were all alive, but Beatrice, Silje, and I were completely drained of celestial power and would remain so until dawn tomorrow. Hattie still had some reserve, I think, but she never seemed normal to my senses so I could not be sure exactly what it was I could feel emanating from her.

And Kateri, I stopped. Reaching out to touch her, I checked again, refusing to believe my own senses. But there it was, unmistakable. No longer Fallen, but not Wingless either.

Kateri was human.

Chapter Thirty-Five

"S he's alive," Beatrice gasped out as she slumped onto the floor, her own exhaustion at being temporarily drained of celestial power catching up with her as it did with me.

"You're more correct than you realise, Beatrice," I replied softly.

A puzzled look came over her face at my phrasing. "Joan?"

"She's alive," I stated.

The look of confusion on Beatrice's face gave way to one of incredulousness, and then concern. "This is not some kind of weird joke, is it Joan?"

I shrugged. My strength was starting to return but I had no desire to move more than I strictly had to. "Check for yourself."

Beatrice wearily stretched out a hand and touched Kateri on the shoulder, extending her awareness to feel the life force of our sister. She jerked her hand back as if it were burned, and then spun her head around to look at the peacefully slumbering Hattie. "That's not possible," she uttered in disbelief.

I shrugged again, my voice taking on a slightly distraught tone, despite my attempts at self-control. "Lots of impossible things seem to be happening now, Beatrice. The fact that I dream, the very existence of your daughter, a friggin Archangel trying to kill us, and the so-called 'Lord of Darkness and Lies' doing his very best to protect us. Why should this be any different?"

I stopped talking to take a deep, measured breath. When I started talking again, I was pleased to hear I had regained control over my voice. "Beatrice, when you can move, see if you can wake Hattie and Silje. I'll see to Kateri."

Beatrice nodded and slowly started to shuffle across the floor to where Hattie lay. I moved around so I could see Kateri's face and lay down next to her. Her eyes were open, and she was breathing normally, but her brow was furrowed in pain and covered in perspiration.

"Joan," Kateri spluttered out my name when her eyes focused on me. "I hurt. Everywhere."

"That's understandable, sister. Do you know, I mean, can you feel what has happened to you?" I really hoped her answer would be in the affirmative, I wasn't sure just how I was going to tell her if it wasn't.

The pause before she answered seemed to go on forever, but finally she nodded and looked me straight in the eyes as she said, "Yes. But I don't understand how."

Looking into her eyes was a very strange experience. She was still Kateri, my sister, and at the same time less than what she used to be, and yet so much more. The celestial will that once powered her existence was gone, and in its place...

A soul?

Or at least, a piece of one. I cast a glance over to where Hattie was pulling herself up into a sitting position with the help of Beatrice. Could Hattie have given a part of herself just like Beatrice and Kateri had done for her the night they saved her in the womb? As impossible as that sounded, it made more sense than three Wingless and whatever Hattie was creating a soul from nothing.

That kind of thing was seriously way above our pay grade. And not something we had time to worry about now.

"Kateri," I gently asked my friend, "What did you need to tell us? You may not have much time before your body decides it needs to sleep to recuperate."

Kateri nodded, a lump rising in her throat as she remembered, "It was Michael. He's insane. He kept going on about how he needed to end the war, to finish his work so he could return home triumphant. How it was all our fault, the Wingless, that the gates remained closed."

I shook my head and pulled Kateri up so she could lie in my arms. Her breathing had stabilised, but I could feel her heart beating hard and fast. "I don't know why the Gates are closed," I replied, "I thought it was Michael's doing actually, but either way, you were no longer Wingless, Kateri, no longer a non-combatant. Why take it out on you, especially since he had just killed Toby?"

Kateri uttered a short sob at the mention of Toby, and her fists clenched hard enough for her knuckles to whiten. "There's more, Joan. The reason why he targeted Toby and I. Michael has decided that humans are also to blame."

"What?" I asked incredulously.

Kateri nodded, "He moaned about how he couldn't initially understand how we could not choose a side, and how not knowing vexed him. He decided to watch us over the intervening centuries and was quite proud of himself for finally working it out. It was the humans, he said. We Wingless were the ones who worked most closely with them before the rebellion, so obviously they had 'infected' us with their flaws, their weaknesses. When he saw us behave more and more like them since the war, it became obvious to him. We had been polluted by them."

I couldn't believe what I was hearing. Kateri was right about one thing, at least— Michael was insane. Whether he was driven that way by being cut off from Heaven, by having the very gates he defended closed against him, I did not know. But that still didn't explain exactly how the humans had defiled us in his eyes. "It doesn't make any sense, Kateri. Just what kind of infection does he think the humans could give us, anyway?"

"Free will," stated Kateri softly.

I took a deep breath to avoid exploding with the need to punch something, or to be honest, a certain someone. "Okay, so assuming that in his broken mind, our Father's greatest gift is now something that can be passed on like the common cold, why attack you and Toby?"

Kateri reached a hand up to grip my arm. Her hand was shaking, and I didn't think it was from anger. "Because he's decided that the only way to force us to choose, to remove the pernicious effect the humans have on us, to force us to finally fall and allow him his glorious battle is…to wipe them all out."

Beatrice, Silje, and I all gasped in unison.

"The humans?" Beatrice exclaimed.

Kateri's head drooped. "Yes. And by stealing knowledge from Toby's and my realms, he now knows how to do it without, in his mind at least, violating his oath."

I couldn't believe what I was hearing. This was insane, even for Michael. In order to push for the final battle of his ridiculous war, he was planning the extinction of the very creation we were put here to guide and protect?

Searching for something to make sense of his plan, I looked back at Kateri and asked, "How? How did he think he could possibly succeed?"

Kateri closed her eyes for a moment, tears appearing and starting a slow run down her cheeks. "I'm sorry, Joan, I don't know exactly how he plans to do it; that was the knowledge he stole from me. It was the prize he sought when he chased me across the African continent. But I do know that, somehow, he intends to kill the Tree of Life."

The Tree of Life, yet another of the seven Trees of Creation. I'd managed to go my entire, rather long existence without ever needing to think of them, and now in the space of a short time I had personally met two, and now it looked like I was going to have to seek out, and protect, a third. The seed gifted to me by the last one we met felt excessively heavy in my pocket, and I hoped that was just my conscience metaphysically poking me.

Although, personally, I doubted I was that lucky.

Beatrice looked up at me in horror. "But what would that even do? Are the Trees even contributing anymore? Isn't their job done?"

I shrugged in reply, "Honestly, I don't know. The important thing is that he thinks it will work." We both looked to Silje for her insight.

She was looking off in the distance, her eyes focused on something far away from the little apartment we were in. "I don't think that the humans would just die, but the symphony would be greatly damaged. The best word I can think of to describe it would be that life would become 'unstable'. All the things life fights against like physical cell mutations, cancer, viral infections, and even mental illnesses like depression; instead of fighting, life would instead just give up. In a generation or two, the human world would be on the brink of extinction. That is, if the world governments hadn't already gone to war over it and destroyed it all sooner."

"That sounds bleak," Beatrice commented.

"Armageddon usually is," I said. "But I imagine he will issue his demand that we Fall after he has killed the Tree, promising to fix everything once the war is over. He probably believes that once he's won, and the Gates are open, he'll have the power to do it too."

Beatrice sighed. "Which means we'll never be able to convince him not to go through with it. We will have to fight him."

I reached out and patted the hand Beatrice was resting on Kateri's arm. "He is a *true believer*. He won't listen to reason."

Kateri hadn't said anything in a while. Looking down at her, I could see her eyelids drooping and her breathing slow. She was slowly falling into normal sleep. Beatrice started to shake her gently. "Kateri? Sister, please, we will let you sleep in a minute. You need to tell us where the Tree of Life is. Can you do that?"

Kateri's eyelids closed fully despite Beatrice's entreating, and I held out my hand to forestall any further attempts. "Let her sleep, Beatrice, I know where it is."

Beatrice looked up at me questioningly. "You do? How?"

"Thanks to you, actually," I replied. As she started to frown in response, I went on, "By asking Kateri just now, the image the Tree of Knowledge gave me of the second of the two of her 'sisters' we would visit coalesced for me. It seems the information was placed within me but needed a question to be asked in order to access it. Bloody typical for the Tree of Knowledge, now I think about it. Not that I know anything other than the name of the place, but I can tell you that the Tree of Life is by Lake Karachai, near Mayak in Russia."

I leant over and kissed Kateri's forehead. It felt oddly warm and fragile. "Rest now, Beatrice and Hattie will put you to bed." Beatrice nodded in agreement and she and Hattie started to help Kateri stand in order to lead her to Hattie's bedroom. Automatically, I reached for my phone to call Toby to get him to pull together what information he could about Mayak.

Silje must have noticed my hand start to shake, because she stepped over to me and placed hers around mine, taking the phone from me in the process. "We're on our own now, Joan."

"I was going to call Toby," I whispered, knowing Silje would easily hear me.

Silje simply squeezed my hand tighter and replied, "I know."

I felt my shoulders slump and forced myself to take a deep, measured breath. "Russia. Without Toby, how do we get to Russia without using our powers and painting a target on our backs?"

"You're safe while you are here," Hattie remarked as she came back into the room. The level of certainty in her tone still struck me as uncanny, the words coming as if they were from the body, at least, of a little girl. "While Beatrice is putting Kateri to bed, I will search for the place you mentioned on my laptop. Let me see what I can find."

Silje and I shared a quick glance with each other and then followed Hattie back into her bedroom. I slipped the phone back into my pocket as I did so. Hattie's bedroom looked just as it had the last time we were here, with the addition of a quite tall unconscious woman lying on a bed that was about a foot too short for her.

After a small amount of typing, the small screen of Hattie's cheap notebook computer was displaying the Wikipedia page on Lake Karachai. She highlighted a sentence about halfway down the screen and read from it.

"According to a report by the Washington, D.C.-based Worldwatch Institute on nuclear waste, Karachai is the most polluted open-air place on Earth from a rad-i-o-logical point of view," Hattie read out loud for us.

Silje and I leant in closer to the screen and read the rest for ourselves. Apparently, the lake and most of the surrounding town had been a dumping ground for radioactive and chemical waste from the nearby nuclear plant in Mayak, which had been the first to be tasked with producing weapons grade plutonium for the Soviet atomic bomb project after World War Two. According to the radiation numbers in the article, just standing at the lakeside would deliver a lethal dose of radiation within an hour. That is, if the other toxic chemicals in the surrounding area hadn't killed you first.

Silje and I straightened up from reading the screen. "The Tree of Life is in that?" she asked.

Kateri's soft, groggy voice answered from the bed, "Yes."

"Fuck," I said for the second time that day.

Beatrice still held Kateri's hand as she sat by the bedside. "I think that's the secret," she said. "Michael isn't going to kill the Tree, not in his mind. He's going to lower the Tree's defences somehow, and let mankind's pollution do it."

"Will that really work?" asked Silje.

Beatrice nodded. "I think so. The fact that this place is so physically deadly is only part of it. Add in the spiritual resonance around the reason why the polluting substances were created in the first place, and the arrant disregard for the planet displayed in how they dumped it, and you have a deadly combination."

Tears started to flow from Kateri's eyes and Beatrice leant over to hug her. What Beatrice said made sense. It usually did, but it also gave me an idea.

"Then that is how we get there to stop him," I stated firmly. "Adelita. We'll get her to use her U.N. connections to get us into the country and enough paperwork to get close to Mayak. After that, it is up to us."

Kateri opened her eyes once more. "Joan, you'll lose your powers as soon as you get near."

I nodded, "And so will Michael. At least I hope he will. Either way, we have to try."

Silje gave Hattie a hug and then stepped up beside me. Beatrice also stood, relinquishing Kateri's hand. "Besides," Silje said, "The other Tree must have given us those seeds for some reason. Maybe this is it?"

I looked to Silje for a second, and then back to Kateri. "Good point. Kateri, where is your seed?"

Kateri's eyes opened wide for a moment. "Oh! Of course! You can take mine too, I won't be able to come with you and I certainly can't use it now. I keep it on me all the time, just like the Tree told me to. It's just in my pocket."

As she was speaking, Kateri dipped her hand into her pocket, but when she brought her hand out and opened it, on her palm was just a small pile of brown dust.

"Huh? I don't understand," Kateri uttered.

Silje tentatively reached out and touched one finger to the dust in Kateri's palm. "Nothing," she said. "No power there at all." Looking up at me, she asked, "Joan, do you think that's why our miracle worked, why Kateri is human now?"

I held my hands up in surrender for a moment before answering, "I don't know, Silje, and I am not about to ask. If there is one thing I have learned over the years, it is to never look too closely at just how or why a miracle works. And that goes double if it is one you've woven yourself."

Chapter Thirty-Six

The International Departure terminal of Heathrow International Airport had already appeared in the front windscreen of our taxi as I finally hung up the phone with Adelita. Without Toby to facilitate our conversation, and with Silje, Beatrice, and I all drained of miraculous power until dawn, it had been a laboriously long phone call. At one point, Beatrice had to reassure our increasingly worried taxi driver that we weren't all high on some illicit drug, using the age-old fallback of convincing him we were practicing lines in a play instead.

"Not sure you should be referring to the All-mighty and Angels in a play, it's disrespectful," muttered the driver. "But you young folk will do whatever you want I suspect, pay no attention to me. Not that you will anyway."

It didn't help that Adelita had taken quite a bit of convincing as well that we were not simply hallucinating or under the effects of some malevolent miracle. With my patience wearing thin, I must have barked down the line to her, because I felt Silje's hand on my shoulder and turned to see her slowly shaking her head.

I paused to take a deep breath, apologised, and soon we were organising flights, visas, and U.N. Travel permissions. These were not small things to create in the small amount of time we gave her, and by the time we got to Heathrow, Adelita had also completely drained herself of power.

Beatrice, meanwhile, had phoned Gary, Lennox, and Admonae, the other three Wingless who had seeds from the Tree of Time, and told them to meet us at the airport. Silje texted Damien and Joel to let them know that 'things' had happened, and that they were to contact Adelita for further details.

We were breaking my order for communication silence, the very one that I had only just given that morning, but our need was great, and I was banking on Michael being too focused on his now imminent goal to be worrying about us anymore. It was a gamble, I admit, but so was everything else we were planning on doing.

The only one left to tell was Orfael, but the only way we had to get the information to her was through Azazel. It felt wrong to leave her out of the loop, but telling her meant telling Azazel. I tried to tell myself that this wasn't the old prejudices rearing their ugly heads again, but once he knew he would definitely do something to try to help. In fact, knowing now who and what he really was, he literally would not be able to stop himself. And I couldn't shake the feeling that, at this point, Azazel's help, no matter how well intentioned, would do more harm than good.

It was probably hubris on my part, or a desperate need to give meaning to our Wingless state and exile to Earth, but part of me felt that this moment could be the reason why we were put here in the first place.

Either way, I decided this was something we needed to do for ourselves.

Our taxi pulled away from the curb, its driver smiling brightly from the generous tip Beatrice had given him once he had retrieved our rather meagre luggage from the trunk. To Silje's questioning look, Beatrice just shrugged and commented about spreading some last-minute good will into the universe.

"Besides," Beatrice commented as we headed into the terminal, "If we screw this up, he hasn't exactly got a long time left to enjoy it."

"Inspiring," I jokingly added.

"Honest," Beatrice replied in her usual deadpan way.

We grabbed some coffee from a well-known American coffee chain just inside the terminal and grabbed a table outside the café, which was easily visible from the terminal's main doors as we waited for the others to arrive. The 'coffee' had us all grimacing slightly, but it was worth it to see the look on Gary's face as he saw us and practically did a double take from the sign above our heads to the branded cups in our hands.

"Well," Gary exclaimed as he all but jogged up to us, shopping bag in hand, "If you've given up on the world already you could have given me a heads up. I mean, I can't see any other reason for you to be punishing your taste buds like that." I tried and failed to suppress a chuckle as he continued, "Throw that out. Sorry we're late, but I prepared some proper meals and coffee to bring with us. We're going to need to strengthen our bodies to deal with the area near the Tree and we are not going to be able to do that on airline food or…whatever it is you have in those cups that is masquerading as coffee."

Beatrice, Silje, and I stood and the six of us embraced in silence for a good minute before I disentangled myself and nodded towards the Security screening area that led further into the airport terminal building. As one we turned, and through centuries of practice we all started to walk with the countenance of someone who was exactly where they were supposed to be.

Striding confidently up to the security doorway, we side-stepped the stammering assistant asking for our luggage and up to the Department of Transport Officer in charge of the station. Looking up from his paperwork, he was clearly surprised to be confronted with six somewhat serious looking people standing quietly right in front of him.

You don't work security in a modern airport, however, without developing rather formidable defences to the strained emotions of the travelling public, and so he slowly closed the folder he was reading, stood up from his desk, and looked each of us straight in the eye before saying in a practiced, sceptical tone, "Yes?"

Admonae stepped forward, hand extended, and the officer found himself shaking it before he realised what was happening. I could feel her power delicately manipulating his reaction as Admonae brought her miracle up. "Mr. Havisham, I believe you were expecting us. We're the U.N. Inspection Team that Geneva would have called your office about. They should have delivered our travel documents here by now?"

We could all see him glance at the top drawer of his desk as Admonae finished, and I knew that meant Adelita had come through in time. Admonae released Mr. Havisham's hand and he pulled a key out of his pocket to open the drawer. Released from the small miracle, he fell back on his extensive training, checking our faces against the photos in the UN Passports and Visas, and getting us to sign for the documents in his ledger before calling over one of his people to be assigned to escort us through the terminal.

Within ten minutes we were headed for our plane, being guided through the back ways of the terminal usually reserved for VIPs. There was nothing Adelita could do about flight schedules however, and we arrived at our gate to find an all but empty waiting area and two hours to kill before we could board.

Gary looked back down the main concourse at all the bright lights of the duty-free stores before turning back to me with a wistful expression on his face.

"Go," I said, while waving him away, "Just don't lose track of time."

Cheekily, he winked at me and patted the pocket that I imagined held the seed from the Tree of Time, and then he skipped off in the direction of the shops.

Beatrice shook her head at his departing form. "He'll never change."

Admonae sighed in unison with Beatrice, but Silje rather uncharacteristically disagreed with her sister. "Actually, I think we're all changing. We have been for a long time now, but it is speeding up."

It was a sobering thought, even though thoughts like that were not something we really had been in short supply of recently. "We're in tune with humanity," I said. "We always have been. As they change and evolve it makes sense that it has an effect on us. But Silje is right, something is happening to us, and I have no idea what it is. What I do know is that we are about to do something incredibly stupid, but I can't see that we have any choice."

Admonae smiled softly and gave me a quick hug. "Yes, we do. Perhaps we have always had a choice. What you mean when you say we don't have a choice is actually that you can't see yourself, or any of us, choosing to do anything different under the circumstances."

"But isn't that just because of who we are? We are Angels, after all," asked Lennox.

Admonae shrugged. "Not even I can see the answer to that. Are we choosing to try to keep Michael from destroying humanity, at the very real risk of our own existence, because it is the right thing to do and everything else is anathema to us, or are we doing it simply because we are in some way, hard-wired to risk everything to save them, even from the hosts of heaven themselves?"

"I choose," stated Beatrice bluntly.

"But how do you know?" asked Lennox.

Beatrice shrugged, "I just do," before turning away and walking over to a vending machine to peruse the variety of chocolate within.

"I wish I had her certainty," Lennox softly added as Beatrice walked away.

I reached out and grasped Lennox's shoulder, giving a friendly squeeze as I commented, "Don't we all."

The problem with modern air travel is all the 'hurry-up and wait' that is involved. Rush to the check in counter, wait in line. Get through security and rush to your gate, wait for the plane. Finally get seated and listen to the safety briefing while you wait to taxi to the runway. It gave one far too much time to dwell on all the things you could be doing at that moment, while simultaneously being on tenterhooks for the first sign of your next movement, the next stage of the whole royal command performance that is modern commercial flying.

I don't think I ever missed my wings so much.

Chapter Thirty-Seven

The long straight road we were driving down was lined on both sides by tall, thin poplars, and headed almost directly south-east from Yekaterinburg. Our plane had landed just over an hour ago after thankfully flying into the dawn. The concocted U.N. credentials combined with a smaller than average bribe saw us through customs and into a rental four-wheel drive without needing to expend any of our newly returned miraculous power.

The car trip, much like the plane journey before it, was strangely quiet. Each of us were caught up with our own thoughts on what was to come. Every once in a while, one of us would catch the eye of another and there would be a comforting smile shared, or a hand reached out to connect through a gentle touch.

The silence wasn't uncompanionable. It was just that with what we were here to do, none of us felt the need to make conversation.

After all, how does one plan to go up against the Archangel of War? We had our goal firmly set in our hearts and minds, and we had our determination to save the life this world was home to. We each had a seed from a Tree of Creation in our pockets, but had no idea of what they would do or how we were to make use of them.

And, although it felt strange to admit it, we had our faith.

About 150km away were the old towns that made up the Mayak Production Association, one of the biggest nuclear refining facilities of the old Soviet Union. Originally between the towns of Kasli and Tatysch, only one small plant was still in operation after the accident known as the 'Kyshtym Disaster' in the late fifties. With about an hour's driving still to go, I rested in the backseat with my eyes closed, Lennox having taken over the driving at the halfway mark. I had nearly nodded off in fact when a pressure, slowly building up behind my eyes, caused me to frown and shake myself fully awake.

My fellow backseat passengers looked to be experiencing the same effect, and the rough feel of loose ground under our tires as Lennox quickly pulled off the road, told us she was feeling it too. All the other cars on the road simply sailed past us without a concern, leading me to guess what, or who, was behind this. Seconds later my suspicions were confirmed as Michael's voice filled our minds.

> *"Hosts of Heaven, heed my call to arms. I have discovered the true path laid out by our Father for us. I now know what needs to be done to grant us our victory in the war against his enemies. The puzzle He set for me to solve, the quest I was forced to undertake by the actions of the traitorous Wingless, has been arduous, but it has been fruitful. Soon now, the last barrier to our victory for His glory will fall. Be ready, my brethren. Be ready."*

I blinked as the booming voice left my head and the world swam back into focus. Beside me, Gary groaned, "What an ass."

"There is no way anyone missed that," Admonae stated, rubbing her temples.

Silje's face was still scrunched up in a frown. "The Fallen did. He made sure they would not hear and be forewarned of the attack."

"Then why did he let us hear it?" asked Admonae.

"Spite," Beatrice replied. "He wants us to know he has won. No, more than just won. He wants us to know that he has beaten us, that he now *knows* it is all our fault and he has seen through our plot against him and the Father."

"He's insane," Lennox quietly offered.

Beatrice just nodded, "Yes".

"Or he's trying to play us. If he really thinks we are in league with the Fallen, then he will expect us to warn them," I posed.

"So?" asked Gary. "That sounds like a great idea, why don't we?"

"No, think about it for a moment." I paused, catching the eye of everyone in the car before continuing. "We know how Azazel really feels, and I suspect Michael does too. What would Azazel order the Fallen to do if he knew about this?"

"He'd order them to battle. He would do anything to try to stop Michael. If not to protect all the humans, he would do it to try to protect...us," answered Lennox, stumbling over the last revelation.

I nodded, "Precisely".

"And they'd all just jump to Michael's location and land in the middle of the Tree's influence. They'd be powerless!" announced Admonae, shocking herself with her realisation.

"He'd slaughter them all," added Silje sadly.

"I agree, and he'd enjoy doing it. And then, there is the message he left in the last part of his call, the part he put in there for us." I watched them all come to the same conclusion I had. "So, we say nothing. And one way or the other, we end this. Today."

With a curt nod of assent and a determined set to her jaw, Lennox pulled the car back onto the road and accelerated towards our goal. We still didn't have any real plan for how we were going to win, but now there was no way our determination would falter. Michael believed that the removal of the Wingless would trigger the final battle, allow him his glorious victory, and place him back by God's side. And to do that he was willing to destroy every single human life.

It would be incorrect, however, to say that we had no choice but to fight. He had hidden our choice in his speech to the host. '... the last barrier to our victory for His glory will fall'. That was us. We would either die by his hand, or, in order to save the humans and allow the war to start, we could choose to Fall.

And I honestly think he expected us to do just that. To give up in horror of what he was willing to do. To simply choose to Fall and take our place in the armies of Lightbringer. It was, for Michael at least, quite a clever strategy. Fall in order to save everyone? That was something we would actually consider doing.

The bit he missed in his great scheme came from a simple lack of understanding. He never quite appreciated the sheer stubbornness that came with staying as a Wingless all these millennia. The choice to Fall had always been there for us, and true, over the ages many of us had taken that option. Those of us who were left, however, by either being completely stupid, incredibly recalcitrant, or more likely, a combination of both, had learned one very important lesson.

We could always Fall tomorrow.

If we had to Fall to save everyone, we would. But we wouldn't do it until every other option was exhausted. We'd hold off until the last moment. And that gave us the most terrible weapon of all to use against Michael.

Hope.

As she drove, Lennox tossed her phone to me. "Joan, use this and contact the others. If we have to take that last step, they'll sense us doing it, and they need to know why we decided to take that path. All their contact numbers are in there, and any message will be handled mundanely by my program, so they shouldn't be detected."

"Thanks, Lennox," I said, as I started to key in what I wanted to send.

"All for one and one for all, huh?" chuckled Gary. "Do I get one of those hats with the big feather in it?"

Beatrice replied, "If it comes to that, it has to be. And no."

The car sped down the highway to the sounds of Gary's bad jokes, Beatrice's equally stone-faced monotone responses, and groans from the rest of us. After sending the messages to the rest of the Wingless, along with strict orders against replying, I handed the phone back to Lennox so she could go back to using the map program to find our destination. It was obvious that we were nervous, and each of us was dealing with it in our own way. We were close, we were family, even 'cut from the same cloth' one might say, but we were still individuals, and how each of us dealt with that nervousness clearly displayed that individuality.

The quietest one of us was Silje, sitting in the back and silently watching everyone, much the same as I was. When I caught her eye, she mouthed one word—'changing'—as she indicated each of our friends with a nod.

Raising an eyebrow in response, I nodded back. She was right, but that just led to another question. What were we changing into?

Eventually, we turned off the highway and onto roads that wound gently around the hills surrounding Ozyorsk. Other traffic was now at a minimum, and when we turned off the main road, it was to take a narrow road lined with signs demanding that we turn back. Very soon a checkpoint blocked our path, just under 10 kilometres from the site. Several Russian soldiers sauntered out to greet our car, automatic rifles held suggestively out in front of them.

Lennox wound down her window and started to address the soldiers in flawless Russian, complete with a perfect Moscovite accent. We, of course, could feel the power of her miracle behind what she was saying, but to the soldiers it all made perfect sense that this car full of GRU officers needed to drive unprotected into the most radioactive spot on the planet.

As they lifted the barrier and saluted the passing car, Admonae commented, "We could have tried our U.N. credentials first, you know, rather than use some of our limited power."

Lennox just shrugged as she slowly accelerated the car away from the checkpoint. "I figured that since we will lose all that power once we enter the Tree's influence and we are on a bit of a tight schedule, it wouldn't matter. Besides, you know there isn't going to be any other people closer than this to the town."

"Not unless they like glowing in the dark," added Gary.

"No more guards?" asked Silje.

Beatrice shook her head sadly. "Why bother guarding something that will kill you to look at?"

"Wasn't Chernobyl worse?" asked Gary.

Beatrice nodded, "The initial accident, yes. But after Kyshtym, Lake Karachai was used as a dumping ground for all sorts of radioactive and chemical waste."

The car crested one last hill and before us lay the small dale that held Lake Karachai. Unconsciously, I held my breath as we passed into the area of influence of the Tree. We could each feel its presence, and I couldn't help but feel that it sensed us as well. The dale itself was covered in sickly looking poplars, birch and maple trees, and various small, coarse ground cover plants. On one edge of the lake, however, a small section of trees and grasses looked healthy and vibrant, in stark difference to the rest of the area. Standing in the middle of this copse, completely out of place with the rest of the vegetation, was a quite young but perfectly proportioned beech tree. The Tree of Life.

Gary couldn't help but chuckle, "Hey look! Life's a…"

Beatrice slapped her hand over his mouth before he could utter another word. "Don't! Just. Don't."

Chapter Thirty-Eight

Lennox pulled the car to a stop just after cresting the hill and we piled out. Instinctively, I started to go through the small movements designed to limber up muscles before a fight, stretching my arms, twisting my neck and my upper body, all things I have done so many times that I don't even realise they are happening. Feeling my strength return as blood finally reached muscles too long cramped in a car made me suddenly realise one other vital fact.

I still had my strength. All of it. I silently reached out with my will to that place where I drew on the small amount of power I had for miracles, and discovered that it also was still there.

Admonae was the first to voice it. "We still have our power! We're close to the Tree and we're still Angels. How?"

It took but one moment more before, as one, we were diving our hands into whichever pocket in our clothes held the seed.

"It's warm," Gary stated. "Not burning, it's more like I'm holding the perfect cup of coffee."

"Mine's singing," added Silje, a look of sheer relief on her face. Remembering how much the silence of the other Trees affected her, I couldn't help but smile at this particular turn of events.

"My one seems to be vibrating," Lennox said with a curious tone.

My fingers closed around the seed I carried. It felt smooth and yet somehow also sharp on my skin. There was a warmth around it, tickling the palm of my hand like tiny flames, and yet the seed itself was ice cold. I had a feeling I knew exactly what mine represented.

"This is the gift we were promised," Beatrice announced. "A link to who we are outside of this place."

Admonae corrected Beatrice's statement, "A link to who we are *when* we are outside of this place. It's all got to do with time."

Gary hmphed. "If that's the case, why not link us to a time before we lost our wings? We'd have a lot more power."

I shook my head. "It seems we have been allowed to bring to this confrontation nothing more and nothing less than who we are. We may have been expecting some great weapon or advantage, but I for one cannot think of anything I'd rather have more."

"So," Lennox asked, "Where is he?"

"He wouldn't have had to come by car like us, so he may have landed anywhere," I replied. "Stick together but keep your eyes out for any sign."

Slowly, we started to walk down towards the lake. Rather than head for the tree directly, I led us in a spiral path around the area. I didn't think that even an Archangel would be able to will themselves to appear this close to the Tree, so he must have entered the area from some direction. I was ready for him to come at us from somewhere close to the lake though, so it was Silje, looking outwards away from the Tree, who spotted the first sign of his passing.

Silje attracted my attention before reaching out and gently disentangling a single long, perfectly white feather from the grasping branches of a nearby thorny bush. The expression on her face as she turned to hand it to me was strained, as if just holding the feather was painful to her. I took it from her and immediately relief flooded her features. I felt no such reaction, but I did notice the base of the feather was stained with small red droplets of blood.

Beatrice reached out to hold Silje as she stepped back from me. "Too loud," Silje uttered as she took a moment in her sister's arms to re-centre herself.

Gary, meanwhile, had been examining the bush and the ground around it. He pulled Lennox over to join him, and after a moment's conferring, waved me over.

They had discovered tracks, fresh ones but easy to miss. Hard soled boots had tromped through the underbrush, the type of marks that would come from the metallic armoured boots Michael preferred, although less for any defensive advantage, more for the dramatic visual effect. What made spotting the tracks hard, however, was that the leaf litter and dirt looked to have been swept back over the path as if to try to hide his passing.

Which would have been entirely out of character for the Archangel.

I looked from the disturbed trail to the feather in my hand and then back again. "That idiot!" I exclaimed, far too loud in the circumstances. "What was he thinking?"

"Joan?" Admonae prompted.

I held up the feather. "He forced his wings to stay out as he stepped into the sphere of the tree's power. Maybe because he wanted to rub our faces in the sight of them, maybe he is just that..."

"Pigheaded?" offered Lennox.

"I was going to say inflexible," I continued, "But no matter how much he prepared his physical body for the removal of his power once he got here, there is simply no way the muscles in a human body can hold up his wings. They've been dragging in the dirt behind him ever since he got here."

Beatrice was unconvinced. "But he could have just stepped back out and put them away. Why keep them out after he realised he couldn't raise them?"

"Pigheaded," repeated Lennox.

I found myself nodding in agreement. "Pigheaded."

The trail led directly to the copse of trees that held the Tree of Life, but the impressions in the dirt suggested Michael had walked this track back and forth a number of times. He wasn't one to pace fretfully or second-guess a decision he had made, so each trip must have been for a purpose.

I turned and followed the trail down towards the lake. Whatever Michael was doing with his power once he walked back outside the influence of the Tree would not have left much evidence for us to find, but the other end of the trail would.

As we carefully stalked along the trail, doing our best to remain as quiet as possible, my mind was awhirl with questions. Just what was he planning to do here without his power? Even amongst all this pollution and radiation, the Tree of Life was not some delicate little sapling. It was a living, sentient entity, as old as creation itself. Older, actually, if only by a little bit, although time had little meaning back then. The creator had brought it into being to be a tool in his great work. It hadn't always been in the form of a tree of course, that came later, but it had always existed.

A distracted part of my brain wondered why God had left his tools scattered about the Earth instead of putting them safely away once he had finished with them, but I imagined he had his reasons.

Silje's shocked gasp dragged me back from my musing. We had just come around an outcropping of bedrock and the Tree itself had finally come into view. What had shocked Silje, however, was the thing we had not been able to see from the top of the hill: the base of the tree. Or more specifically, what had been placed there.

It was obvious now what Michael had been doing. At the edge of the Tree's dampening effect, he had been using his own miraculous power to summon various items to him, and then manually dragging each one down to place at the base of the tree. It would have been arduous, possibly even painful work for the powerless Archangel, and from the looks of it he had managed quite a number of trips.

Arrayed around the tree was an odd collection of objects, all man-made, and all heinous. Each one signified an 'evil' of humankind. Nothing as simple a tool as a sword or gun—what Michael had collected here was vile, and from my time on Earth I knew each and every one of them. He had summoned canisters of mustard gas from World War One. Nerve and Biological weapons from more recent conflicts. Slave collars from colonial America sat alongside torture implements used by various Inquisitions. One branding iron in particular made me shudder uncontrollably for a moment when I recognised it. It had been used on me that day I hung from that wall and refused to submit. The day I had burned.

Piles of bones were scattered around the area as well. Complete skeletons, each one of them an animal forced to extinction by the hand of mankind. Alongside them were the tools of their extinction: canisters of chlorofluorocarbons, lumps of coal, piles of soot, a lumberjack's axe. Examples of human industry employed to ease their lives at the cost of the planet's delicate ecological balance.

In one section of this repugnant collection, the dirt had been churned into mud. Those same signs in the ground of dragged wings, now sodden, were leading up from the edge of the water. Sitting there, still dripping from the lake they had originally rested in, were rusted barrels of toxic and radioactive waste. The results of failed experiments to create even nastier bioweapons were laid next to containers of spent atomic fuel rods, and the contaminated by-products of nuclear fuel enrichment.

These were not the holy symbols of a war between Angels, the war Michael was desperate to fight once more. These were symbols of mankind's war against creation, against Life itself.

We could all see what these things were, but it was Admonae's power to see the truth that put all the pieces together.

"He's playing Prosecutor," Admonae explained, "and this is his evidence against humanity. He can't hurt the Tree directly, he's far outmatched for power here, but if he can get it to despair, to give up for just a second, if not on all life, then at least on the humans, then he'll have the opening he needs."

"As Judge," Beatrice added, "I would have to say the weight of argument is on his side."

Lennox nodded, adding, "And he must have gotten the idea of just how to assail the Tree's spirit from Kateri. She'd know better than anyone how it felt about all this."

"It's ingenious," stated Beatrice.

"It's insane," countered Silje.

Gary just raised his arm to point back down to the lake. "And it's time. He's here."

Chapter Thirty-Nine

Michael stood at the edge of the lake, still knee deep in the highly radioactive and toxic water. His now more mundane skin, bereft of his miraculous power, was already showing signs of reddening and blistering from being submerged in that deadly mixture. This didn't even slow down the Archangel, however, who no doubt saw his temporary weakness as a cheap price to pay to achieve his goal.

What pained me the most to see was the state of his wings as they lay stretched out behind him in the muck at the lake's edge. Covered in mud and slime, bloodied from being dragged across the ground, and with enough feathers missing to leave small bare patches scattered across each wing. As he stood there, I watched another feather detach, and as it hit the ground it was as if I felt a knife twist in my own back, as if my own wings, so long denied to me, were crying at the sight.

In his left-hand Michael carried an ominous looking canister emblazoned with the radioactive warning trefoil. Brushing his long golden hair away from his face, he looked up and for the first time, saw us. Rather than seem disturbed by our arrival, his face broke into a twisted, feral grin.

"Finally," Michael uttered. He bent down to place the canister on the shoreline, retrieving his sword from where he had stuck it into the sand before entering the lake. "I was beginning to worry that I would not be able to put you traitors down in person."

"You really hate us that much?" asked Gary.

Michael's manic grin turned into a sneer as Gary spoke. "You? You are nothing. I made sure of that. When you refused my call to arms, refused to fight for His glory, I expected you to Fall like the others. When I saw that you had not, I asked Him what should be done with you."

Michael practically spat his next words at us, and the vitriol in his voice was obvious, "That's when I made you Wingless."

Hearing those words was like being hit by a truck. I relived that very first moment when I called on my wings to extend and they ignored my summons. I could see that my friends were feeling that same moment. It was Beatrice's stoic nature that allowed her to recover first and answer back.

"I don't believe you," she taunted Michael. "Not even you would have that power. How could you possibly pull off that kind of miracle?"

Michael was clearly enjoyed torturing us. "Child, you know nothing. I merely took God's reply to my question and channelled His power through my holy sword, my icon of office." He lifted his sword as he spoke, allowing sunlight to glint off its blade. "I will admit I did not know what final form God's punishment for you would take, but when I spoke the words, they made you what you are."

Michael paused, relishing the pain he was causing before slowly pronouncing once again the sentencing he had passed on us so long ago. "Leave them to Earth."

It was probably just psychosomatic, but I swear I could feel my wings tighten even further for a moment. Admonae's head, however, had snapped up at the pronouncement, and her eyes were clear and focused.

"That's a lie," she stated firmly. The certainty in her voice had all of us, Michael included, holding our breaths.

"Don't be ridiculous," Michael responded after a few seconds, "I am an Archangel, I do not lie."

Beside me, I could feel Admonae raising the power within her, "They were the words you spoke, that is true, but they were not the words given to you."

Michael chuckled, "I assure you, Wingless, they were the—"

Admonae cut him off with a shout, and we all felt her miracle envelope Michael. "What were you told!?"

Michael physically stumbled back, clearly shocked that Admonae could use a miracle here. Still, the will of an Archangel is strong, and through pursed lips he uttered a reply. "It is my job to interpret..."

Again, Admonae interrupted him, the fury in her voice clear as she poured all her power into her command. "What. Were. You. Told!?"

With a stunned expression on his face, Michael repeated the answer he had received so long ago, his voice monotone as he was forced by Admonae's miracle to say the words through gritted teeth. "Leave…Earth to them."

Hearing that answer was like feeling a heavy chain you have been carrying around all your life suddenly just drop away. It was him. It was Michael and his twisted interpretation of God's will that had done this to us. We hadn't failed in our duty. We hadn't failed Him.

I reached my arm up and back, feeling my sword materialise as I did so. Grasping the hilt, I drew it slowly, deliberately from its scabbard, allowing Michael plenty of time to register what I was doing as the plain steel came into view.

His smile returned as he did so, and certain as he was in his own martial expertise, he raised his own sword in mock salute. "Yes, Trazael, let's finish this. If you wish to die by my sword, I will grant you this boon."

"If I die," I replied, "It won't be by your sword, Michael." I poured my will into the weapon in my hand, removing the shackles I had placed upon it back in the car. Immediately it burst into golden flame, lighting the area in a holy glow.

Michael recognised it immediately, agitation and anger clouding his face. "But that's...How did you get your filthy hands on my sword?"

"To be perfectly honest," I stated, as I moved my feet into a duelling stance, "I didn't get your sword."

It was my turn to pause for effect.

"It chose me."

Fury replaced the uncertainty in Michael's eyes, and he took a measured step forward, raising his sword and dropping into his own favoured fighting stance. Even weakened as he was, his body was in peak physical condition, and his experience was more than a match for my own. His arm muscles rippled as he increased his grip on the hilt of the sword, the visual effect part of his duelling strategy. For Michael, combat was just as much about psychologically attacking his opponent's spirit as it was defeating them physically.

And to be honest, he could see in my eyes and small movements that my own analysis of a duel between us agreed with his. "Give up, Trazael," he challenged, "Even with my power gone and you wielding a stolen sword, you have to know you have no chance of beating me."

I nodded, acquiescing to him that point. "You're right, Michael. One on one I doubt I'd be able to take you. But when you made us what we are, when you bound our wings, you also created something else, something far more powerful than miracles."

Sensing a trick, Michael did not drop his guard. "Are you talking about that abomination of a child you are trying to hide from me?"

Behind me, I heard Beatrice gasp. Before he could goad her into making a foolish move, however, Lennox spoke up. "No, you schmuck. You know, I always wondered if you were the inspiration for the Jewish people to create that word, I guess you've gone and proven that now."

I had to stifle a laugh, and Michael honestly looked like he had been slapped. I spared a quick glance left and right, seeing where the others had placed themselves during our standoff and tensed my body for a quick lunge. As Michael noticed my movements and focussed back on me once more, I smiled, and simply said, "You created a family."

I launched forward, closing the distance between us in a single prodigious leap. Around me, I could feel each of my friends creating their own special miracles as I employed my power to physically drive me forward. Silje sang out a note from the universe, a pure note, and one that resonated within my body. Instinctively I could feel that this was our note, this was us, and as much as it empowered us, I could see Michael flinch in pain as it assailed his ears.

Gary had been slowly edging his way around to the water's edge as we were verbally sparring, and with a final jump he reached out and plunged his clay cup into the lake. Instantly, the water began to freeze, a thick white ice sheet spreading out from the cup in his hand and speeding across the surface of the water.

Beatrice had leapt forward with me, although her angle of attack was very different. As she ran, she summoned a long glaive, its blade aimed to block Michael's own sword rather than attack the angel directly.

Admonae had already used most of her power getting Michael to confess, but what little she had left she combined with Lennox, and with that extra boost Lennox reached out with her will. I felt, and then saw, a curved bubble of force appear in front of me, that then formed into a completely weightless shield strapped to my left arm.

I was momentarily confused as to why Lennox had chosen that particular miracle to expend her power upon, as she knew I never fought with a shield. However, as my eyes rose from the transparent shield on my arm to Michael, I saw him draw a huge silver handgun from behind his back and fire it straight at my chest.

Then it was as if everything happened at once.

The shield at my arm shattered, protecting me as it collapsed by sending the miracle-created ammunition Michael had fired ricocheting harmlessly over my shoulder. His sword came up at a dizzying speed towards my neck only to be deflected at the last moment by Beatrice's glaive. As my flaming sword began its downward swing, Michael's attempt to dodge to his left was foiled, as his feet, still ankle deep in water at the lake's edge, were suddenly frozen in place from Gary's ice.

I felt Silje's note hit a crescendo and my flaming blade struck down, severing Michael's sword in two, sundering his shiny metallic cuirass, and his chest beneath it, open from shoulder to hip.

I landed beside and a little behind Michael, cracking the newly formed ice sheet as I did so.

I heard him slump to the ground a moment later.

Chapter Forty

I was still panting from the exertion of my attack as I heard Beatrice and Lennox behind me run forward and flip Michael over onto his back, helping to get his face out of the inch-deep mud and water he was lying in, before dragging him up the sand away from the lake's edge a small distance.

He was barely breathing, and as Beatrice wiped the slime and muck from his mouth, Lennox started to unbuckle the straps on his cloven breastplate. Gary had let the ice dissipate and had started to jog towards them as well, using the last of his power to summon a medical trauma kit.

Admonae had also started to move towards Michael, but Silje grabbed her by the arm and pulled her in the direction of the Tree instead. Together, they quickly began dismantling the twisted effigy to mankind's destruction that Michael had set up around its base, while continuing to cast glances back at where the archangel lay.

I found I was a little ashamed of myself as I watched my friends immediately leap into action to save Michael's life. I realised that I had not thought past the moment of defeating him, regardless of the cost to myself, and certainly not of any cost to Michael. I turned around to face them, flames still lazily flowing up the blade of the sword in my hand. Lennox had just gotten Michael's cuirass unbuckled, lifting it gently off to him to reveal the deep, ugly, and cauterised wound running diagonally across his chest.

They were right in their actions, of course, there was no way we could just let him perish, not even after all he had done. But just what were we to do with the Archangel? As Gary reached him and started to do what he could for the wound, Michael opened his eyes and locked them on mine.

Ignoring the ones trying desperately to save him, Michael raised one shaking finger to point accusingly at me. "Traitor, this is all your fault. Why don't you just finish me?"

"Michael," I started, "You're not well. You have been alone too long. Just let us help—"

He cut me off, while he feebly attempted to stop Gary from seeing to his wound. "I need your help? How dare you? Who do you think you are, that you can talk to me like that?"

"Honestly, Michael, I don't know." My quiet answer stopped his flailing, and even caught the attention of my friends. "I know who I was, I know what you made me, what you made us, but we have changed since then. Grown somehow. I'm not sure what we are becoming, but it is something new."

"Don't be absurd," Michael spat back at me. "You are beginning to sound like them, the humans. Those ridiculous creatures that you were supposed to serve, to protect. They barely understand who they are and so many reject the plan laid out for them. Your good friend 'Azazel' can have them." The vitriol in Michael's voice was plain, as was the implication that he knew more about the truth of who Azazel really was than we did.

I looked sideways at the prone angel and stepped closer, crouching down as I shook my head in disappointment. "Michael, learning how to be a human is a very messy process, even for them. They keep trying new things, getting them wrong, falling down. But each time they fall they get up again. They dust themselves off, learn from their mistakes, and try again. It really is an incredibly powerful, if admittedly painful, way to grow."

Beatrice took up my rumination as I paused. "And they are always doing it. At two years old they start to poke at the world around them, they start to develop their individual personalities, slowly trying to discover who they are. Ten years later they do it again, pushing at their boundaries and exploring themselves as much as the world they live in. And this cycle of growth, consolidation, questioning, and discovery keeps going on their entire lives."

Lennox nodded appreciatively, adding, "In so many ways, they are so much more than us. Perhaps we shouldn't be surprised that they are beyond your understanding."

Michael winced with pain from Gary's ministrations, but continued to argue with us. "They are God's creatures; they belong to Him. That is all I need to know."

I just snorted with disbelief. "You still don't get it, do you? They *are* God!"

"Blasphemy!" Michael croaked out.

I shook my head, "No, it isn't. Listen, there is a little piece of God in each and every one of them. A living spark, experiencing life, growing, evolving...learning."

Before he could interrupt again, I continued, "Who knows, maybe whatever or wherever God came from, coalesced the Universe specifically in order to become them, to be able to experience life. To learn to understand who they really are. They are so much more than us,

Michael, but if we're very, very lucky, we get to be just a little bit like them."

Comprehension flashed in his eyes, not of my argument, but of the decision I had come to while we had been trying to make him understand. "You're going to sever my wings. You are going to make me live like one of them," he said.

Again, I answered him with a shake of my head. "No, Michael, I'm not going to sever your wings, and I can't make you human. To be honest, that is just too large a step up from where you are now. But I can start you on your journey. I can make you Wingless. Not sever, but bind your wings as you once bound ours, and hopefully open your eyes in the process. The rest will be up to you."

"Of course," Michael gasped as his strength gave out and his head fell back to lay on the sand. "You will have your revenge on me."

As I stood once more and raised the flaming sword to carry out the miracle, I replied, "No, Michael, this is not revenge, I wouldn't even call it justice. I promise that we won't leave you alone, we will be there to help. And one day you may just realise that what I do today is a blessing."

Later, with Beatrice and Gary each under one of Michael's shoulders to carry him, and with no wings to drag along behind him, the seven of us reached the top of the small hill that delineated the edge of the Tree's miracle dampening influence. Waiting just beyond the crest was the Lightbringer, and with him were Samael and Orfael.

As we stopped, Lightbringer stepped forward. "Joan, he's my responsibility now. Give him to me. I promise no harm will come to him."

"Sorry, Azazel," I replied, enjoying the look that passed over his perfect features as I used his other form's name. I motioned for our little group to continue moving forward. "No can do. We promised to look after him, and I think you'll agree we're the most qualified."

We covered that last short distance in a few steps and as one we had our wings suddenly and fully open in all their glory. Even Orfael's wings opened synchronously with ours, and humorously accompanied by her squeak of surprise.

And as they did so, a feeling of pride blanketed the area. The kind of pride that can only come from a parent. Lightbringer smiled as well at the sight, before bowing his head in salute. "Well done, all of you," he said. He basked in the sight for a moment before continuing, "I've only felt God this pleased once before. I will take my leave, but one day, when you are ready, I would like to hear the story of exactly what happened in there."

With their full angelic power restored, the others simply disappeared, taking Michael with them. Orfael soon followed, and after a nod from Lightbringer, so did Samael. Once we were alone, Lightbringer transformed himself back into Azazel and reached out his arms, in that request for a hug I used to find so incredibly irritating.

This time, though, I hugged him with a smile, using both my arms and my wings.

"One question," I said, as we broke our embrace. "You said you had experienced that feeling of pride once before."

Azazel smiled again, although this time it had just a hint of sadness hidden behind it. "I have been around the block a few times, Joan. Why do you ask?"

He took a half step back from me, and I sensed he was getting ready to leave. I folded my wings back away, so it would look just like the old 'us', and locked my eyes with his to ask the question I had already guessed the answer to. "Was it when He asked you to lead the rebellion?"

Azazel took another step back and started to fade. He shared a sad smile with me and there was an almost imperceptible nod to his head. As he vanished, a single whispered word was left hanging in the air between us.

"Yes."

Epilogue

To say that it was obvious that we would all just continue with our missions on Earth after regaining our wings would be to miss the point of what we had become. We may have been created from the same mould, but we had grown, each unique experience subtly changing us over time. We were true individuals, possessing something as complex and tricky as it was precious. Free will.

Certainly Beatrice, Silje, and Gary chose to stay where they were. Beatrice had her and Kateri's new daughter to be with, and I think Silje and Gary fancied themselves as the crazy aunt and uncle.

Orfael chose to ascend, feeling a need for time away from Earth, although she had not closed off the possibility of returning one day. Damien also ascended, although he claimed it was just an overdue long service leave holiday he was taking, and he'd be back within the year.

Admonae had, on her own, come to the same conclusion I had about Lightbringer's rebellion and fall from grace, and she decided to indulge in some private discussions with the leader of the Fallen. I warned her that Azazel was probably not going to be as forthcoming as she would like, but Admonae just muttered something about enjoying a challenge and went anyway.

Adelita and Joel ended up travelling with Admonae, as they were planning to make contact once more with all the Wingless who had chosen to fall over the ages. While they said they expected to be back on Earth soon, I was not going to hold them to that. Those sorts of family reunions are not something to be rushed.

Lennox's decision surprised me. While we all felt the loss of Toby, her pain at his death was more intimate, more acute. They had shared so much over so long a time, and the wound left by his passing was not something that would mend quickly. So, when she originally volunteered to be the one to mentor Michael, I forbade it. It took Lennox almost a week of badgering to convince me it was not only something she needed to do, but that she would be the best choice for Michael before I capitulated under the weight of her argument.

And then there is me. Not only had I regained my wings, but I was also now thrust into Michael's position as Archangel of War. Quite laughable, really, except that my time on Earth had taught me that the one sure way to win a war, was to never let it start. Consequently, I effectively split my time between Earth and the Heavens, trying to teach that lesson to human and Angel alike.

Free will, as it turns out, is a hard thing to get right. It was something our Creator had been striving for since the beginning, and I personally believe it was his ultimate goal when He started. The Archangels were his first attempt, and they failed. Next the heavenly hosts, who turned out to be a small improvement, as they could at least make one decision, one choice. Then came us, the Angels whose destiny it was to become the Wingless, because of a war that was arranged by our Creator for that very purpose. After us, it was improved again in the animals of the Earth, and finally, free will was perfected with the humans.

However, in what came as a surprise; even, I'd like to think, to Him, was that once created, free will turns out to be rather infectious. Thankfully so, for us.

Gary would probably say it has a mind of its own.

The End.

ABOUT THE AUTHOR

David M. James is an avid writer and role-player, living in Canberra, Australia's capital city. With Bachelor and Master's degrees in Education, David teaches computer games programming and physics at a senior college in Canberra. When not in front of a class, David enjoys writing role-playing games and LARPs for gaming conventions, something he has been doing since 1986. David also helps run the Phenomenon Games Convention held in Canberra each year. In 2021 he published his first novel, Wingless, an urban fantasy about a group of Angels banished from heaven. His debut novel explored the concepts of free will, family and friendship.

His second novel, Born Without Wings, continues the story of one of the Wingless fifteen years after the events in the first book.

A third book in the series is now also being written.

We hope that you enjoyed this title and look forward to many more to come. Please, leave us a review! Reviews matter to all of our authors.

Take a look at some of our other award-winning series at https://threeravenspublishing.com/series-universes/

Visit us at https://www.threeravenspublishing.com and sign up for our newsletter for the latest and greatest news on upcoming titles and events.

Other series and titles you might enjoy.

AVAILABLE ON
AMAZON
JOINT TASK FORCE
13
HOLDING THE LINE
BETWEEN HEAVEN AND HELL
13

DECLAN FINN
DECLAN FINN
DECLAN FINN
DECLAN FINN
Demons Forever
Honor at Stake
Live & Let Bite
Good to the Last Drop
The Dragon Award Nominated Series
FREE on Kindle Unlimited!

MYSTERY,
MAGIC &
MAYHEM
WITH A TWIST
OF ROMANCE
J.F. POSTHUMUS
ON AMAZON
FIND ME

B.E.N.T.
BIOLOGIC   ENHANCED   NASCENT   TALENT

THE RAVEN
AND
THE CROW
MICHAEL K. FALCIANI
FIND ME
ON AMAZON

STARFLIGHT

IT CAME FROM THE
TRAILER PARK

You can also keep up to date with our latest release announcements on Scifi.radio and get some of the best fandom programing on the planet.

Scifi for your Wifi

And don't forget to check out our other Sponsors and Affiliates

A southern Appalachian jewel for craft beer lovers, Buck Bald Brewing offers something for everyone. With delicious, locally brewed beverages from across the spectrum, Buck Bald Brewing offers craft brews that are consistently amazing.

From the dark and smooth Shesquatch Scottish ale, to the intense hops of Hippibilly IPA, to the puckering sour of the blackberry and cinnamon in Berry My Heart at the Trailer Park, and more than 60+ rotating brews, you'll find what you're looking for and more.

With smiling faces behind the bar ready to help you find your next favorite brew, a constantly rotating selection of delicious craft beverages, toe-tapping tunes always playing, and the biggest games on TV, you can kick your feet up in either Copperhill, Tennessee or Murphy, North Carolina and immerse yourself in the Buck Bald Brewing experience. So, come out, fill a pint, fill a growler, and fill your mind at your new favorite family-owned craft brewery.

To discover more visit us at buckbaldbrewing.com or follow us on Facebook @buckbaldbrewing and @buckbaldbrewingmurphy.

Vesper Wren's
TRAILER PARK
PIXIE PUNCH
· A PEACH STRAWBERRY SELTZER ·
BUCK BALD BREWING

And don't forget to check out the latest edition of *Car Wars*

http://www.sjgames.com/car-wars/

Or the other amazing titles from
Steve Jackson Games

http://www.sjgames.com

…or the latest in the Car Warriors: Autoduel Chronicle fiction series.

https://threeravenspublishing.com/car-warriors-autoduel-chronicles/

Comprised of active or retired servicemen and civilian volunteers, Shepherd's Men enthusiastically raises awareness and funds for the SHARE Military Initiative (SHARE) at Shepherd Center in Atlanta, GA.

This nationally renowned program focuses on assessment and treatment for American military veterans who have sustained mild to moderate Traumatic Brain Injury (TBI) and Post-Traumatic Stress Disorder (PTSD) during post-9/11 service.

Find out more at: https://www.shepherdsmen.com/